Being the other woman was never my goal. But loving him made it impossible not to be. A love triangle between lifelong friends certainly complicates the issue.

From the moment I realised we couldn't be together, I hit the self-destruct button. Life gets complicated and tragedy appears out of nowhere. Loyalty is tested. And love is denied.

Our passion is real. Our feelings strong. Our story heartbreaking. He was never mine to begin with, but every moment in his arms was precious. No one is ever promised a happy ending, but for me loving him was worth the risk.

Will he ever choose me?

Trigger Warning: Contains adult themes including infidelity, terminal illness and drug use.

Loving Dr Jones
Copyright © 2022 VR Tennent
ISBN: 978-1-4874-3636-0
Cover art by Angela Waters

Published by eXtasy Books Inc

Look for us online at:
www.eXtasybooks.com

Loving Dr Jones
Moral Dilemmas 1

By

VR Tennent

PART 1

London
May 2006

CHAPTER ONE: BEX

My head is going to explode.
It's official.

I am going to die from an explosion of the brain. Lying in bed, I curse the concoction of alcohol that flowed down my throat last night. Right now, stars — no, *meteorites* — are flying around my skull, crashing into and destroying any brain cells they connect with. Keeping my eyes screwed shut, terrified of the light, the sun beats through the window onto my face. Obviously, I was too drunk to even close the blinds.

Mustering enough courage to open one eye, I snap it shut. Perhaps the other one will be less agonising. No, it feels like someone is stabbing at my eye sockets with a toothpick. Eventually, both eyes open. The ceiling is swirling out of control. My stomach retches.

Another Sunday morning lost to the demon drink. Another weekend ruined.

I moved in two years ago. Nothing has changed. Creating my own home isn't important. Nothing here reflects my personality apart from being unloved. Seventies styling from when the previous owner modernised it all those years ago decorates the walls. The retro flooring running throughout is old and worn. I tell myself this makes the apartment look lived-in, but in reality, it just looks dilapidated. This place can make you feel drunk even when you're sober.

A familiar dread creeps through the alcohol fog. What happened last night? What did I say? More importantly, what did I do? Reaching across to retrieve my phone, I baulk waiting for the evidence of last night's embarrassing antics. It wouldn't be a Sunday morning without a social media tag for a humiliating moment.

Typically, my morning-after newsfeed is littered with photos and comments, evidence of my drunken shenanigans. This would be perfectly normal, even acceptable, for a student or someone in the process of *finding themselves*. But for a thirty-three-year-old Director of English at the prestigious Hilltop Manor Academy, not so much.

Things have become so bad that I'm using an alias on my social media accounts, unfriending and blocking anyone with a link to the school. I considered removing my internet presence, but then monitoring any negativity would be impossible. It would not be the first time I have tracked someone down, appeared at their door, and begged them to remove embarrassing footage.

I lie back on my pillow and hit the familiar blue app. Nothing. Not one photo or notification. My mind tries to recall the previous evening.

We arrived at our local tavern, The Smoking Goat—our usual Saturday night haunt. The first few drinks went down too easy. I could murder for a vodka and coke right now. But after we moved on to shots, it all went fuzzy. Nope, nothing. I shake my head to try to clear the fog. What happened? How did I get home? Why the fuck is there nothing on my socials?

I *always* get a group picture.

I *always* post it.

I click onto my best friend and long-suffering sister's page. Amy is my rock. No matter how embarrassing I become, no matter how loud, how unbearable, she scoops me up and takes me home. Her page is empty; she was definitely there last night. I vaguely recall her shrugging her shoulders at me. No doubt I asked the same question I've asked her ten times before.

As Amy's page is giving me no clues, I jump over to Kelsey's. Saturday night is always spent with the same people. We drink, dance, fall, and ultimately, vomit together. Squinting at the screen, her page looks different. I can only see limited information and her profile picture: an old photo of her and her late mother sitting out the back door drinking tea. I smile at the sweet memory. Scanning the page, I try to make sense of it. A new button has appeared that wasn't there before. Add friend? She must have unfriended me as a prank. I smart at the cheek of her. Bitch! Add friend, my arse. She can add me.

Half-cocked, I flick through the photos on my phone, in search of answers. I find nothing useful. There are a few from early on last night, the usual posed group photos. Nothing out of the ordinary.

At the top of my page, the message box is blinking with one notification. I perk up. I love getting messages; it massages my ego. On the other hand, if someone doesn't respond to a message promptly, I panic. In ten seconds, I can convince myself they hate me, I've offended them, and I will die alone. The scenario plays out in front of me, and I recoil. Beating myself up is my favourite hobby.

The message pops up on the screen. It's Terry. We've been friends for years; he would've been there last night. My face falls on reading the first line.

Bex, where are you?

Confused, I read on.

You disappeared with him. Please come back. Don't do this to us. To our friends. You are being completely selfish.

My heart starts to race, and blood rushes through my ears. Screwing my eyes shut, I try to remember what the hell happened last night. Nope, nothing.

What I can't remember, my mind makes up. Never truly knowing what is real. I remember being in the bar. We were all there. Kelsey, Amy, Ben, Terry, and myself. Singing karaoke, I think. The boys were downing pints, and the girls, apart from Kelsey, were on the wine.

Kelsey and Ben don't get out much, having two little ones and another on the way. When they go out, Ben goes big. The shots arrived . . . then nothing. I race through my memories: drinks, crisps, laughing, falling over. Pulling back my sheet reveals a purple bruise on my thigh. I fell again.

Fuck, what if I was drugged?

Every Sunday morning, I play the same game. What did I do last night? Then I try to convince myself my sinful behaviour was someone else's fault. The answer normally lies in my newsfeed.

My brain starts to go over the evidence. Waking up to concerned messages and no social media posts means I have done something bad.

Really bad.

My head continues to pound. I need paracetamol. Lots of paracetamol. Bracing myself, I swing my legs out of bed and sit on the edge. The room spins. I swear the teddy my parents gave me for my eighteenth birthday is waving at me, his beady little eyes judging. That bloody bear is always taunting me.

Perhaps sitting up was not the best idea.

I'm debating whether standing up would be a near-death experience when a noise draws my attention to the other side of the bed. The sound is deep and throaty. Whilst I'm praying I'm imagining it, the groan sounds again, and my eyes widen.

Who is in my bed? Rubbing my eyes to clear away remnants of sleep, I hope he might disappear, a figment of my imagination.

He doesn't.

A beautiful man is lying there — dead to the world — in my bed.

His back is to me, and his dark hair is messed up over the

pillow. He wears it long. Not long enough to tie it back, but in a cool, relaxed look. Recognition washes over me. Not again. I put my head in my hands. Will I never learn?

My eyes move down the lean, muscular back. My breathing rises, and my heart tightens. I had promised myself I would not go back there. The last time was the final fling. My body shakes with panic. It happened again.

I have no self-control.

The sheet is pooled across his trim waist. Memories of him on top of me flash before my eyes, my greedy hands running down that taut, toned body, pulling him down onto the mattress with me. With guilt-filled eyes, I see his tattoo, a band around his upper arm. It's a Celtic design that twists and turns — it's a hundred percent recognisable. The name it incorporates, I know well. She's a person I used to consider a close friend. A name loved by everyone, a name seen to never hurt a soul. Wholesome, honest, and trusting. A person who should be cherished, not cheated on.

He starts to fidget and reposition himself, attempting to get comfortable on the mattress. He flips over powerfully to face me, the strong body I am so familiar with on full display.

He is the most beautiful man I have ever seen; no one has ever come close.

Toned stomach muscles continue down from a broad chest that is smattered with dark hair. His happy trail leads to a place I have worshipped and yearned for.

Bright-blue eyes open sleepily, flying open when they see me. Shock changes to anger then fury as he realises where he is, who he is lying next to.

"Fuck, Bex, what happened? How did I get here? Did we fuck? Not again!"

Jumping out of the bed, wrapping the duvet around his waist in a feeble attempt to keep his dignity, he runs around the room, hauling discarded clothing into his arms. As he spins to face me, my heart sinks and tears burst to the surface. The dam is breaking and flowing free like so many times before.

His icy eyes lock onto mine, fixing me to the spot, his voice cold and dispassionate.

"Bex! Bloody answer me. What did we do?"

I drop my head in shame.

"Bex! Fucking tell me we didn't!"

I shrug my shoulders, my emotions all over the place. What I want to say is "Of course we fucked, you absolute tool!"

But I can never bring myself to upset him.

I love him.

Any time with him is precious. Even though it cuts me to the bone that he regrets it and discards me like a used condom.

"How the fuck could you let this happen again?" he shouts.

Dr Benjamin Jones throws open my bedroom door and storms out of my apartment into the morning air, never to be seen again.

I crawl back under the covers and let the alcohol-induced tiredness engulf me as I drift back into a restless sleep.

I'll deal with it tomorrow.

CHAPTER TWO: BEX

Monday morning again.

Trying to piece together my recollections of Saturday night, I've failed miserably. My memories of sex with Ben could be from a previous encounter. No one is speaking to me, including Amy. My sister wouldn't ghost me without good reason. Judging by the limited communication, I have a very public reason to be ashamed.

Standing at the bathroom mirror, I screw my eyes shut in a pathetic attempt to clear my mind. I can't change the past, only deal with the consequences. This mantra is close to my heart, and regularly used as an excuse for my terrible behaviour.

Every day, my routine to get ready for work is the same. Leaving without following the steps means my day will suck.

Brushing my teeth violently, trying to remove the bad taste lingering in my mouth, I spit viciously into the sink. The water turns red. My gums always bleed after a heavy weekend.

I need to sort myself out.

Looking in my wardrobe, I run my tongue over my teeth, considering my options. Today, armour is required. I have a job to do, and I need to feel invincible while doing it.

Being an English teacher is in my blood. Taking on the directorship was daunting, but I have grabbed the challenge by the balls.

I am proud of myself.

I may not be able to handle my drink, but I can fucking handle my job.

My platinum-blonde curls are piled high on my head, my eyes dark in stark comparison to my pale-pink lips. The grey power suit clings to my curves, finishing just above my knees, making the most of my assets. My heels are high and classic black.

Today, I look like a woman in control. If only I felt the same.

The weekend has rattled me.

In looks, I am about average, probably scoring a good six out of ten. I make the most of what God gave me, but overall it's a little disappointing.

I don't hate my appearance.

I don't love it either.

My shape is a textbook pear. Boobs too small compared to my voluptuous butt, clear skin which doesn't tan, and tall for a woman. Plus, I carry a few extra pounds. My long, strong nose gives me a masculine look, but this is softened by my soft chestnut-brown eyes.

I am one of those girls who looks soft and feminine from the back, but when I turn to face someone, people are surprised by my coarse features. Applying another coat of lip gloss to ensure my mouth looks as ladylike as possible, I grab my briefcase and head out.

Hilltop Manor Academy sits proudly on the green outside Heathersedge village near London. The building is antique, almost four hundred years old. Each brick was placed with attention and care. Every time I drive up the long, winding entrance road edged with rosebushes, my mind wanders to days gone by.

What this building must have witnessed over the centuries. Lords and Ladies courting on the front lawn, horse-drawn carriages arriving for private functions. Perhaps a great deal of scandal, too. Smiling, I picture myself as a Lady, waiting patiently on the lawn for her Lord to appear.

I'm a hopeless romantic, waiting on my knight in shining armour to save the day. The devil on my shoulder chooses this moment to point out that being a dirty whore is not going to help snare my knight. I hiss at her to piss off, this is *my* fantasy.

She can go ruin someone else's dream.

Snapping back to the present, I swing my little sports car into my space. It's a highlight of my day. If a teacher is considered important enough to require a parking space with their name on it, they have made it.

RESERVED – Miss Rebecca Corrigan – Director of English

The solid brass plaque sits proudly on its wooden stake, telling the world a teacher with clout parks here. A teacher who can't be delayed while cursing every twat for parking like a cockwomble. I must consider resubmitting my proposal for fining poorly parked members of staff. That would stop the idiots in their tracks.

Hilltop Manor Academy opened in 1920 as an all-girls boarding school. Times have moved on, but the old principles remain. Girls must be dressed demurely in the official uniform and always maintain the ambitious standards of the school. Teachers are expected to maintain this ethos. Any misbehaviour which could bring the school under scrutiny is considered a sackable offence.

I stand at the bottom of the stairs and smile up at the grand old building. Built from bricks made in the past, it's still serving the community now. It doesn't matter how many times I come here; this old building engulfs me.

The heavy wooden door creaks open, aged with time. Rows of old-fashioned wooden desks and chairs—the kind where you lift the lid and store your stationery inside—fill my classroom. Most have their own unique sound. This is not only charming but handy when students try to hide mobile phones or other contraband. I asked for this style of furniture to be kept in my classroom. The old-world style encourages creativity and expansion of the mind. Pupils need to fall head-first into an ancient world of dreams and desire, absorb the words of Austin and Brontë in surroundings that cuddle them with warmth and love. For me, modern, sleek alternatives have no soul to draw on for inspiration.

I love my classroom.

Long green curtains frame the huge bay windows that face the school grounds. It's a chilly summer morning. The log burner is already stoked, crackling away in the corner of the room. I walk over to my traditional blackboard proud on the wall. It spins around on the roller, making a fantastic squeal as it does. Other classrooms were upgraded to modern smart screens. I prefer the feel of chalk between my fingers. It's infuriating when it breaks mid-sentence, but the fragrant smell under my fingernails is divine. I feel like a teacher.

I do not feel digital; I feel real.

Standing at the old window, I watch the ocean of burgundy and gold. Girls run around, enjoying the morning sunshine. They look like something from an era long gone in their long burgundy skirts worn with white shirts and striped ties embellished with the Hilltop Manor crest. Traditional burgundy blazers trimmed in gold, all topped off with a matching boater.

Hilltop Manor Academy not only demands high aesthetic standards, but student results must match the image presented by the school. Parents do not pay £20,000 per year for their beloved child to be a down and out. My class grades are exemplary. I always have students receiving grades in the top five per cent of the United Kingdom's league tables.

Being Director means I don't have as much teaching time, but it allows me to oversee more girls. I have some influence, no matter how small, on the outcome of their education. If I can make a positive impact, my job is done. My team is encouraged to teach English as a subject to be loved, a subject to get lost in and enjoy. Above my desk, a poster with a positive affirmation is displayed proudly.

Learning opens the doors to a life worth living.

My mind returns to the phrase down and out, automatically thinking of Terry, my much-loved friend. He's fiercely loyal, always happy, but never achieves more than an extra parking ticket or final warning at whatever job he has. He messaged me yesterday, concerned. I've not replied yet, not wanting to hear the lecture he will be preparing for me. The last thing I need today is Terry and his advice. At least my life has a clear purpose.

To teach, to lead, to encourage.

The electronic bell rings throughout the school grounds—a modern sound in an old situation. Twenty giggling teenagers burst through my classroom door. Now we begin our journey into the world of English Literature.

I smile at the young, creative minds surrounding me. At this age, they are filled with hope of what life has to offer. It makes me smile.

The world is wide open to them.

We have enjoyed our meandering journey through *The Prime of Miss Jean Brodie* by Muriel Spark. I love this novel, recognising myself in the lead character. Our discussion is volatile, the girls are passionate in their debate. Some loved the novel, while others found it tedious. The ability of books to create controversy amazes me. Two people can read the same piece but develop completely different views. All are valid. It makes for an interesting hour of teaching.

Lost in my thoughts, I notice one of my quieter pupils is sitting and staring into space. The rest of the class has packed their belongings and are skipping out the door to put Mr Wise, the physics professor, through the wringer before break time.

Waiting until the class departs, I settle myself next to my wordless pupil. Sometimes girls, especially teenage girls, need time. I still need time to zone out with my thoughts, recollect myself, and move forward. We sit in silence for a few minutes, contemplating each other's next move.

Sad eyes turn to me.

"I just can't do it anymore, Miss," she says, shaking her head and dropping her shoulders. "It's all too much."

"How can I support you, Amelia?" I ask after considering my words, using a softness in my voice I'm usually too animated to maintain. "What is worrying you so terribly?" Speaking softly is something I struggle with due to my strong Birmingham accent. It doesn't matter how physically refined I become; the roughness of my accent will not disappear.

Standing, she quickly throws her belongings into her bag and turns for the door, eyes wide. She thinks she's said too much, reasoning bringing her weakness into view will be her undoing.

"Amelia," I say calmly, "you are not invincible, and you are not expected to be." I smile. "When you need me, I am here."

She turns and scurries from the room to her next anxiety-filled lesson. Amelia Jane first came to my attention last summer. She was a bright, outgoing girl. Top of every class and loved by her peers. Over the past twelve months, with her moving into year ten, exams have become a reality, and she has fallen into a state of fear. She's frozen by her dread of failure. I tried to talk to her parents about my concerns a few weeks ago only to be fobbed off with an excuse that she was just being a drama queen. Amelia is on my radar. I will do everything in my power to support her in these trying times.

Finally, my favourite part of the day arrives: lunch! Unlike most schools, our cafeteria is stocked with freshly made meals and quality treats. I can have a bistro standard meal any day of the week. Our dinner ladies wear a smile, taking pride in their daily duties. They are integral to our success here at

Hilltop Manor Academy. Well-fed brains create successful students.

I love sitting with my colleagues, hearing about the antics of family life or supporting any challenges they may be facing.

Being a small team with few pupils and high enrolment costs means we have a lot of disposable income, giving us the enviable position of being able to treat our pupils to educational trips away and stock the classrooms full of equipment.

I grab my soup and sandwich.

"Popped an extra slice of ham on your sandwich, Miss Corrigan." Hazel smiles.

I blow her a kiss in gratitude. She is one of the most nurturing people I know. Hazel is big and cuddly with greying, tightly permed hair and a wide mouth that lends itself to putting people at ease with kind words.

The teacher's table is full. There is a lot of chatter which is increasing in volume as the minutes pass. Mrs Wendy Carter, my fellow English teacher, is talking animatedly.

"Well, I heard the principal on the phone talking to someone. I can only assume it was the police. They were discussing inappropriate conduct." She lifts her eyebrows to accentuate her statement.

My eyes meet hers, my ears tuning into the conversation around me. Wendy is always a reliable source of gossip; I half-suspect she is sucking Principal Fraser's dick for the information. She carries on excitedly.

"Well, it sounds as if someone is going to get their balls booted!"

A beaming smile covers her face. Her hair is black, short, and spiked. She is waif-like with the features of a pixie. A bad-tempered pixie, I giggle to myself.

Bitch! I hate those people who glow at someone else's bad fortune. If I had a voodoo doll, I would call it Wendy and stab the cow through the eye. But I do not believe in that shit, so I zone her out and return to my double ham sandwich.

"I hope this gossip you are spreading, Mrs Carter, is not classified information."

All eyes turn to my favourite colleague. Max Gordon's booming voice vibrates around the dining hall. I smirk as Wendy's hackles rise. Max has the uncanny ability to project humour into any situation. A class clown who takes no shit, he is tall and broad with a strong nose and a sharp tongue.

My heart lifts and falls every time Max enters a room. I adore him. My feelings toward him are platonic. I have tried to make them more. It's not happening.

"Hello, gorgeous!" He snuggles in beside me, kissing my cheek. I know he wants more, and a pang of familiar guilt hits me. He's a beautiful specimen of a man. Strong hands with fingers that I know can bring a woman to the edge easily, but my body will not respond.

My heart lies with another.

"Hello, darling," I whisper in his ear. "How has your morning been?" We drop into a relaxed conversation about this morning's events.

Wendy's voice grates on me while still banging on about an illicit incident occurring.

"What are your thoughts on this, Bex?" A smile touches her lips then disappears. I'm surprised by the direct question; Wendy never speaks to me if she can avoid it. Since my promotion three months ago, she has ignored me. We used to be close. Ten years older than me, she was a massive support when I was a newly graduated teacher, helping me find my feet and nurturing my confidence both inside and outside the classroom.

I'm careful what I say to her. She has this ability to twist any response into criticism and take offence.

"I have every confidence that the correct procedures will

be followed, Mrs Carter, and the best outcome achieved," I say flawlessly. Wendy's frenemy relationship makes me feel uneasy.

"Yes, dear, I'm sure they will." She grins and winks to intensify her point.

A cold shiver runs down my spine.

What the fuck does that mean?

Max taps me on the shoulder again to restart our conversation, I smile gratefully at him. He understands things have not been easy. Being the youngest ever director of a subject in the school's one-hundred-year history has come with a huge helping of the green-eyed monster.

"So, gorgeous. How was your weekend?" he asks.

Having spent years in southern Spain, Max is a linguist — well, in Spanish and English — and he finds it remarkably successful in bedding the birds. His words, not mine.

I roll my eyes. "I don't remember." I cringe, and my cheeks flush red.

His good humour vanishes, replaced with anger. "For fuck's sake, Bex! You can't keep going out and getting gassed. It's going to catch up with you!" he hisses at me under his breath. "I worry about you when you get into that state. You're never in control and could end up anywhere."

I pale slightly at his words. It's true. Alcohol is dangerous for me; I'm regularly having blackouts. But I won't be admitting that to this jacked-up hypocrite! Giving him my best glare, I shoot back, "You concentrate on your fucking geography books and sluts, and I will worry about me." Standing to leave, I spit out, "You are not my fucking boyfriend, so do not cast your opinions on my life!" Visibly stung, he recoils, and I storm off in the direction of my classroom.

Prick!

The day has been good if you ignore the argument at lunchtime.

The final minutes tick down on the old school clock. The girls have been dismissed, and I sit down at my desk to wrap up for the day. My computer pings softly to alert me to a new message on the school's inter-message system. Briefly, I consider ignoring it.

The message pops up on my laptop screen.

Principal Fraser sent you a message at 16:40.

Miss Rebecca Corrigan,

You are summoned to attend an investigative meeting with Principal John Fraser on Tuesday the 12th of May at 9 a.m. Your classes have been allocated to a substitute teacher for the duration of the day. Please bring with you your ongoing professional development folder and school identification cards.

Regards,

Cynthia Smith (PA to Principal Fraser, Hilltop Manor Academy)

My head spins, my heart drops, and a sense of dread engulfs me.

This can't be good.

CHAPTER THREE: BEN

Being a high-profile oncology consultant is a high-pressure job. Living with stress is something I've become accustomed to in my day-to-day life. Today's stress, however, is not due to a patient with an inoperable tumour. My stress levels are through the roof, and it's my own fucking fault.

Sitting at my wide mahogany desk, drowning in patient files, I let my hands cradle my head as I rerun Saturday night. My slightly-too-long hair flops over my forehead.

"I need a fucking haircut," I grumble to myself. Even my hair is pissing me off today.

We were all having a few drinks at The Smoking Goat as we sometimes do at weekends. The banter was high, and the drinks were strong. My wife, Kelsey, kissed my cheek before she headed for home, leaving me to continue enjoying the fun. I should have gone home. I should have put my family before my social life.

Waking up in *her* bed again sends a shiver of shame through my body. A few drinks and a sexy song, and my dick falls into Bex Corrigan's vagina or ass, whichever she offers. Her beauty is unique. She's not beautiful, but with wide hips and a round backside that sits on top of long, slender legs, I'm crazy about her. An image of her bent over the edge of the bed pops into my mind. I'm riding her hard. My whole length is engorged within her tight, creamy cunt. She squeezes, almost breaking me in two, and I feel her juices flow down my balls.

Her face is strong; she has a look that says *don't fuck with me*. On Saturday night, she was wearing a skin-tight red dress

17

with a neckline that cascaded down to her breasts. I remember my tongue running over her erect nipples. Her nipples so large, they are almost too big. My cock hardens. Bex Corrigan is my Achilles heel, an on-off affair for over a decade, physically and emotionally. We don't discuss it. It doesn't happen often. A few times, we have gotten drunk and ended up in bed.

I had promised myself that last time was the last hurrah, but alcohol-induced insanity had taken over on Saturday night. My wife was at home, tucked up in my bed, while I had ridden that vixen rotten in her dingy little flat. The iron bed had rattled off the walls and I enjoyed every damn stroke.

A strong rap at my door surprises me. My esteemed colleague and friend, Dr Eamon Reynolds, enters my office in his usual happy manner. He's a short man, stout with a rotund belly that hangs over his suit trousers. His green eyes are bright with mischief as he scans my office for any havoc he can create.

"Well done, Jones! Sexiest Doctor Award! Really thought I had it this year." He gestures with his free hand at the award on my desk; his other is clutching a takeaway coffee and doughnut. My eyes move to the award perched precariously on the edge. It is in the shape of a stethoscope wrapping around a heart inscribed with *Sexiest Doctor awarded to Doctor Benjamin Jones for giving us all something to look at.* My nursing team presented it to me during my rounds this morning.

"Did you have to fuck that witch, Staff Nurse Neilson, to win it?" Eamon raises his eyebrows and waggles them playfully. He wears a broad smile that can't be seen because of a huge moustache overhanging his top lip. All his hair is on his face, not the top of his head.

I shrug and declare, "What the fuck can I say? Sometimes we have to take one for the team."

He erupts in a bellow of laughter.

On more than one occasion, Eamon came to my rescue with the voracious nursing staff. He was my mentor and allowed me no extra leeway for sexy smiles. He rode me hard and manhandled me into the oncologist I am today. Without him, I would probably be wrapped up in an orgy of nursing graduates at Flat 5B

Now we are on the same team, heading up the specialist oncology unit at Royal London Hospital. For many of our patients, we are their last resort—their last chance at continuing in life. When you deal every day with people who are facing death, it gives you a different perspective on life. I tend to live in the moment and grab opportunities with both hands. The safe option just doesn't seem so appealing.

Eamon throws a cheese sandwich wrapped in foil at my head, turns on his heel, and waddles off out the door. Pulling back the foil, I see a note. His wife, Melissa, is a wonderful woman. She is loyal, loving, and worships the ground her husband walks on. She's of similar stature to her good man with bulbous features, giving her a homely look with her greying hair. They match perfectly. Slipping the note from its hiding place, I read it.

To our darling Ben and your beautiful family, we would love it if you could all join us for Sunday Lunch.

My stomach growls hungrily at the thought of Aunty Mel's roast dinners, and the day starts to look better.

Pulling to a stop outside our tranquil home, my girl purrs underneath me. I love this car. She was a gift to myself after my promotion within the oncology department. With her I feel powerful and successful. My focus drops to the luxurious leather, taking time to appreciate the slick surfaces surrounding me. Slung low, her sleek curves wrap around you as you travel. She's impressive, filling the eye with her long body and elongated nose. People notice her. People stare.

I came to the sad conclusion that my car is yet another woman in my life. Another person I would rather be spending time with instead of my wife. My gaze flicks toward our little cottage. I know Kelsey will be waiting for me.

She always is.

Our little white house sits in a traditional English garden full of rosebushes and peonies. The thatched roof looks like something out of a fairy tale. When we first moved in, I expected a talking rabbit to pop his head in the door and welcome us to the area. We live on the edge of a small village, about one hour's drive from London on a good day. It's a typical English village surrounded by rolling fields. It comes complete with a village green, a small school, a corner shop, and a customary English pub. A family trip for the Sunday roast at The Stag & Rabbit is one of my favourite pastimes. The children can play on the soft green grass while we sit at picnic tables and enjoy the delicious food.

I continue to waste time in the car, picking things up, putting them down, rearranging crap, and dusting away invisible specks. Kelsey will be there with dinner on the table and two small children at her feet. The children are our world. Kelsey is my partner, but I am struggling to settle.

From the outside, my life looks damn near perfect. I have a beautiful family, a good job, and a safe home. But I have a nagging suspicion I've done something wrong. A nagging suspicion that won't go away, that I've made a wrong turn in life. I'm always attracted to the naughty, the bad, the erotic. I seem to get my shit together, then I fuck it up again.

The wonderful woman by my side is not deserved. I know that. She doesn't know the man she's married to. The man who bounces from her bed to another. It's not every week, it's not every month, but it has happened multiple times over the years. And it's wrong.

I rub the back of my neck to release the tension building up my spine. It spreads up my back like fire. This always happens when I've had one of those nights. When I've overstepped the mark. When I've ended up back in Bex's bed. My body punishes me with pain for the ecstasy I've enjoyed.

Not able to put off the inevitable any longer, I swing open the car door and grab my leather briefcase embossed with my name. A gift from my wife. Making my way up the quaint little path and through the sage-green front door, I could not walk any slower if I tried. My world has turned to slow motion since pulling up outside.

Uncertainty of what I'm entering stirs in my chest. I'm nervous. I've never been so brazen in my actions before Saturday.

Kicking off my shoes, I place them in the carved wooden box at the door marked *shoes,* then hang up my work jacket on the wooden peg marked *Daddy's Jacket.* The children are playing, chattering between them. The house sounds peaceful. I wonder how long that will last.

For all our home looks traditional from the road, we have spent a small fortune upgrading and modernising the living space. The large space is edged in gloss cream cabinets topped with a sleek black marble. Every modern kitchen appliance known to man is in this kitchen. Not that I use them. But when Kelsey agreed to become a stay-at-home parent so I could continue my career, this was the payoff.

Kelsey fills the role of housewife and mother amazingly. There are always fresh meals on the table and clean clothes in the wardrobe. The children are played with and loved. Our family is a happy one. I perplex myself as to why I continue to risk the ultimate dream for a cheap one-night stand.

Huge roof windows allow light to flow into the room. It has an expensive but lived-in feel, and there are a few children's toys scattered around the floor. They have been playing with cars while Mummy prepares the evening meal. Fresh flowers of pinks and whites are on the dining room table. Kelsey loves flowers and creates all her own arrangements. Our house is usually decorated with at least five displays at any time.

She is standing with her back to me at the kitchen island, tossing a salad while she keeps watch over our two cherubs. Her chestnut curls roll down her back as her hair flows free. She's wearing a soft white summer dress with thin straps. It's loose, just skimming the curves of her body. When she turns to see me, her face lights up with a rosy glow, and soft hazel eyes lock on mine. Her belly is swollen through the soft material, six months gone with number three. A boy this time, we hope, as we have our two beautiful girls already. My heart swells in appreciation. I do love this woman. We have been together since we were teenagers, except for a break in our twenties.

"You're home, darling," she squeaks and runs forward, throwing her hands around my neck. I drop a soft kiss onto her pink lips. "How was your day?" She smiles.

Kelsey always asks about my day, always interested. I am a lucky man to be so respected and loved by my wife.

"It was a quiet one, honey. I was mostly in the office. I had a few consultations." A sense of sadness fills me. She realises and hugs me a bit tighter.

"Tell me when you're ready, sweetheart. I know some days can be tough, and today seems to have been one of those days," she says.

This woman astounds me. Her understanding is breathtaking. She knows when I've had a bad day, when I need to talk, and when I need to be left alone with my thoughts.

I squeeze her tight. "I do love you, Kels. You know that," I whisper in her ear. "Forget about me. How is my perfect wife today? Have you been resting enough? Have you eaten?" I question her softly.

During her first two pregnancies, Kelsey did not take good enough care of herself, always running around after everyone else. She can be quite dramatic in anxious situations, and it always concerns me if she isn't resting enough.

During her seventh month with our second, Rose, she ended up in the hospital overnight, dehydrated, and exhausted. Being so busy looking after the house, caring for our eldest, Savannah, and baking for a local charity bake sale, she had completely forgotten to eat. My temper rises at the memory. I had been furious with her for risking our little family by not taking care of herself.

Hypocrite! I bark at myself internally. *What you're doing is a lot worse.*

My mind flicks back to that phone call I'd received from Eamon: "Don't panic, Jones. But Kelsey is in the maternity ward. She's ok, but she's tired."

The terror and fear that had coursed through my body had been palpable. I had sprinted from the oncology ward through A&E across the cafeteria to maternity, retelling the situation to colleagues on my radio as I went. I'm surprised no one from the mental health team popped by to check out the crazed Doctor Jones in the days after.

She rolls her eyes and lifts them to the heavens.

"Don't you roll your eyes at me, Mrs Jones," I whisper darkly. "You know what that does to me?"

She frowns, shakes it off and acts as if I said nothing. I kick myself. She hates any kind of dirty talk or anything remotely dirty at all. Our sex life is very vanilla. A means to an end, as it were. Enjoyable, but not explosive or abundant.

"Dinner's ready," she calls. Savannah and Rose come scrambling through from the conservatory. They are the apple of my eye. Both under five, but Savannah will be off to school after summer.

"Daddy! Daddy! Dinner time!" they shout.

I smile at their enthusiasm for such a basic part of the day. They are the spitting image of each other. Both have baby-blonde messy curls that seem to go everywhere but where they are meant to. Their mother is always trying to tame their manes. As I laugh to myself, my wife raises an eyebrow in question, and I rub my hands over my hair to mess it up in answer. She smiles lovingly at our daughters.

Four bright-blue eyes look up expectantly at me over sweet button noses. I lift them both into my arms and swing them around. My girls squeal with delight as I carry them toward the dining table.

The long wooden table is laid with our ornate cream crockery and a feast of chicken cacciatore is spread out before me. The smell of homemade bread lingers in the air. I spot a freshly made strawberry cheesecake waiting on the worktop for after. No doubt Kels will have picked the berries fresh from her kitchen garden this morning. So much love has gone into making this meal for us, and it's only Monday night. My heart sinks as my guilt surfaces. Perhaps my brain is wrongly wired somehow.

The four of us sit as a family around the table, stuffing our faces and chatting idly. The girls keep us entertained with their eating habits; one is as bad as the other. No items can touch each other on their plates, and everything must be eaten in a certain order. Heaven forbid there is a sauce; this would cause World War Three in our home, as full-plate decontamination would be required. Two little mouths chew vigorously at whatever they have chosen to put in there.

"Well done, girls." I beam at them. "Keep up the good work, and I think Mummy has pudding for you!" I raise one finger across my lips as if this bit of information is a secret. They burst into fits of giggles and excitedly stuff more food in their mouths. I feel my wife's eyes on me; glancing over, I see a sadness that isn't normally there. My heart constricts; she knows, or at least suspects, all is not well. I move my focus back to my plate and then to her again. The sadness is gone, replaced by the soft, loving look she gets when I interact with the children.

As Kels has the children all day, bedtime tends to be my duty. I scoop my two little cherubs up, and we walk hand in hand up the wide staircase to the bedrooms. You would never know this cottage had an upstairs until you walk around the back. We extended into the loft space and replaced that with a glass box extension to maximise the space. By the time I've bathed them, brushed their teeth, looked for missing socks, read three bedtime stories, and found Mr Bugsy the stuffed rabbit, the girls are fast asleep. Looking at them, lost in childish dreams of unicorns and fluffy clouds, I think, how can I risk it? This perfect family.

After changing into my soft check pyjama bottoms, I wander downstairs. Kelsey looks up from her iPad at my bare-chested appearance and then returns to her reading. She's wearing a cotton pyjama set. It has baby-pink shorts that finish just above her knee with a slogan T-shirt that reads *Mummy is my favourite person*.

This is as sexy as Kels' nightwear gets. I consider myself lucky when she has shorts on and not trousers. I smile sexily at her, wink, and hold out my hand for her to come with me.

"What?" she asks, wrinkling her nose.

"Come with me. Please, Kels," I plead.

She sighs and wanders over to me.

"Let me give you a massage," I cajole her. She wants to say no. She would rather spend the time with her iPad. Conceding, she follows me down the hall to our bedroom.

Our bed is huge. I had to get the downstairs windows taken out just to get the base in. It has a strong wooden frame with four posts draped in white organza. The whole room is swathes of white linen with heavy wooden furniture. We spared no expense in this room. I wanted it to be our haven, a place my wife and I could enjoy.

Having already set up the room, with a throw to protect

the spotless sheets and a bottle of aromatherapy oil on the bedside, I slowly strip her out of her mummy pyjamas. I go to remove her panties, beginning to slide them down her legs, but she freezes. My heart drops, and I leave them in place. I motion for her to lie on her side; she's too big now to lie on her stomach.

"Close your eyes, honey," I suggest, rubbing the oil between my hands to warm it. As I start at her shoulders, massaging the oil into her skin, she visibly relaxes underneath my touch. My cock hardens in arousal as I run my hands over her body. My wife is a stunning woman, all big brown doe eyes, soft curls, and womanly curves. I love the softness of her and the innocent side of her personality. Sometimes, I think Kels hasn't developed beyond our innocent teenage romance, swinging from a loved-up teenager to a drama queen.

I work on her body gently, starting in the safe zones away from her breasts and sex. From experience, if I go straight to getting down and dirty, she will clam up and shut me out. After caressing her back along her spine, my hands move sideways until I can run my fingers over her breasts. She doesn't reject the touch, so I continue and get into bed behind her so we can spoon, wrapping my arms around her, which gives me access to her erect nipples. Laying my chin on her shoulder and slowly caressing each nipple between my fingers, I hear her breathing start to quicken. My body responds eagerly, and I struggle to contain myself. What I really want to do is pull her to the edge of the bed on her knees, ass in the air, and fuck her hard. Sex with Kels doesn't work like that. If I ever become too eager, she shuts down and won't let me in. On numerous occasions, our sex session has ended with me in our downstairs bathroom jerking off to dirty porn on my phone.

But tonight, she is responding positively to my touch. My confidence rises, and I run one hand lightly down her stomach. It is large, swollen with my precious cargo inside. She is so damned sexy. This wonderful woman has given me two beautiful children with a third on the way. My fingers arrive at her clitoris. I hesitate. This tends to be the make-or-break point in our lovemaking. With Kels, it is always making love. We never fuck, and bloody hell, I wish we would. Inserting one finger through her swollen lips confirms she's wet. My heart rate quickens as I pump in and out. Her lips part, and a small moan escapes. My second finger starts to work and stretch her wide in preparation for my cock. I lean across to kiss her gently.

"Get on top of me, baby" I whisper. "Kels, I need you."

I lie back on my pillow, and she moves the sheets off my body, exposing my hard cock, ready for her. My balls are throbbing, waiting for her to take me, to give me the release so desperately needed. She straddles me cautiously and lines herself up to my length. Nerves dance in her eyes, mixed with arousal. Laying my hands gently on her hips, I help lower her down onto me.

Fuck, she's tight and wet. This is what my wet dreams are made of. I close my eyes to enjoy the sensation of her going deeper, millimetre by millimetre, wiggling her hips to let me in. Then I'm balls deep in this beautiful pregnant woman. She feels familiar and safe. Holding her, I encourage her to move. She pumps me slowly. Her breasts are full, and her nipples are dark now in the later stages of pregnancy. It's so fucking hot. My hands become a bit more forceful to encourage more movement, but she stills, and I release my grip, knowing I must let her move at her own pace. She falls into her regular rhythm to bring me to my orgasm with love and care.

We lie together in the dark. Kels has drifted off into a deep sleep, relaxed and content. My mind reruns our lovemaking. I'm ashamed to say I feel unfulfilled. As much as I love my wife, our sexual relationship is not satisfying for me. I have no idea what I am going to do about it, but something must change.

Chapter Four: Bex

Tuesday morning arrives and I'm not looking forward to the day ahead. After receiving the summons from Principal Fraser yesterday afternoon, my good humour vanished. The weather outside is like my mood, cold and grey. My evening was spent stressing over what the hell the meeting could be about, alongside necking vast quantities of wine to block out the sheer fear coursing through my body. Deep down, I know something is completely off. Shit is about to happen.

It's 5 a.m. and I'm incredibly hungover. Pulling myself out of bed, I stagger over to the mirror and take in the sight before me. Makeup is running across my face like tram lines, my skin is gaunt with huge black bags under my eyes, and my hair isn't even worth mentioning. I fill my lungs with as much air as I can to take a breath, steeling myself for the day ahead.

A shower. That's what I need. A good long shower will fix everything. Stripping everything off and stepping under the streaming hot water, I can feel myself relax as the water carries away my anxiety for the time being.

One hour later, my hair is styled into a neat bun, and my makeup is natural and elegant. I'm wearing a fitted black dress, plain, simple, and classic. My shoes only sport a small heel. My look is professional and in control. Lifting my briefcase which I have checked three times to ensure it contains the documents I was requested to bring, I square my shoulders, hold my head high, and leave to see what turmoil awaits me.

It's 7:30 a.m. and I'm in my classroom not doing anything,

just passing time until my dreaded meeting with the principal. There is a rattle on my door, and Max pops his head around it with a warm smile on his face.

"Can I come in?" he asks.

My eyes rise to meet his, ready for round two of our argument.

"I'm not here to fight, Bex." He holds his hands up in surrender. It makes me laugh, and I soften immediately.

"Of course, darling, come in." I smile, gesturing to the seat across from me. To be honest, with the way I am feeling, I need all the support I can get. As time marches near to my meeting with the principal, my nerves are rising tenfold.

"Bex, what's going on? I heard your classes have all been subbed today. So, what are you doing here? I just assumed you were on a course or something. Then I saw your light on," he says.

The concern on his face is obvious as he watches me. What does he know?

"You may know better than me," I admit with a shrug. "I received a summons last night for an investigative meeting. I have to take all my documents."

He drops his focus guiltily, then it rises to meet mine.

"Do you know something, Max? You would tell me if you did, wouldn't you?"

He doesn't respond but thinks about his answer as if warring with himself about what to say. I look at him pointedly. He simply rises from his seat, leans in, kisses my cheek, and then leaves the room. Whispering over his shoulder, he adds, "I'm here if you need me."

My heart sinks. This is bad. Really fucking bad.

For the next hour, I wander around my classroom picking things up, dusting them off, and putting them down. My collection of classic novels has been rearranged three times. First in alphabetical order, then in chronological order, and finally, because I don't give a shit anymore, in my fucking favourite order. I glance up at the old clock on the wall. It's 8:50 a.m.—ten minutes to go. I gather my belongings and take a quick look out the window at the gaggle of girls outside playing. Squaring my shoulders, I set off for Principal Fraser's office on the first floor with a sense of dread hanging over me.

The principal's office is in the west wing of the building. It feels like visiting the President of the United States rather than a school principal. To get to the office, you must walk a long corridor lined with doors on either side. This is where all the administration staff work. We call it *The Oval Office,* as most of us never come up here unless it is on important business. I stride along the corridor and hold my head as high as I can to portray false confidence.

Portraits of school principals and key figures of yesteryears hang proudly throughout this part of the school. The ceilings are high and ornate, the decoration stuck in a time long gone. At the end of the corridor, Cynthia, the PA to Principal Fraser, is sitting at her huge wooden desk. It's more like a dining table. Every inch is taken up with paperwork or personal memorabilia. She has a frame with pictures of her kids, various school art projects she's been given, and what looks like hundreds of cheap plastic figures. The whole desk is completely at odds with its traditional and classic surroundings. I smile to myself at the absurdity.

"Good morning, Miss Corrigan." Her sharp voice brings me back to my current situation.

"Good morning, Cynthia." I smile sweetly. "Please call me Bex. I think we know each other well enough now, don't you?"

She glares at me, running her tongue across her bottom lip and sneers, "I want nothing to do with someone like you."

Taken aback by her harsh words, I stammer, "Is he in?"

"Yes, but wait till you're called. Take a seat over there." She points her finger and gestures with her chin toward the waiting area. I turn to go when Principal John Fraser appears from his office.

"Come through, Miss Corrigan," he instructs, and I follow him.

Sitting on a green leather wing-back chair, I survey my surroundings. The space is huge and organised to perfection. A large desk sits in the centre of the room with big leather chairs on either side, one of which I am currently sitting in. Bookcases filled with leather-bound volumes line the walls, and the remaining areas are painted a strong blue and covered with portraits of the previous tenants of this office. There are two chesterfield sofas surrounding a coffee table, obviously meant for relaxation or less official meetings. As I was not directed to take a seat on one of the sofas, I assume that means my meeting is an important one.

Principal Fraser takes his seat opposite me, tenting his fingers in front of him, looking at me with eyes so dark that I'm sure he can see through me.

My resolve begins to waver, and nerves dance in my stomach.

"Good morning, Miss Corrigan," he says, "Do you know why I have called for this meeting?"

The door opens, and Cynthia totters in on heels so high, I've no idea how she walks. She sits herself down at a small side table with her laptop, poised to take notes, looking at me over her broad-rimmed glasses on the end of her nose. Principal Fraser waits patiently for my answer. I open my mouth to respond but nothing comes out. Rubbing my hand across my forehead, my temperature starts to rise. Taking a deep breath, before trying again.

"In all honesty, sir, I don't," I stammer. Clear eyes meet mine, strong and taking no prisoners. He sits back in his chair, getting comfortable, then stretches his arms out in front of himself. He is collecting his thoughts, weighing up the best course of action.

"Would you say you have a problem with alcohol, Miss Corrigan?" he asks simply.

His question stops me dead in my tracks. I was not expecting this. "Well, sir. I enjoy a drink, but no more than the next person, I would say." He eyes me speculatively. "Can I ask why you felt the need to ask such a question?"

"Miss Corrigan, yesterday morning the school was emailed some footage of yourself at The Smoking Goat Tavern on Saturday evening."

My stomach free falls.

"This video shows you in a state of total inebriation, acting carelessly and unprofessionally in the bar." His eyes meet mine. "Quite honestly, what I saw was disgusting and certainly not the kind of behaviour I expect or tolerate from a director, or any staff member, for that matter, at my school."

My world stops, and time freezes. The office starts to swirl around me. He continues to talk, listing all my bad behaviour from the weekend. Devastatingly, he has watched every bit of footage from the bar.

His next words grab my attention. "I was enlightened by your dancing skills, as I believe I saw you gyrating on the lap of a man. A married man, I may add."

Heat engulfs my face, and I feel like a beacon ready to guide a ship in from the sea.

"Miss Corrigan, your personal life is your own until it affects the school, and your behaviour is concerning." He pauses. "But what was the deciding factor on calling this meeting was the footage from outside the bar."

I wince.

Phoning my sister had crossed my mind last night. But she still hasn't spoken to me and I'm being stubborn. If I had, at least what he is talking about would not be a complete surprise to me. Right now, I'm completely in the dark.

"You were filmed by the premise's CCTV on your knees in the back alley, giving a married man a physical act in his private areas with your mouth," he states, deadpan.

I have no words. What can I say? Now I know what Ben and I did on Saturday night.

We ruined my career.

His face softens slightly when he sees the distress in my eyes. "I am sure you can understand, Miss Corrigan, that I must take this information seriously. I try not to encroach on my staff's personal life, but when it becomes known to me, then I must act. I would suggest you take some time to consider your life choices and your extracurricular activities."

He takes a deep breath.

"Therefore, with immediate effect, you are suspended from your post. Please hand in your pass and any sensitive files on your person to Cynthia. There will be a full investigation into your conduct before any further action is taken. Your classroom is empty. Please clear out any personal belongings you require for the time being. You will be paid in full during this time." He stands, and it is obvious the meeting is over. There is nothing to say anyway.

Jumping out of my seat, I bolt for the door, holding back the tears about to fall.

Cynthia gives me a snide smile. "See you later . . . maybe," she calls to my retreating back.

I scurry down the long corridor back to my classroom. The room feels tiny, like all the walls are closing in. I throw what I can get my hands on into a waiting cardboard box. My colleagues knew this was going to happen, someone was trying to be helpful. Or rub it in. I sit behind my desk with my head in my hands and let the tears fall. Being a teacher is the best part of me. It is the area of my life where I feel alive and strong. Desolation washes over me at entering a completely unknown stage, one where I need to get myself sorted out. Back on the straight and narrow. I know in my heart that my time at Hilltop Manor Academy has come to an end.

In my dingy little apartment, I sit in silence, looking around the cramped space and taking in the terrible, dated design. The cardboard box containing my life as a teacher is sitting on the kitchen worktop between the open bottle of wine and a huge bar of chocolate. It's 11 a.m., and I'm on my second glass of Pinot Grigio.

Today is a bad day.

It's mid-afternoon, I think, and I'm on to the next bottle whilst lying on the sofa, watching a celebrity dating show. How pathetic are these people's lives that they need to date on TV to make money? My mind is turning these thoughts over when I recognise I am just as sad and pathetic to be lying here, watching them, due to being caught giving head to a married man at the local bar. Shame is seeping into every bone. I will never get over this. Maybe it would be better if I wasn't here at all.

A knock at my door takes me by surprise. I stagger over, attempting to spy through the peephole. Being two bottles of wine down makes this task a difficult one. Closing one eye, I stare through the hole with the other. My balance is off; I stabilise myself by leaning on the door with my forehead. Max is standing on the other side. His hands are in his pockets, and he is in casual clothes. Is it that time already? Has school finished for the day?

I swing open the door, plastering a huge smile on.

"Max, I take it you're here to check up on the new lady of leisure?" His face drops as he takes in my appearance. "What's wrong?" I snap viciously. "Not like what you see?"

He ignores my outburst and walks past me, leading me back into the apartment and closing the door quietly behind us.

"Bex, I'm really worried about you." His statement is simple, filled with concern, his brows furrowed with worry. "I heard what happened."

Before he can continue his little speech, I cut him off. "Stop! Just stop! I bloody know you heard what happened! You probably knew this morning that I was going to get fired!" I scream irrationally. "Some friend you are, letting me walk into the lion's den. To be shamed by my boss for drunken Saturday night shenanigans. For all I know, you could have been the bastard who sent the fucking footage in!"

On a roll, I continue. "We both know you're a jealous bastard, Max! You hate the fact I love Ben and not you! You hate what we have together!" I storm around my apartment, not knowing where to look. Then I see it, a small glass that I had my morning orange juice in, inscribed with *World's Best Teacher*. I pick it up and hurl it at the wall. It smashes into a thousand pieces.

Max looks at me with so much pity that I almost feel guilty. He walks toward me and puts his hands on my shoulders. His face is sad, so unlike the happy-go-lucky Max, I know and love. He's worried about me. I can see that.

"Bex, I love you. I hate this downward spiral you are determined to take. We have been friends for a long time, and I can't watch you self-destruct." His eyes meet mine. "Ben is not yours. He never has been. You're his booty call. *Irregular* booty call."

My eyes burn with anger, but Max soldiers on. "He has been with Kelsey since he was a boy; they are married with children, for fuck's sake. When will you start having more respect for yourself? You need to get fucking real." He holds his hands up to ward off any argument. "I'm not here to fight, Bex, but I'm here to tell you, you need to wake up."

He goes to leave then turns back. "And Bex," he says

quietly. "It's actually Friday today."

With that, he walks away.

Friday!

Fucking hell. What happened to Wednesday and Thursday?

The last thing I remember is getting back from work on Tuesday, cracking open the wine, and drinking myself to oblivion. I've never lost days before. Hours, but never days.

Scanning my apartment, all I can see are discarded bottles and takeaway containers. I don't need to look far to know what I've been doing. Shaking my head and inwardly hating myself, I do the only thing I know that numbs the pain. I head for the fridge.

CHAPTER FIVE: BEN

Eamon and Melissa's apartment in the city is modern, high-tech, and completely at odds with its two residents. Surrounded by restaurants and nightclubs, it is noisy at all hours of the day. My friends love the buzz of city life. Both can be found amongst it every day, sitting in pavement cafés, watching the world go by. They love the variety of people, the constant stimulation of living here, and the fact that they are surrounded by people but anonymous at the same time.

Even after having lived in this very home for twenty years, they don't know their neighbours' names. Instead, they identify them by recognisable features. In the basement, an older gentleman who lives with ten cats is known as Catman. On the first floor, a young woman with long blonde hair, always carrying loads of shopping bags, was given the name Serial Shopper. I smile to myself thinking of the various residents of this building I've heard about over the years. There always seems to be a good story to be told.

Sunday lunch at the Reynolds home is a fantastic affair. Melissa spares no expense to put on a full spread for us. My girls love them; they have become additional grandparents to our daughters. London traffic is busy today. I shouldn't be surprised; it's always gridlocked around here. I couldn't live here. I need space and fresh air. One night in the city is enough.

We are all staying over tonight. I can enjoy a few drinks while we watch the game. Kels is starting to tire easily. She doesn't like driving in the city, so Melissa suggested we all stay. She loves to pamper my girls with beauty treatments after lunch. Mel used to own a high-end boutique beauty parlour not far from their apartment. A large chain bought it, meaning they were able to pay off their hefty mortgage. Now she spends her time looking after Eamon and baking for charity events.

Pulling into the underground parking, I look for a guest parking space. Eamon said he had prebooked one for us so my name will be written on the message board with the relevant space number. I hate parking my car down here. The last time, some idiot gifted my baby with a lovely dent on her driver's door. Manoeuvring into space number 109, I breathe a sigh of relief; there is a pillar on each side that should protect her from any bumps or scrapes.

Climbing out of the car, I extricate my pregnant wife and two squabbling children from the low-slung seats, then grab the bags out of the boot. "How many nights are we staying, Kels?" I groan, seeing two huge suitcases in the boot.

Our argument leaving the house was uncomfortable. I had nipped in to work to check on a patient in critical condition. When I returned, the car was loaded, and she had lifted the heavy cases in herself. I was furious. She was told no heavy lifting, but now that Kels is on baby number three, she's stopped listening to anyone, especially me.

She smiles and rolls her eyes. "Just you wait till we are packing for five. We are going to need a minivan." I cringe at the thought. We have spoken about changing my car to something more practical, but the idea devastates me. I don't want to be one of those middle-aged default dads with an SUV, wearing tracksuits every day and having a pint at The Smoking Goat on a Friday being my highlight of the week.

Having collected all required humans and baggage, we head for the lift. Cramming everyone in, Kels hits the button to the penthouse apartment. Up we go.

You know an apartment is expensive when a card needs to be swiped to exit the lift. Eamon and Melissa's apartment is the only one on this floor. The lift opens into a swanky reception area. A console table displays a huge vase of fresh flowers. Surrounded by soft-pink walls, an ornate chandelier hangs in the centre, sparkling light around the room. There are three paintings of the countryside hanging on one wall. They bought these at an art auction a few months ago. It was a good investment, I was told.

They stand in the opulent doorway to their home. Both the doors and their arms are open. My heart swells. I love these people. They are my greatest supporters in life. Melissa would be so disappointed if she knew what I was capable of. The familiar feeling of shame overwhelms me as I walk forward to embrace them.

Lunch has been delicious. We have eaten our fill of roast chicken with homemade gravy, mashed potatoes, and vegetables. Mel has truly spoiled us by presenting a homemade caramel cake for dessert. I think I may need to unbutton my jeans soon to accommodate my full stomach.

Retiring to the lounge, the children are cuddled up on the sofas watching cartoons while we chat quietly between us. Kels and Melissa are sitting on one sofa discussing our plans for the new addition. I haven't quite got the nursery finished yet, and it's stressing her out. I make a mental note to get it finished this week. My wife deserves it. I am a terrible husband.

The excitement in her voice is palpable. Kels loves babies, she is a fantastic mother. But this is the last one. She was very unwell after having Rose and was warned against any more children. Watching her lying in intensive care fighting for her life while I held our newborn daughter was the worst experience of my life.

Without Bex's and Amy's support, I don't know how I would have coped. They looked after Savannah, stayed in my home, and were my shoulder to cry on. Not once did Bex make a move or suggest we have a dirty night together. We used to be such good friends, all of us.

This baby was a complete shock to me. She was meant to be on birth control. However, Kels had stopped taking it. She wanted to let nature take its course. At first, I was enraged. How could she trick me into another baby? But as time passed, my anger disappeared, and my excitement grew. After this, though, I am going to get fixed. Three children are more than enough. I won't risk any more *accidents*. Kelsey is not aware of my plans, and I may not even tell her. A conference for a few days is a good enough cover story for the procedure.

Playing chess is a pastime I don't do often, but my favourite thing to do with Eamon is set up the board, drink whisky, and put the world to rights. We had been slowly making our way through his whisky collection since the afternoon. The girls had all gone to bed and are sound asleep. I could see him lining up his queen to take me out, a slow smile playing on his lips.

"Checkmate, Jones!" He laughs. "Good game."

I slap my hands down on the table in mock protest then raise one to shake his.

We sit back in our chairs as I reset the board. One more game. Maybe I will beat him this time. In all our years playing chess, I've only managed to beat him a handful of times. He is a master of distraction, never mind chess. I feel his eyes on me, surveying me.

"So, Jones, are you going to tell me what's wrong? Or do I have to guess?" His voice is soft enough, but I know he means business.

"Eamon, with work and the baby on the way, I'm just busy

and tired. Worrying we will have a similar situation as when Rose was born. I'm not sure my nerves could survive it."

He raises an eyebrow and shakes his head. "Bullshit!" he barks. "You fucked her again, didn't you? That little whore that hangs around like a bad smell."

I wince at his harsh words. Trying to deny it is futile. He will never believe me anyway, and it's true.

Hanging my head, I shrug my shoulders and feel the tear trickle down my cheek.

"What are you thinking, son? Why would you risk everything you have for a shag with that bit of skirt? You have a beautiful wife and children," he says gently. I know he's trying to understand, but even I don't understand, so what chance would he have?

My haunted eyes meet his, and I whisper, "I don't know, I just don't know. When we cross the line, I just can't keep my hands off her. Our bodies are interconnected. Her response to me is exquisite. When it happens, she is the only thing I can think about. Everything else seems insignificant."

He snorts in disgust but says nothing.

Our last game was played in silence, both lost in our thoughts of my wayward behaviour. After I make my way through to the guest bedroom, I see Kels is lying on her side facing away from me, chestnut curls are splayed across her pillow, her eyes closed in a deep sleep. She has been distant since last weekend, still her loving beautiful self but guarded. I head into the bathroom to have a quick shower.

Under the hot water, I relax, and my mind wanders back to the sex I enjoyed with Bex. We had both been incredibly drunk, fawning over each other in the middle of the bar, making no secret of our attraction. Then she had taken me by the hand and dragged me outside. Our mouths had collided as soon as we felt the fresh air, our tongues trying to overpower the other. I had walked her backwards to the alley while my hands explored her body. She dropped to her knees and freed my cock from my jeans, slowly, one button at a time. My body hardens in response to the memory, and I begin to stroke myself. I want my release; the thought of that woman drives me insane with need, the memory of her blonde hair swaying in the wind as she fucked my cock with her mouth violently.

She had bitten me playfully, and I grabbed her around her waist, pulling her up so she could wrap her legs around me, hitching her skirt up to sink myself into her against the wall. She had been tight, juicy, and full of creamy ecstasy. We had gone back to her dirty little apartment, barely making it through the door before she was naked before me. Clothes were strewn across the floor. Her boobs were perky, and her pussy was swollen, ready for me. Wanting me. She loves sex, I love sex, and we fuck together so bloody well. It's electric. I replay the whole night in my head as I pull myself roughly, building to orgasm and shooting my load in the shower.

It's not until I'm cleaning myself down that I'm aware of eyes on me, watching my every move. Kels' eyes meet mine, sad and broken with tears running down her face. She knows. Fuck . . . She knows.

Chapter Six: Kelsey

Watching your husband pleasure himself is erotic. Seeing his strong hands rub up and down his shaft had sent my body into intense arousal. I was almost stripped off to join him when I heard her name. He'd whispered it quietly beneath the water, but I'd heard it.

Bex.

My heart had dropped, and the blood rushed to my head. I've known for years there was something between them. The illicit glances and her laughing at every fucking thing he said. My anger rises again.

I'm six months pregnant with his third child, and he's messing around with our so-called friend. That's where he went on Saturday night. That's where he stayed. With her. "I stayed with a friend, Kels." That's what he told me. A bloody friend with benefits.

From the outside looking in, we have the perfect marriage. We've been together since we were sixteen, remaining together through university and into our twenties. The break we took in our relationship was hard, but my tragic life brought us back together. We know each other inside and out. If I had to pick a quiz show subject, I would pick Dr Benjamin Fucking Jones.

I know how he likes his eggs. I know what his favourite colour is. I know what his dreams are. I know how particular he is about the way he cleans his car. And I bloody well know what brand of boxer shorts he prefers. Together, we work. We have a beautiful home and beautiful children. A successful family. We are what many people aim to be.

But I am so bloody bored, part of me doesn't blame him for straying.

Thinking back to the beginning, when we were full of teen-age hormones, we couldn't keep our hands off one another. Our time was filled with stolen kisses and loved-up moments. That initial lust was addictive. A drug. I couldn't get enough. I was drunk on his obsession with me.

Between the ages of sixteen and twenty were the happiest years of my life. We studied hard because of our ambitions. We were planning to take on the world together. Moving on to university, we didn't grow apart, but we lived separately so as not to put too much pressure on our relationship. We talked every day for hours and supported each other through our darkest days. When we met up, we laughed and made love. It was our routine. It was familiar, and it was safe.

Our final year was incredibly pressurised as a trainee doc-tor and nurse. The realisation that we were going to be re-sponsible for saving people's lives was both terrifying and ex-citing. I fed off the adrenaline of a shift in accident and emer-gency. That buzz you got when someone's life was on the line, and you played your part in pulling them through. Hooking up that essential IV line or administering CPR at the crucial moment.

It was during one of those shifts I met Sam, a newly quali-fied nurse on my team. He was tall with soft-brown curls and the deepest hazel eyes. Sam had a kindness about him. When he spoke to our patients, it was with love and genuine consid-eration.

Being a male nurse, he was in the minority. It was obvious as I got to know him that he was smart. I asked him once why he chose nursing instead of being a doctor. His answer was mind-blowing, telling me he wanted to be on the front line with the patients and nurture actual relationships with them.

My heart melted. His point of view was doctors were removed from the actual people more than we were as nurses. I understood him completely.

Ben and I had many conversations about our days, and I always felt his experience was somewhat more aloof than mine. A doctor analyses and prescribes, whereas we nurses feel with the patient. As trainees, we walked side by side with them.

The ward alarm was blaring; a critical case was on the way to the hospital. The information coming through was sketchy. All we knew was a young boy, five to eight years old, had run into the road and been hit by a car. He had multiple broken bones and a severe head injury. The trolley blasted through the doors and my team started running to meet them. We worked like a well-oiled machine, doing whatever was necessary to save this child's life, setting bones and taking scans as required.

After three hours, our patient was stable and settled in his room. His little body looked tiny in the huge hospital bed with one parent on either side, gently holding his hand, terrified to touch their son in case they inflicted pain on his delicate body. I was exhausted and emotional. We almost lost that poor little soul. His life was almost snuffed out, far too young.

My mind wanders back to that night after my shift had finished, sitting in the staff room with my head in my hands. Tears flowed freely down my face. Ben was still working. I couldn't call him. I needed a hug. As I shrugged into my coat, desperate to go home, Sam wandered into the room, and his face fell at the sight of me.

"We are going for a drink," he declared. I didn't argue, following him like a sheep from the room.

Sitting in a cosy little bar down the road, we cracked open a bottle of red, going over our shift in minute detail, analysing every decision made and the near misses our patient had gone through. He wasn't out of the woods yet. I knew I would lie awake tonight worrying until work the next day.

Sam was witty and funny. He distracted me from the worry overwhelming my mind. With another bottle of red down, our hands touched across the table. An electricity bolt ran through me. The next thing I know I'm straddling him on his chair, hands in his hair and my tongue down his throat. He pulled me onto him, grinding his hard length against my sex. The manager had approached us and asked us to leave; that had brought me swiftly back to my senses. I jumped from his lap and ran home, cursing myself to the heavens. Pure little Kelsey wasn't so pure anymore.

The next few weeks passed in a daze of guilt and hatred. I was angry at Ben for not being available when I needed him. I was angry at Sam for being so appealing. But most of all, I was angry with myself for being completely promiscuous.

Sam and I avoided each other for a few months, working on the same team but only communicating directly when necessary. The incident almost felt as if it hadn't happened. I couldn't deny my attraction to him. It was the first time I had been interested in another man. I mean, I had always noticed when men were attractive. What young woman doesn't? But I found myself fantasising about him, and thoughts of him crossed my mind at the most inappropriate times. I felt confused, starting to doubt my relationship with Ben.

Then we had another high-pressure case involving a child. This time, we didn't get a happy ending. I crumpled into a heap at the end of the day. Ben was unavailable again. Sam scooped me up and took me home. We talked. We cried. We ended up in bed. Perversely, I felt more alive than I had in years. It felt like Sam was the only person who got me. He was living practically the same life as me. We were dealing with the same cases, and ultimately, the same losses.

Ben was so busy he barely noticed the nights I was home

late or how many girls' lunches I was having. I'm not sure who he thought I was out to lunch with, because I had no girl-friends except Bex and her sister, Amy. Perhaps he was too distracted by the pressure he was under as a medical student, or perhaps he just didn't care enough to notice.

The guilt rises within my chest at my dismissive thoughts. Back then, all Ben thought about was work and us. He would always talk about when we had graduated, when we had a few years under our belt, when we could finally have this idyllic life he so craved. I suppose being with the same person since you were sixteen means you are ready for more at a younger age.

Well, some people are. At this point in time, I was so con-fused. Everything was charging along, and all the events I thought I wanted were happening. Life was progressing the way I had dreamed it would, but I wasn't a hundred percent committed. I had doubts, and that terrified me.

Sam and I had become more brazen in our relationship, es-pecially around work. Ben was based in the same hospital but in a different department. We would occasionally grab lunch together when our shifts allowed, but most of the time I was with my team, and he was with his doctor friends. The divide between the trainee doctors and nurses was real. The doctors projected a sense of superiority, and we were *just the nurses.*

This made me resentful of Ben. My anger boiled under the surface. I distanced myself from him and withdrew, espe-cially in the bedroom. Outside work, he was still the sweet and kind man I loved with all my heart, but inside work, he was one of them. I would sit with Sam at lunch, laugh loudly at his jokes, and touch his hand at any opportunity. We would grab any private moments to steal a kiss.

Our affair had been ongoing for six months when I got the phone call. He asked to meet to talk. My heart sank as a thou-sand scenarios ran through my head. Was he going to break it off? I wasn't sure I could cope; he was like my medicine after a shit day. We arranged to meet at an obscure café near the hospital where we had been a hundred times before.

Sam was sitting at our usual table. It was our day off. He was wearing a fitted black shirt and low-slung jeans with a nervous expression. Leaning down, I gently kissed his cheek, my eyes quickly scanning the room to make sure there was no one we knew there.

"Don't you wish we didn't have to do that?" he asked quietly, a sad smile on his lips.

I looked at him quizzically. "What do you mean?" Feeling my defences rise, sensing danger was on the horizon.

He sighed softly. "Let me speak to the end, Lolly. Please." Lolly was his pet name for me. I loved it. "We have been seeing each other in secret for six months. I like you. I'm in love with you. I want us to make a go of things properly."

Dumbfounded, I gawked at him. "Make a go of things?" I repeated back to him. The words raced around my head. Shit! He wants me to leave Ben.

"Lolly, I'm sick of sneaking around all the time. Having time with you when you can squeeze me in. I want to walk down the street with you and hold your hand. I want to be able to kiss you in public. I want to be able to introduce you to my parents. But while I'm the other man, those things are not accessible to me." He dropped his eyes and then looked at me hopefully. "The thing is Lolly, I've met someone. Nothing has happened, but I'm curious. I'm not prepared to see both of you at the same time, so you need to decide whether you actually care for me or if I'm just a band-aid for your broken relationship."

I sit, looking at him silently with no idea what to say. Leave Ben? The thought had never even crossed my mind. Sam isn't prepared to see me alongside someone else. My head spins. Sam isn't willing to risk a potential relationship for his affair with me. The hatred and anger start to rise. I'm so damn angry. How dare he make me feel so cheap? I push my seat back from the table with force, standing up.

My eyes are wide. I stare down at him, and I see red. "How fucking dare you!" I yell. He looks at me, startled, then his anger surfaces.

"How dare *I*? Lolly, I'm asking you to give us a chance. Stop screwing around and hiding from everyone. Give us a bloody chance. I'm not prepared to be your secret fuck any longer, to massage your ego or pick you up off the floor when you're struggling. You are either with me or you're not. If you're with me, then let's step out together and show the world. If you're not, then from now on we are colleagues and nothing more."

Tears flood to the surface. I feel completely lost. I care for this man, but I don't love him. It's always been Ben. He's my life. A huge wave of guilt fills me. What have I been doing? Risking my relationship while playing with Sam's emotions at the same time. My eyes meet his, I shake my head slowly, then walk away from the table, not looking back. His voice rises behind me. "Oh don't worry, Lolly," he sneers. "I won't tell the poor bastard your dirty little secret."

Escaping the café and onto the street, my lungs fill with fresh air and I take off toward my apartment, walking as fast as my legs will allow. Climbing the stairs two at a time, I arrive at my front door never having been so relieved to be home. Walking into the apartment, I kick off my shoes. My flatmates will be at work. I have the place to myself.

Blazing blue eyes are staring at me from the sofa. He sits perfectly still. He is fucking furious.

I just look at him dumbly, unsure what to say.

He holds a letter up and waves it in the air. "Is it true?" he yells.

I walk over and take the letter from him; my terror rises as

I read it.

> *Ben,*
> *I'm sorry to have to write this letter.*
> *We don't know each other particularly well*
> *but I feel it is my duty as a fellow man to tell you.*
> *Kelsey and I have been sleeping together for six months.*
> *We are in love, and I am going to ask her to leave you for me.*
> *I won't be the other man any longer.*
> *You've lost a good one,*
> *and I am sorry I am the person who has done this to you.*
> *But I love her completely. She is my world.*
> *Sam*

He scans his eyes over me, pleading for answers. "Are you leaving me?" he whispers, tears filling his eyes.

My hands shake uncontrollably as wetness covers my face. I shake my head.

"Is it true, Kels? Have you been sleeping with him?"

My heart breaks as I nod my head.

"Do you love him?" His voice is strained. I can hear the pain this conversation is causing him. I can't bring myself to speak, so I simply shake my head, keeping my focus on the floor.

I'm filled with shame, embarrassment, disbelief, and anger at being caught. How did I think this was going to end? Am I going to lose them both? The thought is soul-destroying.

Blue eyes meet mine. "Let's talk. How can we fix this?" he asks.

My thoughts return to the present situation. This time, the boot is on the other foot. He is the one cheating, and I am the one who has found out. What am I going to do about it? We are older now with a lot more responsibilities. But am I ready to let Dr Benjamin Jones go, once and for all?

PART 2

London
September 1996

CHAPTER SEVEN: BEX

Today, we moved into our grown-up apartment, all newly graduated and stepping into the big, bad world of full-time employment. The four of us have been friends since high school, spending most weekends of the past decade together. Located in the centre of a lovely little bustling community in London, our apartment is spacious and bright. Within metres of our front door, there is a pub, The Smoking Goat, an express supermarket, a budget off-licence, and a beauty parlour. Everything required for a twenty-three-year-old graduate teacher to live, work, and enjoy life in this fabulous city. Never mind the fact I'm sharing this experience with my three best friends in the world. I can't wait to be lounging around the house having TV dinners and putting the world to rights with them.

My sister, Amy, has just graduated in Kinesiology. What that means to you and me is she learnt how the human body moves at university. She is working at a local gym while studying toward her personal training qualifications. Amy is an all-out health addict, and her dream is to own a gym one day. Being the success-driven person she is, I have no doubt she will achieve everything she wants.

My sister is the sweetest person you will ever meet with a core of steel. I have seen her bring grown men to tears with her tongue after they deliver a terrible pickup line. Men fall at her feet everywhere we go; you can see their tongues hit the floor. She is tall, fit, blonde, with the face of an angel. Unlike me. I used to be jealous of Amy; she was the sister who won all the trophies and had all the friends.

Feeling like the odd one out is something I became used to. With my masculine features, it was harder to be one of the girls. It still is. I don't have the same feminine beauty to work with, never finding a method to make the best of my canvas. But Amy always makes sure I'm included. She's looked out for me since we were in our teens and I didn't have a date to prom. Being a twin isn't easy, especially when you're the ugly one.

Ben and Kelsey were high school sweethearts. It's a bonus, because it meant we only needed a three-bed apartment, but the rent is still split four ways. Winner! In school, they were *the beautiful couple*, Prom King and Queen, captains of the football and netball squads, etc., etc. How they ended up friends with me, the class geek, I will never know. Ben is a graduate doctor, and Kelsey is a graduate nurse. I mean, they are so fucking textbook perfect, it's cringeworthy.

My parents think it will be strange living with a couple, but I don't see why. We hang out together all the time anyway. We are all friends, and it just so happens two of us are fucking. Not me, obviously. Chance would be a fine thing. But it works. We support each other and will have a great time. I think this living arrangement can only go well.

Our first night as flatmates is a Friday, the ideal pizza and beer night. I pin a note to the fridge telling everyone to be there.

The party is starting tonight! Pizza and beer!
Rendezvous in our living room at 19.00 hours!
Wear your pyjamas!

I laugh at myself as I read the message back. We are so boring, years of partying have made us dull. None of us start our new roles until Monday except Amy, who is already working, so we have the weekend to unpack and settle in.

Right now, our flat looks as if the delivery men dumped all the boxes in our living room and we have made castles out of them. That's exactly what Kelsey, Amy, and I did this afternoon. We drank wine and built castles then pretended to be princesses waiting for a dashing knight to save us.

When Ben got home from his induction meeting at the hospital today, he was not impressed at all by our lack of productivity. But he did enjoy being Kelsey's knight, dragging her off to the bedroom to save the day. Note to self, I must look at soundproofing options for their room or perhaps noise-cancelling headphones for me.

Stuffed to the brim and well-greased on beer, we all lounge on the sofa. Pizza and beer night has been a huge success. Not that it wouldn't have been, as the four of us have done this a hundred times before. But this is the first time we have had pizza and beer in our own home. We had the same argument over which pizzas to order, and as usual, we ended up ordering one of each. My favourite is ham and pineapple. Ben says pineapple on pizza is bloody diabolical. Personally, I feel the Hawaiian pizza is a much under-appreciated delicacy.

I feel lucky to be living my best life surrounded by my best friends. We have so much to look forward to. I am excited about the year ahead. Sitting in my half-drunken state, I survey the scene before me. I am happier than I have ever been.

"Oi! Sis! What's with the halfwit smile on your face?" Amy slurs from her couch.

"This halfwit is happy to be here with all you roasters," I respond.

Ben and Kelsey stick their fingers down their throat in unison and make sick noises. "Urgh, pass the sick bag." Kelsey laughs, and we all fall into fits of giggles.

Our festivities are interrupted by a loud bang at the door. We all sit and stare at each other.

"Does anyone know who it is? Or anybody expecting someone?" I ask. They all shake their heads, eyes wide, wondering who is at the door. Kelsey and I watched too many

London crime documentaries before moving here. In the process of our research, we had also terrified the shit out of ourselves. I hadn't been able to sleep for a week, dreaming of masked men, and not in a good way.

A booming voice erupts from the other side of the door, "Come on! I know you're in there! Come and meet your neighbour." Ben jumps up, running toward the noise. He's wearing his tartan pyjama bottoms with a terrible character T-shirt. He does not look like the hotshot trainee doctor tonight.

Ben graduated top of his class and is destined for great things in the medical world. He was offered various positions across the UK, and even in the States, but turned them all down so he could stay with Kelsey. A lot of people called Kelsey selfish for keeping him here, but that wasn't the case at all. She told him to go, but he couldn't bear the thought of being without her.

Kelsey wouldn't move due to her dad being on his own now; her mum passed away when she was in her teens. I don't think either of them has ever gotten over the loss. She speaks to her dad every day at least once, and she organises fresh meals to be delivered and cleaners to keep the house spotless. It's almost as if she still lives with him but from a distance, overseeing his well-being from day-to-day. I've seen her going as far as to phone his friends if he's been stuck in the house for an extended period. The black cloud hits him hard and fast; one day he is the cheerful man we all know and love, and the next he is like a bear with a sore head. Snappy and downright vicious with her, he knows what buttons to press to expose her vulnerabilities. I wouldn't like to think of the number of occasions that Ben has had to scrape a distraught Kelsey off the floor due to her dad having a bad day.

A giant suddenly enters our living room, followed by Ben. He is huge, filling the doorframe. A broad smile is plastered across his face and bright green eyes full of mischief survey the room. This man is attractive in a loveable way. He's not classically good-looking, but he's interesting, his sandy-blond hair worn long and falling over his forehead. You just know by looking at him, your day just got better. He holds his arms wide.

"Welcome to the building, folks," he bellows. I wonder if he has volume control. "I hope you lot are more exciting than the last boring bastards who lived here."

We all sit, taken aback. He reminds me of a Nordic Viking. Big and brawny. No one utters a word, so he continues with his introduction.

"Well, as none of you are forthcoming, I will go first." He smiles. "I'm Terry Trodden, yes, Trodden, like you stepped in something."

I can't help it; I burst out laughing. He winks at me. "You have no idea how good a pickup line that is." He laughs, and it's infectious. "I've lived here, Flat 6A, for five years. It's a two-bedroom, but I live by myself. Moved to London to chase the dream with a mate, but he lost his mind and got married." He waggles his eyebrows and smirks. "Anyway, I'm thirty-one, single, and looking for the perfect woman. Any takers?"

At this point, I'm not sure if he's joking or not. I sit quietly on the sofa and sip my beer.

"I work at a double-glazing sales company while I'm trying to make my name as an actor," he continues. "Maybe you saw me in the haemorrhoids advert I did last year?" We all look blankly at him, shaking our heads. "Enough about me!" he roars. "Who are you all?"

One by one, we give him a brief history of ourselves. Name, place of birth, job, and our hobbies. My hobbies don't account for much; drinking beer and watching TV seemingly don't count. I sit, watching the proceedings in awe. How can a stranger barge into your home and take hold of the reins so easily? An hour later, we are all chatting like old friends, having sunk another case of beer. He has got us to disclose some of our most embarrassing secrets. So far, he knows about Ben being caught tied to a lamp post with his pants down during a university prank day, my close encounter with a male professor in his office, and Amy being caught shoplifting in the supermarket. Kelsey is so pure that not even Terry Trodden can get any dirt on her.

It turns out the haemorrhoid advert has been Terry's only mainstream TV appearance so far. He has made a few appearances as the drag queen, Vixen Vicky, in three low-budget porn movies but apart from that, he's spent the past five years bouncing from one pointless job to another, having a hell of a lot of fun in the process. Terry Trodden lives life in the moment. He says he considers himself pansexual. Seemingly that means you look beyond gender and are attracted to the person, not their sexuality. To me that seems a positive way to live, not restricting yourself to a box, living the way that feels right to you. Loving who feels right to you. Since I was a teenager, I've been trying to tick off a checklist.

Exams, tick. University, tick. Graduate, tick. Get a job, tick.

But have all those ticks been what I wanted, or what I *thought* I should want?

When I was a little girl, I dreamed of being an air steward and travelling the globe, waking up in different places while seeing the wonders of the world. My family told me an air steward was nothing but a glorified waitress, a *trolley dolly*. I accepted that judgement and moved on to a more appropriate career with *prospects*. What I would give to live a day in the life of Terry Trodden, to be as carefree and to not worry about what is around the corner. Just to experience life in its raw state. I have a good feeling about Terry Trodden; he is going to be a wonderful addition to our little group and to my life.

Chapter Eight: Bex

Thank fuck it's Friday!

My first week is over as a real teacher in a real school. If I'm being honest, I nailed it. The kids are fantastic, we had a brilliant week getting to know each other. A few pupils are going to test me, especially with me being a newly qualified teacher. I am considered fresh meat since I'm young. Some of my students are only five years younger than me. But when I walked through cling film stretched over my door, didn't lose my temper, then returned the favour in their next lesson, I did my credibility a lot of good.

To me, being a teacher is about being approachable and having a good sense of humour but not being a walkover. It's a fine line. Over the past four years, I've completed placements and a probation year, but it's not the same as being fully in control of your class. Having to get all your plans signed off by your mentor is time-consuming and restricts your teaching. I always taught in a way I believed the system wanted me to, not how *I* wanted to. Of course, there is a curriculum to follow, but there is plenty of flexibility within it to put your stamp on your lessons.

Sandbank High is an inner-city secondary school. It's low on funds, so budgets are tight. This means we must get creative with our teaching material. But the kids turn up and most of them want to succeed. The school has managed to instil in the pupils a desire to learn, something a lot of schools fail at, no matter whether they have big budgets or small.

It's four o'clock on Friday afternoon, and no one else is

home. I'm enjoying the peace. This week has been stressful. I have been up an hour earlier than required each day, arriving in my classroom by 7:45 a.m. My teaching schedule is packed. Having only four free periods in the whole week, I'm already bringing work home. Ben and Kelsey's sex life is having an impact on my sleep. With my first pay packet, I am buying those noise-cancelling headphones. I mean, what man can get it up at 3 a.m. every day and still function normally?

Not that I'm at all jealous, it's just been a long time since I've had sex with anyone or anything not shaped like a rabbit.

Everyone starts arriving home around six. I've thoroughly enjoyed my alone time, but our big night out tonight is calling. Terry promised he is going to show us the local hotspots. I'm not sure my idea of a nice place and Terry's idea of a nice place is the same. But having got to know him this week, we will have a fantastic night wherever we end up.

Terry has camped out in our living room every night. He is lonely and normally goes out on his own. I can just imagine him tagging onto whatever group is in the pub then dragging the poor people along to a random club with him. Most of Terry's friends are married and have children now; nights out for them are few and far between. Plus, from what he's said, most of his friends' wives don't like him and see him as a bad influence on their perfect, domesticated husbands. I find the differences between people in their twenties and their thirties terrifying. Please never let me be so boring that I don't see my friends more than once a month.

Operation: Night Out gets underway as soon as Amy gets home. She is our glam master, ensuring we are all suitably turned out to be in her presence during a night on the town. I don't do glam. No part of my body is allowed to be on display. I prefer long-sleeved tops with jeans. My figure is very straight with little curvature apart from my huge ass. My hair is long and platinum blonde, hanging limply down the sides of my face. As for makeup, it frightens me. Amy did my makeup once, and I ended up with black eyes teamed with whore's red lips. Never again. I hide in my room until everyone else is ready to go then tag on at the end so she can't "do me up" against my will.

Nine o'clock rolls around, and it's time to go. I emerge from my hiding place, dull and drab as usual. Amy rolls her eyes at me but says nothing. I ignore her. She's not ruining my night by starting the same argument we've had a thousand nights before. *Be more confident, Bex. Flaunt what the big man gave you, Bex.* I've never been one for flaunting my body. I have nothing to flaunt.

It's easy for Amy. She's perfect. I'm the ugly twin, and I know it. All the crap-looking genes from our parents came to me, while she was blessed with all the good-looking ones. When I cover myself in makeup and wear a short dress, I look like a pretty boy in drag. It's sad, it depresses me, but I accept it. No one will ever want me the way men want my sister.

Kelsey looks so pure; that's the only way to describe her. She has this serene look about her. Wholesome and honest. Always wearing flowery dresses that skim her body but don't cling to her curves. She can pull off classy-sexy with such style it's sickening. On a night out, I stand as far away from her as possible, as a petite, feminine girl next to my macho appearance only accentuates my ugliness.

Next to Kelsey, Ben is as dashing as ever. He rocks the definition of tall, dark, and handsome. Those blue eyes of his see through you and make your heart flutter. I would never admit it to anyone. He's one of my best friends, but you would have to be dead to not find him attractive. He's always dressed sharply in expensive jeans and fitted T-shirts with a sleek jacket to complete the look. He turns women's heads wherever he goes, but the most endearing thing about him is he never notices. He only has eyes for Kelsey, and it's been that way since they were sixteen. They have nailed the first-love thing. It's both wonderful and sickening to watch, knowing that will never be me.

The five of us head out into the bright lights of London, completely reliant on Terry's knowledge of the nightlife. Our first stop is the local pub, The Smoking Goat. It's warm and cosy, packed to the brim with locals. The barstools are filled with old boys and tradesmen who have been here since they clocked off at four this afternoon. Pints of heavy ale sit on the bar alongside a shot of whatever their favourite tipple is. Most are still dirty from a day's work, or they lack personal hygiene. I'm not sure which.

In one corner of the pub, there is a group of clearly underage schoolies, hiding and sending the oldest looking one up to get the next round for them all. The girls hardly have any clothes on. The boys are drooling over them but trying to act uninterested. I cringe to think that was us not long ago, and I was always the one that got the drinks. My looks are so odd, I could be any age, and no one dared to ask.

Finally, there are the young professionals; I suppose that's what we are. I smile to myself at the thought. We are at that stage in life where we look good but can't afford a pot to piss in. We need to hang out in this kind of bar to afford the drinks. Hopefully, in a few years, we will be able to frequent the classy cocktail bars in the city centre, but right now, The Smoking Goat will have to do. I suppose that's why Terry still comes here. He's in his thirties but stuck in his twenties at the stage where he should be moving forward in life, but he's making no progress.

Terry nabs a table in the far corner of the pub, a booth. It has a brilliant view for people watching. I get a full-on show of a not quite sixteen-year-old girl giving her boyfriend a lap dance. I assume it's her boyfriend. Her makeup has run because she's been crying, but he is enjoying himself immensely.

We all get settled in, and Terry heads to the bar to order the first round. Ten quid each in a kitty and off we go.

The woman behind the bar is older, maybe in her fifties. She has blonde bobbed hair and is caked in more makeup than a drag queen. Her smile is broad and welcoming. It's clear she knows him well as he leans over the bar to kiss her cheek. She's wearing a low-cut top, showing her breasts off to full advantage, I assume in a bid to sell more pints. I don't need to see Terry's eyes to know where he is looking. She takes his hand across the bar and a realisation hits me: he's been there. I can see him whispering sweet nothings in her ear as she hands over the drinks. She waves away the money, and he promptly puts one of the notes in his pocket. Sly bastard.

He struts back to the table like the cat that got the cream, and he bloody well did — our money. The tray is full of various liquids, including a jug of a drink with no name but which is a fetching shade of green. We distribute the drinks liberally with a Russian roulette-style system. What you get, you drink. No personal orders are being taken tonight. The drinks continue to flow, and we become merrier by the minute.

Conversation flows easily between the five of us; it's as if Terry has been part of our group for years. It crosses my mind that he is refreshing. He isn't trying to get into anyone's pants; he's being completely platonic. Previously, anyone who became part of our little gang was quickly ousted because they tried to sleep with one of us — that shit is not allowed — apart from Ben and Kelsey who have been fucking since before we started hanging out together. Their relationship became common knowledge when they were caught bumping uglies in the store cupboard at school.

The hours pass fast, and several rounds of tequila later, we head off to the club. The Chequers nightclub looks dismal from the outside. It's just a single open door with a simple sign lit up in pink neon. There is a burly bouncer who fills the door, managing the long queue that stretches around the corner of the next street.

Terry walks confidently past all the waiting punters outside. "Barry!" he yells to the burly bouncer. The large bald head turns to face him and splits into a broad smile.

"Terry, good to see you, mate. Go straight in." He lifts the red rope with one hand while gesturing with the other. I can hear heckles and pissed-off comments behind me as I begin to skip up the stairs.

The music is eardrum-bursting loud, and I can feel the floor vibrating under my feet. I love to dance. My body naturally moves to the music before we get to the top of the stairs. The club is dark, and laser lights are swinging around the room. It's quiet now, with only a few groups of people hanging around or sitting in booths. I notice a large group of maybe twenty professional looking guys in the corner. They are the kind of guys I avoid, entitled and arrogant. They frighten me.

We grab a booth near the bar, and the drinks start to stack up. The music continues to blare through the club, and my head bounces along to the beat. It's starting to fill with people. I can feel the atmosphere building. People are happy and excited to be out. The thing about alcohol is it lowers your inhibitions while increasing the joy you feel in that moment. I love the freedom it gives me on a night out. It reduces my nervousness about being in social situations out of my control.

Amy and Kelsey stand up and shimmy out of the booth. "Come on, Bex, we're dancing."

They totter on their killer heels in front of me. I giggle at the sight. We head down to the sunken dance floor and dance in a small group, facing each other. The girls sway from side to side, barely moving their feet. They look sexy and in control. Every so often, they swing their ass a bit more. I stand opposite them and dance wildly to the beat of the music. I mash the potato and cut the cheese like a madman. Alcohol and music turn me into a different person. Wild, fun, and out-going. I love me as a drunk disco dancing babe, though I very rarely remember the next morning.

I'm in my little bubble when I notice a cute guy at the bar waving in my direction. I look over my shoulder to check there is no one behind me. There is no way that guy can be waving at me. He's one of the suits, and guys like that do not engage with me. He smiles, points at me, then gestures for me to come over.

No freaking way!

Wobbling my way across the club I do a happy dance in my head. I'm not wearing heels. I'm just drunk.

This guy is tall, hot, and blond. His dark eyes seem to be undressing me as I walk across the room. There is no way this stud is into me, but why else would he be calling me over? I hold my head high and look him straight in the eye, Dutch courage flowing in my veins. Well, I try to look him in the eye, but right now, he is kind of moving in clockwise motions, swirling around in my head. Oh, he is dreamy.

"Hello, gorgeous." He smiles. "Fancy a drink?"

I smile idiotically at him. Ignoring his question completely, I blurt out, "I'm Bex, and bloody hell, you're gorgeous."

He laughs and strokes my cheek. "You're cute, do you want that drink?" I nod my head enthusiastically, and he raises his hand for the bartender.

Half an hour passes and I'm drooling over this man. He's chatty, confident and massaging my ego with every word. He leans in to kiss me, and I submit willingly, his tongue dancing with mine. Arousal courses through me, and my stomach lurches in excitement. Lifting my hands to his face, I run my fingers through his hair. My nipples harden in response, and a wetness appears between my legs. Oh, it's been a long time since a man touched me there. I need it so bad.

Suddenly, he pulls back. My eyes spring open—one of his

suit friends is standing next to him waving a fifty-pound note. Confusion enters my brain. I'm trying to connect the dots. They are all laughing. Laughing at me. The friend has tears trickling from his eyes then full tears as his laughing becomes harder.

"Oh, my fucking god, Joel! You did it! You kissed the ladyboy!" he shouts. "You earned this fifty!" He passes the dirty note over, and Joel kisses it. He turns to me.

"Sorry, love." He shrugs. "You're a bloody good kisser for a boy, though."

The world stops, and my head spins. A feeling of complete disbelief overwhelms me. I stand abruptly, then I'm running blindly around the club. My friends are nowhere to be seen. Embarrassed, ashamed, and made a fool of yet again, I charge down the stairs into the fresh air. My head spins. I fall hard on my knees, then stagger to my feet and rub my hands on my legs. They come away bloody. The tears start to fall, and I feel a hand on my shoulder. It's the burly bouncer.

"Want me to call a cab for you, honey? Looks like you've had a shit night."

I look into his kind eyes and nod.

CHAPTER NINE: BEX

Waking the next morning, I feel lost.

Was last night a nightmare?

Did that really happen?

Those assholes thought I was a ladyboy. They challenged their mate to fucking kiss me. That is what I have become, a cheap dare. With my head in my hands, shame washes over me at the realisation that the whole sleazy event was real. This is my life. I am a boyish girl who must rely on men paying each other to get attention.

Sitting up in my bed, I notice blood on the sheets. Pulling the duvet to the side, I stare down at my legs. They are covered in scrapes and bruises. I remember myself running from the club. I remember falling. I remember the pain. Internally, I shudder in response to the memories.

The taxi ride home had been deathly silent. The burly bouncer had piled me into the car, double-checked my address, and confirmed it with the driver. We had pulled up outside my apartment, and the driver had helped me to the door. I must have looked ghastly. Once safely inside the communal hall, he had turned on his heels and run back to the safety of his car.

The apartment had been empty when I got home. Everyone else must still have been at the club. Making a beeline to the fridge, I had taken a bottle of white wine and one of the extra-long party straws then headed to bed. That's the last thing I remember before the oblivion of alcohol flooded my brain. It had been pure relief.

I check my mobile. There are no missed calls, so they must know I'm home. They would be so angry with me for bailing out. I broke our code last night. Don't leave the club on your own. Don't leave without telling someone where you are going. Sitting on the edge of my bed, I listen for signs of life outside my bedroom. Nothing. The apartment is silent. I glance at the small alarm clock on my bedside cabinet. It's bright pink with Minnie Mouse in the centre, her arms pointing to 9:15 a.m. I love that little clock; she reminds me of happy times playing with my dolls in my bedroom at home.

Swinging my legs out of bed, I place my feet on the carpet. They sink into the deep pile, and it feels snug against my toes. My head is not sore, but it's spinning. It crosses my mind that I may still be drunk. It was only a few hours ago I was drinking wine through a straw directly from the bottle. Pinot Grigio, if I remember correctly. Looking at the evidence on the floor, I confirm it was Pinot. My headaches don't tend to be too bad when I drink that. It's the harder stuff that makes me ill. I stagger to my bathroom to survey the damage, my mind racing over last night's events. It's the worst I've been made to feel in my whole life. Gullible and embarrassed.

The best thing about this apartment is that every bedroom has an ensuite. Whoever designed it was a genius. It was the key selling point for us, and not having to share a bathroom with three other people was a necessity for me. I don't like to share my personal space. I want to leave all my crap lying out; I know where it is, then.

Woeful eyes look back at me from the mirror. Oh hell, I look like I've just stepped out of a horror movie. My mascara has run down my face with my tears. As I have wiped them away, the rest of my eye makeup has been pulled across my face to form a bandit mask. My lips are pale, and my skin is gaunt. The bird's nest on my head looks as if little eyes should be watching you from it. I really am a mess.

Roughly washing the muck from my face and viciously brushing my hair into some sort of style, I berate myself for being so damn stupid. To believe a man like that would be interested in someone like me. *Of course it was a joke, you idiot.* A soft knock at the door distracts me from my self-loathing.

Amy pops her head around the corner.

"Bex, can I come in?" Her eyes full of worry.

"Sure," I mumble.

"Where did you disappear to last night? We were worried about you." Her voice is firm but kind. She is giving me a chance to come clean.

I'm trying to collect my thoughts. Do I want to tell her what happened? That a group of dicks made me their dirty bet for the night? Embarrassed and not knowing what to say, I sit, mute.

"Bex, when we couldn't find you, we came home." My guilt rises. They cut their night short because of me. "We asked the bouncer outside, and he said you had a fall, that he put you in a taxi."

I nod because that part is all true. I stay silent.

"We got home," she continues, "and you were passed out on your bed, covered in blood with a tear-stained face." Her eyes widen and she reaches for my hand, encouraging me to speak. "Bex, what did you do?"

I look at her, wordless. What did *I* do? No, I'm not going to tell her. I hate the fact she's looking at me with pity in her eyes. Screw her. My sister should be more fucking dependable. Shrugging my shoulders and faking a smile, I sneer, "Oh, you know me, Amz. You can't take me anywhere."

She sighs and gets up, leaving the room, saying nothing, only closing the door softly behind her.

Monday morning came as a welcome distraction from the disaster of the weekend. Saturday and Sunday were spent avoiding everyone by sitting in my room reading, only emerging to meet whatever takeaway delivery man that was expected. London is amazing for delivery service; this weekend, I have managed to get every meal prepared and delivered to my door. It's been a relief to not run the gauntlet of meeting anyone in the kitchen. I don't need their pity or words of wisdom. I just want to wallow for a few more days or weeks, whatever it takes.

This is my second week working at my new school. I'm looking forward to it. My plan of how I want to take my students forward is clear in my mind. My colleagues appear to be supportive and don't take themselves too seriously. Walking into the staff room, I meet one of the other English teachers in my department. Wendy gave me a great impression the moment I met her last week. She was warm and open, welcoming me into the team enthusiastically. She has taken me under her wing, fussing around to ensure I am settling in and have everything I need to conduct my classes. She was very liberal with her advice, pointing out the disruptive students and the teachers to keep at arm's length. I think Wendy and I will become good friends.

"Happy Monday, Bex," she calls from her seat on the sofa. It is only the two of us in the staff room. "How was your weekend?" she asks.

I grimace at her question, shake my head, and raise my eyes to the heavens. "Don't ask," I say, trying to sound light-hearted and failing miserably.

She frowns. "That bad, huh? Come sit down. I will get you a cup of coffee. Then you can offload on me. Can't start the week down in the dumps." She smiles, and I sigh in defeat.

This woman makes me talk. I can't help telling her what's on my mind, and it concerns me as I've only known her a week, but I already trust her implicitly.

"Black, two sugars?" she calls over her shoulder.

"Yes, please," I respond. The thought of a good cup of

coffee lifts my mood. She appears back from the tiny kitchen, which is in what used to be a storage cupboard. The staff room is bleak, grey, and boring. Old uncomfortable sofas sit around coffee tables that are on their last legs. The grey walls are littered with posters and leaflets about meetings or school events, most of which are at least two years out of date. Most of the window blinds don't work anymore, which doesn't matter as the staff room is in the darkest part of the school that barely receives daylight, never mind sunshine.

With us taking a sofa each, Wendy sets the two cups down on the old, worn table. "So, Bex, what happened on Friday?" She smiles warmly to encourage me to talk. "You were so excited about it. What went wrong?"

I remember rabbiting on about our plans for Friday night. How Terry was going to show us the places to go in the local area. Her eyes survey me, but she stays silent, waiting for me to speak. I know she isn't going to utter another word until I tell her what happened. How can she read me so well?

"Where do I start?" I say. "Friday night turned into an absolute crock of shit. I would award it the title of the worst night of my life." My mind does a quick flick through all my terrible and embarrassing nights out. There are plenty. But it agrees that, yes, Friday night was the worst ever.

Wendy sits quietly and waits for me to elaborate. I take a deep breath, roll my eyes, then jump into the story in all its embarrassing detail. How the bunch of jumped-up suits used me for a bet in the nightclub. My disgust at being stupid enough to think someone like that would be interested in me. Falling and hurting myself. The pity from the bouncer. The pity from my friends. How I hate feeling like that. The fact I hate the way I look. My complete lack of confidence. I ramble on and on, my emotions raging to the surface as I continue to talk. Getting angrier and more upset with each word.

Wendy takes my hands in hers, giving me a kind smile.

"Bex, honey," she says, "we are going to fix this." I narrow my eyes, confused. She continues.

"Stand up and let me look at you." I do as she instructs, and she walks around me. "You are a striking woman, Bex, you just have to know how to use it. This Friday, after work, we are going shopping. Clear your diary. I won't take no for an answer."

With that, she turns and strides from the room. I watch her depart, and a sense of relief washes over me. This woman is going to make me do something radical to myself. She won't take no for an answer. Excitement and fear bubble in my stomach. What have I just let myself in for?

The week has gone well overall. I had a few issues with a challenging student in year ten, but after some negotiation, we are moving forward. The girl was lacking focus in class, disrupting her classmates by talking or passing notes. I kept her behind after class yesterday to discuss the situation with her. After some posturing and talking around the houses, it turned out she can't hear me when I speak. She has recently been prescribed a hearing aid, but at the moment, she does not feel comfortable wearing it in front of her peers. Her position in the back row of the class was not conducive to her limited hearing. We agreed that she will move into the front row, until such time as she feels able to wear her device in school confidently. Strictly speaking, I should have been insisting she wear it, but the lines of communication are now open. Hopefully, over the next few months, she will come to that conclusion on her own. I pat myself on the back for a situation handled well.

Wendy and I are heading off shopping today. I'm terrified. All she has told me is to bring an open mind and my credit card. I wait patiently in the staff room. Half of me wants her to arrive, the other half hopes there will be a diabolical incident so we will have to cancel. My stress started this morning when I was deciding what to wear on our shopping trip.

Right now, my bedroom floor is a sea of discarded clothing after trying on what felt like three thousand outfits. I decided on my trusty black fitted pencil skirt and pink satin blouse teamed with thick black tights and flat black ballet pumps. This outfit says professional and feminine. Wendy took one look at me, half smiled, half laughed, and declared, "That outfit is bloody awful. You will be a different woman tonight, Bex, and not just in the way you dress."

My stomach had lurched in fear at her words; the words themselves were mild, but the tone was fierce. I knew I was in for an interesting night.

Ten minutes later, Wendy struts in wearing a fitted dress that sports a bold blue and white chequered pattern. The neckline is cut low enough just to expose the top of her breasts. Sexy, but professional. She's wearing heels, not quite high enough to be called too high for a work environment. Her legs are bare, and her black hair is styled into short, sharp spikes. She wears makeup that is relatively natural apart from a set of strong red lips. She looks like a woman in control and at ease with her body.

Within minutes, she has me marched down the three flights of stairs to the staff parking. Her bright-red sports car with only two seats and a soft top sits waiting. She beeps the button to unlock it, and we climb in. The inside is the complete opposite of the spotless exterior. The floor of the passenger side is littered with fast food containers and sweet wrappers. She moves a pile of paperwork off my seat by throwing it on the floor, telling me to watch where I put my feet.

We head off out the school gates to a shopping centre on the edge of the city, one of those huge places that has everything from a supermarket to hairdressers to high-end restaurants. She spins the car around the car park at break-neck speed, parking as close to the doors as physically possible. Turning to me, she gives me a megawatt smile. "Come on, then. Let the fun begin." She beams. We get out of the car, and I follow her to see what future awaits me through those sliding doors.

First of all, she takes me to a large glass-fronted unit. The sign above it is neon yellow and flashes. *Heathers*. Inside it is a bustling hive of activity. It dawns on me: this is a hairdresser and beautician. Wendy winks. "First things first," she says, "let us get the basics right. You will be here for two hours. I've arranged for you to get a haircut and then any required beauty treatments they think you need."

I look at her blankly and raise my eyebrows. "Beauty treatments?"

She stares at me as if I'm an idiot which at this moment I am. "Yes, Bex, like manicures, pedicures, and waxing. Trust me, this is the first step in the journey to being a new you. The best version of you."

"Waxing? Where?" I squeak. Her eyes drop to my crotch. "Wendy, my bits are for my eyes and those I choose only."

"Don't be such a baby, regular waxing eliminates the stress around constantly having to shave, is more hygienic, and means you are always ready for a fuck, if the opportunity arises," she says.

"The notches on my bedpost, or lack of them, is none of your business."

Ignoring my protest, she leads me into the shop.

Two hours later, I have been prodded, primped, and preened within an inch of my life. My platinum-blonde hair has been cut to shoulder length and is sitting in soft, beachy waves. I now have a fringe that doesn't quite reach my eyes. I'm told this style frames my face beautifully, accentuating my large brown eyes. My nails are long and hot pink; I love seeing the bright colours swishing around every time I move them. The waxing was as painful and humiliating as expected — having your fanny on display, while holding a leg in the air so a woman you have never met could cover you in hot wax and rip it off again. The past few hours have been a learning curve. I am happy when it comes to an end.

Wendy is waiting for me at the coffee shop across from the salon. She stands as I approach. "Right, Bex, no time for coffee. Let's get shopping," she declares and marches off in the direction of the women's fashion shops. After what feels like hours later, I am in the changing room of a huge women's department store. It's been over an hour since wearing my own clothes. Wendy and two of the store assistants are bringing me a steady stream of garments to try on. So far, we have decided on purchasing four items, while around forty are on the discarded pile. They are pushing me out of my comfort zone, encouraging me to try on bold, bright colours, much more fitted than I'm used to.

"You have a fantastic figure," one of the assistants says. "Those curves deserve to be shown off." I giggle nervously at her compliment. "It's true. You are a striking woman, enjoy it."

"That's exactly what I told her," Wendy adds, and I roll my eyes at her.

At last, my basket is full to bursting, Wendy is satisfied I have enough clothing to nail my new look. "Ok," she says excitedly, "final surprise." She jumps up and down on the spot, clapping her hands. "We are going to a makeup workshop, and it starts in fifteen minutes."

With that announcement, she grabs my hand and drags me off in an unknown direction for the final phase of *Operation: Beautify Bex*.

Arriving back at the apartment in a sea of bags, I plonk myself down in exhaustion. It's eleven o'clock at night, and I left the house at seven this morning. I'm officially fucked. A huge smile spreads across my face as memories of the day play in my head. What a fantastic fucking day.

I already feel like a new woman, and I've not even started putting what I have learnt into practice. Silently I bless Wendy for being an incredible friend, making a mental note to take her a small present on Monday. Like a bath bomb or something.

After wrestling all my goodies from today into my little room, I lie down on my bed and immediately fall into a dreamless sleep, ready to start a new day as a new me tomorrow.

CHAPTER TEN: BEX

Tonight will be my first social event appearing as the "new" me. For the past few weeks, since our shopping trip, Wendy has spent hours helping me perfect my hair and makeup. Using a scoring system out of ten, we have rated every hairstyle my poor hair has been subjected to. Once we found the winner, I agreed to never change my hair again or face banishment from our friendship. Extreme, I thought, but necessary, according to Wendy.

My new full hairstyle accentuates my cheekbones while minimising my nose. The colour is still blonde but has been relaxed with a subtle golden tone. Makeup tutorials are my new obsession. I faithfully read how-to-guides in fashion magazines and spend my evenings practising. I never knew that you could change your makeup depending on the occasion. Rather, I had assumed you found a style you liked — in my case, as little as possible — and lived with it. I have practised faithfully in my room every day. Deep down, I am finally feeling feminine.

Wendy has been my cheerleader every step of the way, squealing with delight at every appropriate or inappropriate moment. In hindsight, she will squeal at any opportunity. She has kept me focused on my goal, often saying, "The goal of the process, Bex, is for you to feel comfortable in your own skin. To own your look and wear it with pride." I hear her sharp, strong words in my mind. It makes me smile. My confidence is building day by day as I try on another new outfit and study myself in the mirror. My bedroom is cluttered with clothes, makeup and hairstyling products. No surface has escaped being used as a dressing room.

My door starts to rattle violently. Someone is banging viciously on the other side.

"Bex! How is my pet project coming along? Are you nearly ready, gorgeous girl?" Wendy screams through the door. "Hurry up and let me in. I have supplies. I can't wait to see you!"

Laughing, I walk over to unlock the door to let her in. "Supplies? What on earth have you been buying now? Hopefully not more beauty products. I don't think my poor room could store anymore."

She stares at me as if I'm an idiot. "Don't be such a buffoon," she snaps, then breaks into a huge grin. "I have wine!" She holds up a pink bottle and shakes it. "Right, you get the glasses," she orders. "Let's get this party started!"

For the next hour, we sit in my room and discuss the fun we have had the past few weeks. I have loved spending time with Wendy; she has been a refreshing and much-needed addition to my life. It's wonderful to have a buddy who has no preconceived ideas of who I am, who will just accept me for me. She seems to like me a lot; we have spent every evening after work together. To most people, I'm boring Bex, quiet and subdued. The Bex who needs a good serving of alcohol to get out of first gear. I have never understood what my friends see in me. I bring nothing worthwhile to the party. I certainly don't attract hot men. My conversation sucks, sticking to subjects I know like teaching or reading. The reason they keep me around is a mystery to me.

Wendy's voice cuts through my thoughts. "I'm so glad you went for that sexy nurse costume; you look incredible." She's smiling at me coyly. The way she runs her eyes excitedly over my body makes me nervous but gives me a thrill.

Terry has invited us to his annual Halloween Hooley. He

promises it is going to be one hell of a party. From what he has described, if the police are not called to his flat, then the party is a flop. I invited Wendy along to be my plus one. I need her support to step out in this outfit. The dress, if you can call it that, is short, so short that if I lean forward, the bottom of my butt cheeks are on show. It is tight and clings to my curves. The neckline is cut low to my belly button and exposes my bra. Of course, the lacy bra had to be red because, according to Wendy, that is what sexy nurses wear. Accompanying the dress is a pair of red fishnet stockings with lace tops fully on display. The killer red patent boots make it impossible to walk. Wendy says they show off the shape of my legs and make my arse look totally fuckable. This assessment did surprise me, but it was positive, so I just smiled goofily at her. I wasn't allowed to do my makeup tonight. Wendy is currently applying two tonnes of the stuff. Once she is finished, I close my eyes and she leads me toward the mirror.

"Ta-dah!" she shrieks while jumping up and down on the spot.

I stare at the woman looking back at me. Wow! She's stunning. After a moment, the realisation hits me: the woman is me. My skin is clear and golden, my eyes are huge with smoky tones and strong eyeliner. My cheeks are pronounced with blush, and bright-red lips complete the look. This woman is smoking hot!

A huge smile crosses my face, and I laugh, feeling emotion overwhelm me. Turning to Wendy, I hug her fiercely. "Thank you! You absolute angel. I look incredible."

She stares at me and smiles softly; the look in her eyes makes me feel uneasy, like she's looking at me with longing. She whispers, "Don't you dare cry. You will smudge your makeup." The tension in the room breaks, and we both laugh softly. Something has changed between us at this moment, or maybe I have just woken up to the situation in front of me.

Putting the awkward thoughts to one side, I decide to enjoy the night we have put so much effort into preparing for. Wendy is dressed as Catwoman, encased in black leather that leaves nothing to the imagination. She is a good-looking woman with curves in all the right places. Her makeup is dark and brooding. It comes to me that she has never mentioned a man in her life or any of her previous partners, which does strike me as strange. I have divulged every past conquest in detail, not that there are many. She has extracted every bit of information on me over the past few weeks during our time together. Maybe it is just me that's been rattling on, selfishly focusing on myself. I make a mental note to ask her more questions in the future and not to be so damn self-centred.

Terry's apartment is on the top floor of our building and has direct access to the roof terrace. But London in October is not ideal for an outside party. It would be feasible for a drunk partygoer to be blown over the side in the autumn winds. So, Terry has promised that all celebrations will be indoors.

When we reach the upper hallway, there is no doubt which apartment the party is at. Michael Jackson's *Thriller* is playing loud and proud through the door covered with cobwebs. Orange eyes welcome you on approach and tell you to have a "Happy Halloween."

Wendy pushes open the door, and we walk in. There is no point knocking; no one would have heard us anyway. The room is crammed with people in Halloween getup. With one scan of the room, I conclude that Halloween is a serious event here. The Queen sits on the arm of a chair, drinking a pint of lager with her legs spread wide. I assume so her crown jewels have some room in her dress. Many celebrities are in attendance alongside ghosts, goblins and monsters. Fun and hilarity are everywhere; everyone is here to have a good night. For once, I feel confident entering a room.

Wendy strides into the centre, looking hot as she swings

her hips in time to the beat of the music. She grabs two drinks from the side table, turns to me, and winks. People are watching us; I can feel it. The flute she hands me is filled with a red gooey fluid; a vampire stuck to the glass informs me the drink is named *Blood Lust*. The taste of strawberries fills my mouth; it is sweet and delicious. I guzzle it greedily. When I look up, Wendy's eyes pop wide open. She passes me her compact mirror and a tissue. I take a quick look. My lips and around my mouth are bright red.

"Bloody Terry and his piss-taking. What does he get out of mocking innocent partygoers?" I hiss at her, and she giggles while fluttering her lashes. I dab at my mouth to remove the residue.

"Holy shit, Bex! You look bloody delicious!" Terry hollers, grabbing me into a bear hug. Then he turns his eyes on my companion. "And who is this feline fantasy you have brought with you? I will be dragging the guys off the two of you."

I laugh and peck him on the cheek. "Oh, Terry Trodden, your patter is bloody awful. This is my colleague, Wendy."

He takes her hand, bends low, and kisses it like a knight of the round table. "It is a pleasure to make your acquaintance," he drawls and flashes her a wide smile. "I cannot wait to get to know you better." He leans forward and whispers in her ear, "preferably on your back in my bedroom."

My eyes widen in horror, and I give him the dirtiest look I can muster. He laughs while disappearing into the party. "Until later, ladies," he calls over his shoulder. We watch this mammoth man walk away in sky-high heels and a pencil skirt; Terry Trodden makes walking in heels look damn easy.

If the first ten minutes are anything to go by, this is going to be one hell of a party. I am here to flaunt my body for the first time in my life. Tonight is my rebirth, the birth of the Bex I like and am proud to be. I'm going to flirt, dance, and have fun. Tonight, people will notice me. I know I look damn hot.

CHAPTER ELEVEN: BEN

For the past five years, Kelsey has dressed us up in matching Halloween costumes. She spends weeks, if not months, preparing for the parties we attend. "It has to be amazing," she repeats over and over while deliberating on the theme for the year. Halloween is not a holiday I look forward to. It is always stressful and about one-upmanship.

Kelsey's father normally hosts a massive Halloween party with champagne, canapés, and live music. For me, it is boring as the average age of the guests is well over sixty. Kelsey feels we should attend to support her father now that her mum is not by his side. This year, her father has been unwell, so he decided to cancel the party. Terry's boozy bash is a welcome change.

My costume is not unbearable. Danny from *Grease* is miles better than the *cute* sheep she dressed me up as last year. My balls itch at the memory of those god-awful wool shorts. I was left fighting off old ladies who wanted to pet the lamb, while Kelsey had been swanning around as Little Bo Peep, dancing with all her father's friends and collecting compliments on her outfit. My skin prickles at the memory.

Tonight, I'm comfortable in a leather jacket and all-black ensemble. My hair has grown slightly longer than usual, as I was ordered, so it could be styled into the required quiff. Kelsey is dressed as the *Innocent Sandy* before she found the skin-tight jeans and red high heels at the end of the film. I had tried to convince her to be the *Sexy Sandy*, but she replied that wasn't her style. Her A-line dress is a soft yellow teamed with a knitted cardigan and ballet flats. Her chestnut hair is down and soft, held in place with a pink headband. Kelsey looks every bit the girl next door.

I am standing with the guys; we are huddled around a table talking women and sport. Seemingly they all live in the building on the second floor and have known Terry for years. They are a mixture of lawyers and accountants, but from the stories they are telling me, they certainly know how to have a good time. As much as I love Kelsey and the girls, it would be nice to have more male company. Lads to go out for a few pints with, talk about the game on the weekend, or discuss the hot chick who lives a few doors down.

A tall, blond guy opposite me, I think his name is James, suddenly stops talking. It is noticeable, as he has not stopped laughing and joking since I joined the group an hour ago. His eyes are pinned over my shoulder at something behind me.

"Hold on to my pint, boys." He passes his beer to his mate and stands up. "The talent has just arrived." We all turn in unison to see who he is staring at.

Next to the front door, Terry has a blonde woman in a bear hug. Her back is to me, so I can't see her face, but she is barely dressed in a nurse's uniform. Standing beside her is a female wearing a black PVC jumpsuit finished with a set of pointy cat ears. Her hair is short and spiked. She looks both amazing and terrifying. Terry is speaking to them animatedly. Both women look incredible.

My focus moves back to the sexy nurse—something about her is familiar. Her legs are long and shapely, and the skyscraper heels she's wearing show them off to perfection. The little nurse outfit scarcely covers her behind. I'm sure if she leant forward, I could see her ass. My mind wanders to what that ass underneath looks like. Is she wearing a thong under there, or perhaps nothing at all? My cock twitches at the forbidden thought. I imagine myself bending her over to find out. I am sure I have seen her before. I try to place her but fail. She turns to talk to her friend.

In profile, I know exactly who she is.

Bex looks unbelievable. I can see her makeup is dramatic, dark smoky eyes and ruby lips. I find myself willing her to turn around. I want a better look at her. I need a better view of her. She whispers something in her friend's ear, and they both laugh. Her head is thrown back and exposes her long throat. I imagine my tongue there, licking and sucking. I can't tear my eyes away.

An annoying tapping on my shoulder brings me back to now. "Ben! Ben! Ben! Oh, bloody listen to me!" The voice is shrill, and I stare down into Kelsey's eyes. "Bex is here, and she looks like a whore. Like a bitch in heat!"

I look at her, confused, trying to string a response together. I can't, so I say nothing, concluding that telling my partner I think Bex looks incredible is probably not the best idea. My head nods as I half-listen to her ranting on about "having no decency." My eyes keep straying back to the naughty nurse. She has turned around fully now; I can see the full length of her. Her red lacy bra is on show, hinting at the fullness of her breasts. She lifts her drink to her lips and gulps greedily. It's so fucking sexy. My brain misfires. I imagine her kneeling in front of me, her red lips wrapped around my hard cock, and my hands in her hair.

The night continues like any other party. One drink follows another, cheesy music plays loudly, and people start to peel off in secret together. I've watched Bex from a distance. She has been fending off a constant stream of admirers. Her confidence is high, she's had a huge smile plastered across her face all night. Tonight, she has laughed more than I have ever seen her. She's mesmerising. Catwoman hasn't left her side, always standing close to her. She touches Bex at every opportunity. She finds her attractive, the same as every man in the room.

The Black Cat's eyes meet mine, and I see her nudge Bex then point to me. Bex looks across and smiles, waving shyly. She leans down to whisper in the cat's ear. Taking this as my cue, I walk over to them and introduce myself to the lady in black.

"Good evening, ladies. I'm Ben." I smile, holding out my hand to shake the cat's paw.

"Well, well, well," she beams at me. "So, you're the *Doctor Jones* I've heard so much about. I'm Wendy. I work with this stunner here," she says, gesturing toward Bex. Her comment takes me by surprise. This woman is bloody confident. Older than us — maybe in her thirties — but as sexy as hell with it. She sees my discomfort, grins, and carries on. "Your eyes really are as blue as Bex said they were."

I look to see beetroot red Bex standing beside me and giggling nervously. Why the hell would she be discussing my eye colour with this woman? Moving my attention to my friend, I take a sip of my beer to contain my thoughts before I speak.

"You look gorgeous," I tell her and feel my heart rate accelerate. "It's wonderful to see you looking so confident in your own skin," I continue, and she stares at me, unsure what to say. She drops her gaze away from mine, suddenly shy, but I see a small smile on her red lips.

Leaning in toward her, I whisper in her ear, "You do look amazing."

A hand on my arm demands my attention. It's Wendy. She pinches me softly and says, "Your girlfriend is watching, and she doesn't look so happy."

I look across to see an enraged Kelsey watching my every move. She saw something she didn't like, and I am going to hear all about it. Flashing both these sexy women a smile, I walk off in her direction.

The next morning, I lie awake going over the night before. Bex looked like a different person. My body was filled with arousal from the moment I saw that naughty nurse. I don't think I have ever felt more attracted to someone in my life. All these years of being loyal to Kelsey, and temptation has stayed away until now. If Bex had given me the go-ahead last night, though, I am certain that I would have jumped into bed with her.

Kelsey and I had left the party immediately after my conversation with Bex and Wendy. She hadn't spoken to me beyond saying she was ready to go. I asked her umpteen times what was wrong, but she ignored me, immediately locking herself in the bathroom when we got home. Fifteen minutes later, she emerged makeup-free, wearing the most sexless fluffy pyjamas she could own. She climbed into bed and turned her back on me. Still, not a word was spoken between us. I had lain in bed, rock-hard and dying to touch a woman, but not the woman lying next to me. My mind was still with the naughty nurse at the party upstairs.

CHAPTER TWELVE: BEN

My reaction to Bex last night has me completely unsettled. Kelsey and I have been together a long time, and I'm in disbelief of my attraction to Bex. I'm more than attracted; I'm *lusting* over her. After getting home last night, I lay awake, running over the indecent thoughts going through my head.

She looked completely and utterly fuckable. I have never looked at Bex in that way before. She has always been our geeky, weird-looking friend, tall and gangly with no shape and a long nose. To me she's never been attractive. Even the odd time she made more of an effort on her appearance, I've always looked at her platonically. But last night ignited a fire in me. A fire I didn't even know was there. I was aroused and carnal. I wanted to grab that woman and bend her to my will.

Kelsey is still giving me the silent treatment this morning, not even looking in my direction over breakfast. She had laid out my bowl, milk, and cereal as she does every day. We cleared the cereal bowls once we finished eating without saying one word. It strikes me how old our relationship seems. Suddenly, I am looking from the outside in. We act like a couple that has been married for twenty years, not young professionals in their twenties and in love. There is no spontaneity. Everything is functional and works, but I'm not sure either of us are truly happy.

I love Kels, and I know she loves me, but the question is whether we are still *in love* with each other. Our relationship quickly moved to not being one of lust and ripping off clothes. There is no throwing her over my shoulder and having my wicked way. Everything is tranquil and calm, full of organisation and planning. We live the life we were brought up to believe we should.

A few hours later, I am sitting on the sofa watching the match. There has been no sign of Amy or Bex today. Perhaps they are both sleeping off a hangover. A sinking feeling in my stomach makes me suspect that, perhaps, Bex didn't make it home at all last night. She looked incredible; someone would have taken her home. Bile rises in my throat as jealousy courses through my veins. I'm bombarded with images of her having sex with a mystery man. In my head she moans as she orgasms in ecstasy underneath him.

Feeling myself redden in anger, I try to bring my emotions under control. This is ridiculous. Before last night, I've never thought of Bex in that way. It's a complete overreaction. I've been watching too much porn with nurses taking the starring role. It's skewing my perception; there is no way she looked that bloody hot last night. I sit and stew in my thoughts for a while.

Feet padding softly down the hall tells me that someone has woken up. There is a slight cough and then, "Ouch! Fuck, that bloody hurts!"

I stifle a giggle as Bex appears in the living room. "Bloody door. Stubbed my toe," she smarts. I smile at her; she looks a mess but edible. Her blonde hair is messy and unruly. She still has last night's makeup on, and her skimpy nightie hangs over her full breasts, her nipples erect and poking through the soft material. Tired eyes meet mine, and she smiles softly.

"Morning," I say quietly.

"Is it still morning?" she asks. "I haven't had as much fun as I did last night in a long time. I need to wear a nurse costume more often." She laughs, and it is completely infectious. I can't help but laugh along with her.

"What?" she questions, taking me off guard. "Why are you

looking at me like that?" She frowns slightly as she watches my face for clues of what I'm thinking. Bex has little confidence, and she will be automatically jumping to the wrong conclusions.

I look her square in the eye, trying to control my heart rate. "I'm just enjoying seeing you so happy. It's nice to see you smiling the morning after a night out. Normally, you're quite down and brooding."

Her eyes widen and I realise that comment was deep. Bloody hell, I didn't even realise I'd noticed that much before. She's looking at me curiously, obviously thinking the same thing.

A few minutes later, I'm just sitting there staring at her. Drinking her in. She is beautiful. My body starts to respond to the vision in front of me, and I harden beneath my sweats. My mouth goes dry. All I want to do is kiss her. She looks at me uneasily, completely at sea with my bizarre behaviour. Pulling my focus away from her, I pretend to go back to watching the game, needing to break the connection, to get my body back under control. No one has ever affected me like this, and I've not even touched her.

She wanders round to the other sofa and sits down, curling her legs up underneath her. "Who's playing?" she asks.

Her words surprise me. Bex is no more interested in football than swimming the channel. I raise an eyebrow and she laughs, deep and throaty, her head thrown back, accentuating her shape. "Ok, ok, that was crap small talk. I don't care." She smiles and winks.

I snigger and shake my head in response, then we both settle down with our eyes on the TV, but neither of us watching it. There is electricity, a buzz in the air. I'm not sure what is happening, but it feels like something has changed between us. The attraction is mutual. That both excites me and terrifies me.

Kelsey stalks into the room, demanding our attention and still wearing a pissed-off look. My eyes meet hers, but she snaps hers away. I can almost hear her growling at me from the other side of the room.

"Morning, Bex," she snaps, angrily. "Good night last night?" Her tone is sharp and judgemental. "Perhaps next time try wearing more clothes, then you won't get every creep fawning over you," Kelsey says with a sneer and marches off in the direction of the kitchen.

Bex turns to look at me before bursting out laughing. "Jesus Christ! Did you piss in her cereal this morning? Someone got out of the wrong side of the bed," she says and raises her eyebrows.

I look at her, blown away by this confident, sexy woman before me. Gone is the insecure teenager. This woman knows she is bloody gorgeous, and she loves it.

There is nothing sexier than a confident woman. The past few weeks have proven it to me. Every day, Bex emerges from her room dressed in a new figure-hugging outfit and heels. She leaves for work with her head held high and her boobs on full display. At night, when we all sit on the sofas, her phone is constantly vibrating with calls from her seemingly constant stream of admirers. Each time she gets herself dolled up to leave for a date, my jealousy increases a notch.

Today was the day that my worst fear from the past few weeks was realised. It is nine o'clock on Saturday morning. Kelsey and I had been out for dinner at a Chinese restaurant the previous evening. A pleasant enough night, we had eaten the two courses for fifteen pounds and shared a bottle of wine. Arriving back at our apartment, we had a customary shag and fell asleep, relaxed but not fully satisfied. It's not easy to get Kels to orgasm; she holds back. I have spent years trying to relax her and find out what she enjoys, but have concluded she just does not enjoy sex, so now we tend to get the act over and done most efficiently.

Walking into our living room, I find a dark-haired man sitting on my sofa. He's only wearing an extremely small pair of boxer shorts. The strain on his crotch tells me he is well-endowed. I mentally smack myself for even noticing that. Is checking another man's junk out normal? He looks up and sees me.

"Who the fuck are you?" I snap, feeling completely thrown to have a random man in the flat. His eyes widen, taken back by my outburst. Then, I hear her voice.

"It's ok, Ben. He's with me." Bex appears in the living room, carrying two mugs of tea. "Ben, this is Eric." She smiles at me, thinking I will be polite.

To hell with that! Jealousy rages through my body, and I feel my temperature skyrocket. I'm livid. How dare this idiot be in my flat with my girl? The sensible part of my brain is pointing out that my girlfriend is still in bed, but the irrational part of me is in full support of my anger. I spin round to face her; my voice is hard and venomous. "Is this what you have become, Bex? The local bike? Bringing random guys home because you've learnt how to put a bit of makeup on?"

Her eyes harden, and I see the anger bubbling below the surface. Then, it bursts through the barrier of her self-control. She hits me hard across the face.

"How fucking dare you? You asshole!" she spits.

Eric looks between us, completely confused by the outburst. Bex turns and grabs his hand, leading him back toward the bedroom without a backward glance. Their two cups of tea sit untouched on the coffee table. They won't be drinking them with what she has in mind.

I sit back on the sofa and run my hands through my hair. It feels slick with sweat, and a few beads trickle down my forehead. My muscles are taut, as if ready to fight. The game is still playing in the background. My gaze drifts back to the little men dressed in red and blue fighting over a black and white ball. I stare at the TV for a while, contemplating what to do next.

Confusion overwhelms me. Normally, I'm an in-control person; feelings and emotions don't tend to get in my way. I'm good at compartmentalising situations, popping them on the shelf until I have time to deal with it. Or never dealing with it at all, if that is easier. But this situation is living with me every day, in the home that I share with my high school sweetheart. I go to bed every night with the same woman I have been with for nearly ten years and have planned a future with. But my mind is with the woman two doors down, imagining all the dirty things I could be doing to her.

Suddenly, I'm aware I'm being watched. Kelsey is standing at our bedroom door. She's dressed in her gym gear, ready to head out for a run. She's quiet and viewing me silently. "What was all that about?" she asks.

Before I can think of anything remotely comforting to say, Amy bursts into the room dressed ready for their run.

"Kelsey!" she shouts. "You ready? Let's get hitting the tarmac, baby!"

"Do we have to, Amz? The thought of walking anywhere this morning is torture, never mind running. I'd rather just lie in bed with mountains of chocolate."

"Don't be such a lazy bitch. You promised," she says and slaps Kelsey hard on the ass, causing her to grimace.

"Amy, if you lay a finger on me again, I will kill you," she growls.

Normally I would laugh at their exchange. A similar conversation happens every time they agree to go running. Amy is always full of beans and dragging Kelsey along with her.

Her interruption was a relief. Kelsey knows me better than anyone, she knows something has changed. My guilty eyes can't hold her gaze when it returns to me. I drop my focus to look at my fingers which are entangled with each other. I need to get my shit together and get control of these ridiculous feelings.

Bex is still the same awkward platonic friend I've always had. I have zero attraction to her. But even as I tell myself these things repeatedly in my head, I know I'm lying. Not only to myself, but also to Kelsey. This makes me an absolute bastard. That is something I am one-hundred-percent sure of.

CHAPTER THIRTEEN: KELSEY

Something has changed.
Something massive.

A sense of unease has hung around the apartment since that bloody Halloween party a month ago. The only person completely oblivious to the awkwardness is Amy. She skips in and out from work to the bar, to the gym, and she doesn't notice the deathly silence. No one talks, it's just Amy who rabbles on about all the insignificant crap that is her life. Today, I want to throat-punch her and demand silence.

"Do you want sugar coated cereal or plain?" Amy asks me, again.

"Fuck's sake Amz," I hiss. "Neither. I'm on a fruit diet, remember." She rolls her eyes at me. "And don't start with all your lecturing about a balanced diet." I add to stop her before she starts.

"Kelsey, what you put in your body is your business. But get your ass in gear, we are on the supermarket run this week. This list is bloody huge, so you're coming."

"Can we not just live on pasta this week?" I whine.

"No, get a bloody move on. And put a smile on your face, you look like you've swallowed a wasp," she announces, before skipping off in search of bags to bring the shopping home.

My life is fucking falling to pieces around me. Everything I thought I knew feels off. My precisely planned future is under threat. Sitting on our bed, the sheets are soft beneath me,

I grab handfuls and twist them in my fists. Silent tears run down my cheeks, as I quietly fall to pieces. Nothing has happened yet, but carnage is just around the corner. The rising panic of loss fills me, and the necessity to take steps to protect myself from the pain is at the forefront of my mind.

When I lost my mum in my teens, it was the most frightening experience of my life. My mum was my support system, a constant fixture. To me, she was a superwoman, keeping our home life stable and putting everyone else's needs before her own. My dad has never been good at looking after himself, always needing a woman's influence to navigate day-to-day tasks. He is capable at work and a clever man, but common sense—not so much.

Mum always said he would have put the washing tablets in the dishwasher then wonder why the kitchen was full of bubbles. I remember the day he did that, trying his best to help around the house and creating more mess. Then there was the time he set the grill on fire cooking toast; the scorch marks were on our kitchen ceiling for years. I smile sadly at the memories, bittersweet all of them.

When Mum died, Ben was there for me by my side through the tears and tantrums. He would hold me close and rock me gently to sleep, never once complaining or running away from the girl falling apart in front of him. We were so young back then, barely adults, trying to navigate our way between school and university. Without him, I don't know how I would have survived. A few times, I did think about ending the pain, weighing up the consequences of the most final decision I could ever make. But I couldn't leave my poor dad alone in this world. He needed me. His mental health plummeted without Mum, and he struggled to get up each day.

I remember sitting at the kitchen island with him on a rainy midweek afternoon. He was still signed off work with stress. We sat and nursed our cups of tea, not speaking, both lost in our thoughts. The house felt incredibly empty with no Mum running around, ordering us about. There was really nothing to say.

Six months previously, she had found a lump on her breast and immediately booked an appointment at the local clinic. The doctor had taken one look at the imperfection and referred her straight to the hospital. Dad and Mum had attended the appointment together to get the results of the tests. I try to visualise the scene.

They were sat across from the sympathetic doctor in the hospital. He had broken the news firmly but with compassion. There was nothing that could be done. Her cancer had spread to untreatable levels. We were talking weeks, not months. Two weeks later, she was gone. It had been so rapid that I hadn't had time to process the initial diagnosis before she was dead. I think it took all those six months for Dad to accept she was gone permanently. It was that rainy afternoon he broke down for the first time and cried. Long heartfelt sobs echoed through the empty house.

Losing Mum so quickly and unexpectedly has made me terrified of change. That is probably why I have held onto Ben so tightly. Even when he found out about my infidelity, I had hung on with a death grip, using my tears, and ultimately, my loss of Mum to keep him around. He had struggled to move on from my affair with Sam, but I had promised him it was a stupid mistake. I had begged him to give me another chance. Then I had blamed him for it happening at all, telling him if he showed me more attention, I would never have strayed. Neither of us had believed that. Ben has always been my rock, and I can't imagine life without him. There was no way I was letting him go without a fight.

To my relief, he stayed.

The tables had now turned, and I was doubting Ben's feelings for me. He wasn't as in tune with me recently. Since

Halloween, his mind had been elsewhere. I thought I was imagining it at first, the glances toward her, the way his breathing increased ever so slightly when she entered a room.

Bex has never been beautiful. She was the woman that was dismissed by the men in a room. But something had changed in recent weeks. Her confidence was growing, and she held her head up with pride. People were noticing her. I couldn't deny it anymore. My Ben was noticing her every day. He watched her as she walked around the apartment.

Then, there had been his outburst when he was confronted with Eric in the living room last week. His face had been riddled with jealousy. I had watched in horror as my partner reacted so badly to another woman's lover. It had cemented the niggling suspicion in the back of my mind. Ben had developed feelings for Bex. He wanted her.

Knowing him as I do, after almost a decade together, I know him well enough to be confident that he has not acted on his feelings. But I must protect myself from the loss. I need to be in control of this situation. I need to make the next move on my terms. The lack of control is frightening, that feeling when the world is moving around you. When you are standing, watching it spin, and you can't reach the stop button.

I have never doubted his feelings for me until this moment. Anger bubbles to the surface again. How dare he lose interest in me this way? How dare he not want me? As irrational as it sounds even in my own head, I am at a loss as to why on earth he would prefer her over me. We are meant to be together. We are the ultimate teenage dream. He has no right to ruin the story, but I can feel him slipping away. I must hurt him first.

Three suitcases and ten carrier bags. That's all I needed to pack up all the worldly possessions I have in this apartment. Ben is on shift today for twelve hours; I have plenty of time to clear out all my stuff. I haven't decided how I am going to tell him it is over yet and that I'm going back to my dad's. The taxi is organised to arrive in one hour's time, I will be long gone before he gets home. Part of me is excited about the on-coming situation. I love a bit of drama. It's a trait I don't par-ticularly like about myself, but one I like to indulge in every now and again.

My suitcases are heavy and crammed full. Hauling them, one at a time, down the three flights of stairs is back breaking. Time is marching on, and I panic someone is going to appear home early, ruining my escape. My keys are lying on the din-ing table alongside an envelope marked *Ben.* I want my exit to be worthy of a soap opera. I want to shock him. Just to be gone. I want him to want to know why. To chase me for an-swers.

The taxi pulls up at the kerb, and the tall, lanky driver un-folds himself from the front seat. He lugs my three suitcases into the boot of the car. I'm glad he has an SUV-style vehicle, as I doubt all my crap would have fitted in a normal saloon. Opening the rear door, I take a long final look at the building I have called home, and before losing my bottle, climb into the car. The door slams shut, and we pull out into the late morn-ing traffic.

We come to an abrupt stop in front of my childhood home. Everything looks the same as it has for the past fifteen years. The roses in the garden are pruned to perfection, and the small fishpond has a fountain that bubbles happily away. The house is a standard two-up, two-down semi-detached in the suburbs of a small town near London. There is nothing excep-tional about it, but it's home. Dad didn't want to change any-thing after Mum died. I believe the house will remain the same until he takes his final journey to meet her.

My feet slow on the path, and I stand looking up at the only house I have ever really called home. My father is standing in his usual position at the living room window, his brow creased with concern. Next thing I know, I'm running up the path and jumping into his arms at the front door. He's warm, cosy, and safe. My defences drop and tears fall freely as I let myself melt into the safety of my dad.

"What's happened, Poppet?" he whispers into my hair. "Has someone hurt you? Where's Ben?"

I look up into his worried eyes and shake my head. "We've broken up, Dad. It's over. I'm home." Then, my sobs start again. Big wet tears fall as I lay my head on his chest, soaking into the cheap shirt he wears. He wraps an arm around my shoulders and leads me up the stairs into our home.

Sitting on the sofa in the front room, my breathing finally starts to steady. I've been crying for around an hour, but I can't really be sure. The room is clean and warm, the decoration subdued, and most items are in tones of cream and beige — the walls, the carpets, the furniture. A bright orange cushion piques my interest; there is a slogan written across the front in squiggly black writing. I squint my eyes to try to make it out. The words *Hot Stuff* followed by *Cuddle this and think of me* throw me completely. Why the hell would my dad have a cushion saying that? It must be a joke from his pub friends. I return to my self-pity.

Dad plonks a cup of tea down in front of me, but not before carefully placing a coaster with a picture of our late pet dog, Bertie, underneath. Mum hated rings on the table from mugs; it drove her bananas. I wouldn't like to count the number of times the dining room table had been sanded and stained to remove them. Our house may have been dull, but it was always kept in mint condition. Mum had borderline OCD. A lot had slipped since she passed, but Dad tried his best to maintain her high standards.

Concern percolates from every pore of him as he watches me. I'm normally the one who is in control and sorting situations. This reversal of roles is making my dad uncomfortable. He is struggling with what to do next.

"So, Poppet," he ventures, "what is Ben saying about this? You two are such a team. This has come as a shock."

"Well, the thing is, Dad, he probably doesn't even know I've left him yet." He looks at me dumbfounded but stays silent. Taking a deep breath, I continue. "I'm not sure what I want, and I need some time to think. It was easier to pack up my stuff and leave. The letter I left for him explains it all." My admission is embarrassing. I brave a glance in his direction.

My dad looks as though I've slapped him hard. His eyes survey me, unsure what to say to this revelation. He stares at me for what feels like hours then sits down on the sofa opposite me. The old seat creaks under his weight; my father is a big man and has gotten huge since my mother passed.

"I just couldn't deal with the conversation, Dad. I needed space," I stammer.

His demeanour is low, and he turns disappointed eyes on me. "And you don't think Ben deserves a bit more respect than this? How many years have you been together?" His voice is quiet, but I can hear the anger. "Or is there something you're not telling me?" he continues, trying to make sense of the situation.

I shake my head. "No, Dad. I just didn't want to have the conversation, so I decided to walk away. I will talk to him, but just not yet."

He stands and walks back into the kitchen. I can feel his disapproval from here.

My phone has been buzzing all night. Twenty-five missed calls and twelve voicemails. That was the kind of reaction I was hoping for. I smile to myself. Bloody hell, it worked. Ben obviously found my letter around five o'clock in the afternoon, because at half-past five, my phone started ringing.

Frantic messages asking me to call him and begging me to respond so he knew I was alright. I hadn't told him I was coming here, knowing the unknown would freak him out more.

God, I'm such a bitch, but a snarky smile crosses my lips. I love this control. He doesn't even realise I have it. Finally, he gave up and called my dad. He would put this off as long as he could stand to because he wouldn't want to cause Dad unnecessary worry. Ben and my dad have become close since Mum died. During that awful time, Ben not only supported me, but he supported my dad as well, helping around the house or taking him to the odd football match in an attempt to encourage some normalcy. Ben had turned into the cliché — the son my father never had.

Once he spoke to my dad and realised I was safe, not wandering aimlessly around the city, the voicemail arrived. He was angry. He was fucking raging.

"Kels, what the fuck are you playing at? To up and leave, not even speaking to me. Not even telling me there was an issue?" I can hear his voice starting to break. *"How could you just walk away and leave me a poxy half-arsed letter as an explanation?"*

I stopped listening after that. Not wanting to listen to him droning on and on about how unfair my behaviour had been. Ok, so maybe I could have handled this better, but at the end of the day, he has not been fully committed to our relationship recently. If I had felt secure and loved, then I would have not wanted to leave in the first place.

This is completely his fault, and he deserves this anguish.

My phone hasn't rung for about an hour. It's eleven o'clock at night, and he has obviously given up. The earlier excitement of him chasing me has died away. I sit, staring at my silent phone. It's goading me, laughing at me. Oh, he obviously doesn't care that much if he's given up already. I switch the bastard off, not wanting to look at it anymore. My dad hasn't ventured up to see me since Ben spoke to him, so I don't know what was said, but I can only assume he is not too pleased with my behaviour either. I crawl under my covers and cuddle my pillow. Perhaps I will feel in control tomorrow, but right now, I'm not so sure.

Chapter Fourteen: Ben

The white envelope sits on the dining room table where she left it, next to the set of apartment keys with the rose key ring. Kelsey's keys. Her writing is so neat like everything about her. All small, neat, and tidily in place. I can tell this letter is important because she's used her, as I call it, posh writing, all squiggles and flicks.

When I got home from work, the apartment was empty. I assumed I must have been the first person home. That makes a change. Normally, the girls are sitting all spread out on the sofas when I walk through the door. The chatter is usually animated, concerning a colleague at work or some celebrity's new haircut. After a day in the hospital, I find their endless gossiping comforting. Taking comfort in the insignificance of what concerns them is relaxing after a stressful day. Normally, they all smile, and Kels will go make me a cup of tea. It was disconcerting not having my usual homecoming.

Bex had got home then, skipping through the door with her new upbeat confidence. She had come to an abrupt halt when she saw me. "What's wrong?" she asked.

I shrugged my shoulders. "I don't know yet," was the only response I could muster.

Picking up the letter, I had turned it over in my hands. This was so Kelsey; she loves a bit of drama. If it had only been the envelope sitting on the table, I probably wouldn't have been too worried, but the fact the keys were there had made my stomach flip. Slowly, I had peeled it open and slid the letter out. It was short and sweet.

Dear Ben,
There is a problem with our relationship. You have changed.
I can't stay here and watch you drift away.
So, I must go. I must protect myself.
Love, Kelsey x

At first, I wasn't sure what to make of the letter, if you can call it a letter. A note, more like. A little short note to end our relationship of almost a decade. I read and reread the note. Then, I panicked. *I must go.* What does that mean? I had called her phone over and over, but she didn't pick up. Then, I left voicemails, begging her to let me know she was ok. The worst-case scenarios were running through my mind. What if she did something stupid? It wouldn't be the first time she considered it.

After no success in tracking her down, I'd called her father, the man who had been to hell and back with the death of his wife. It was only in recent months his mood had improved, and I was sure that was because of his new friend. Once when I had dropped some homemade biscuits round from Kelsey, I'd seen her. He had asked me not to say anything as he wanted to keep things private for now.

He picked up on the first ring. "Ben," his calm, cool voice answered, "she's here."

My heart rate immediately started to slow, and relief washed over me.

"What's going on, Ben? All she will tell me is there is a problem at home, and she needed to leave." His voice is confused. I consider my words carefully, though I am as lost as him.

"I'm not sure. Things have been a bit strained recently, but I'd no idea she felt like this. The first I knew she was leaving was when I got home and there was a note with her keys on the table."

He sighs deeply. "Well, she's safe. I knew you would be worried. Give her a few days, and I will get her to call you."

I thanked him and cut the call. Then, the anger started to rise. How dare she? Nearly ten years, and she dumps me with a note. Disappears from our home with no explanation or warning. Kelsey can be the most selfless person in the world, but she can also be the most selfish. She's a paradox. She has completely flummoxed me this time.

"Do you want a hot drink?" Bex's voice cuts through my misery. She has a strong Birmingham accent, so soft isn't a word I would use to describe the way she talks, but I'm pretty sure that is the tone she is going for. Her eyes are scanning my face, and concern oozing out of her.

I shake my head. The last thing I want is to eat or drink. I feel physically ill. The disbelief that Kelsey walked out on me without as much as a backward glance is haunting. I hold the note between my hands, turning it over repeatedly. The simple words hold so much hurt. I feel a tear running down my cheek.

Bex's hand passes across my shoulder. Her arms wrap around me and squeeze me tight. "It's going to be ok, Ben," she whispers. "She'll come home. Maybe she just needs some time to get her head together."

The tears fall now. I'm not sure if I'm crying for the loss of Kels or the fact that I'm relieved. It disgusts me that when I read the note, a strange happiness filled me. *Freedom.*

Kelsey and I started dating as teenagers. I've never been with anyone else. Part of me is curious as to what it would be like. My recent temptation toward Bex has meant I have been considering this more often. I doubt I would ever have ended it with Kelsey. But now, perhaps I can investigate something or someone different.

Fuck's sake, Ben, the bed is still warm from her body, and here you are getting excited about other women. I chastise myself.

Kelsey never called. I spoke to her father a few days after

she left, but she refused to come to the phone. He sounded like he was dealing with the Devil; her mood swings were fierce. One minute she was declaring she was happy and free at last from her boring boyfriend, the next she was crying hysterically. She has requested a transfer to a nursing post in the hospital near her father's house. She has no intention of coming back to London. I packed her remaining things and sent them by the courier as requested. It was a bittersweet task, but her complete refusal to talk to me meant I had to just move on.

My ability to move on so quickly, according to Bex, is the key difference between a lot of men and women. She tells me that she would procrastinate and go over the situation in fine detail, jumping to conclusions or just making things up to increase the pain. From the hours of chatting with her, I have discovered that many women love to hurt themselves, especially when it comes to relationships. They love to rehash a situation repeatedly. She assures me for some this can go on for months.

Unsure if the fact I've returned to my normal self a few days after my ten-year relationship broke down is a good thing, I've been enjoying listening to Bex and Amy discussing the subject between them. I only have to grunt so they think I'm listening, and the conversation continues. They have done all my worrying for me.

Bex has been my rock these past few weeks, eating dinner with me every night and joining me for coffee at lunch when she can, listening when I need her to or just filling black space. She is as beautiful inside as she is outside. It's as if she found herself recently and knows who she wants to be. In all the years I've known her, Bex has always been underwhelming, and if I'm honest, a bit boring. She was loyal to her friends, but I always thought that was because no one really wanted to be her friend, so she held onto us like glue.

Amy and Kelsey were close in school, hanging out together all the time. Bex was the added extra, always sticking with her twin sister. She was smart—I knew that—but she never seemed to bring anything to the party, always living in her sister's shadow. Amy was clever, funny, and sexy. Every teenage boy followed her around like a lap dog. It was Amy I was after when Kels and I got together. Amy had shot me down in flames and told me I was too pretty for her with my baby blues. It had made me laugh, then knocked my confidence completely when I realised she was being serious. I had been licking my wounds when Kels had approached me, and we started talking. We were inseparable within weeks. I fell hard and fast. There was no going back.

This weekend, the girls have planned a big party session. The *Get Ben Back Out Into the World* challenge is well underway. Terry and I have been ordered to be ready to leave at 8 p.m. on Friday. No excuses. The punishment for not being ready had made both of us hold our crown jewels out of harm's way. I am very concerned about Amy's fascination with male genitalia and nutcrackers. We are in for a fantastic night out.

Chapter Fifteen: Ben

Her blonde hair bobs along to the music, completely lost in the beat of the track. The dance floor is sunken in the centre of the club. It's busy, and people are bunched up, swaying in their small space on the cramped dance floor. Amy and Bex have been up dancing for what seems like hours while Terry and I watch on from the security of the bar. The girls are having a fantastic time; they look confident and sexy. A few guys have them on their radar as they slide up to them on the dance floor and whisper in their ears.

I feel my stomach tighten as a tall blond chap with bouncy curls comes up beside Bex. She's a tall woman, but this man is a giant, standing a head and shoulders above her. He leans down to her level and says something. She smiles, then laughs back at him and places her hand on his arm. Jealousy runs in waves through my body as I watch them. This feeling has been coming more frequently over the past few months, getting harder to control.

Since Kelsey walked out sixth months ago, the four of us have been spending a lot of time together. Our relationships appear completely platonic. We have dinner, go clubbing, and spend every weekend in each other's pockets. Sometimes it feels like we are part of one of those American sitcoms where a group of friends live together and get into all sorts of trouble. Last week, Amy's clothes were stuck in the washing machine; the damn thing wouldn't switch off. Her beloved jeans were spinning round and round for forty-eight hours with no sign of stopping. It took the four of us to switch it off and open the door with a crowbar. Poor Amy was distraught as she looked at her minuscule jeans, now well beyond repair. We all helped drain her sorrows with bottles of wine and terrible rom-com movies.

My focus goes back to my friend dancing with the blond man. She looks so happy and confident, something Bex never looked before. Over the last year, she has gone from strength to strength in her career and personality. Her friend from work, Wendy, seems to have done wonders for her confidence, helping her embrace her looks and use them to her full advantage. Thinking about Wendy, I realise I haven't seen her for a while. Bex hasn't mentioned her. I wonder if they have fallen out. She seemed to become a fifth member of our group until her disappearing act a few months ago. I must remember to ask Bex how she is.

Terry is still talking, but I'm not sure what about. I'm not listening. He's now over his limit as far as his alcohol intake goes, so his words start to blend and become incoherent. Terry is a fun-loving guy, the boy who has never grown up, drifting from job to job, friendship group to friendship group.

Suddenly, he speaks sharply, "Why don't you just tell her how you feel?"

I look at him pointedly. "What the hell are you on about?" I ask.

"Bex." He uses his chin to point toward the dance floor. "Why don't you just tell her you think she's hot?"

My eyes meet with his; he's daring me to challenge him, and a snarky smirk appears on his face. He lifts an eyebrow. "Frightened she will knock you back?" he suggests, then continues, "She's a lovely girl, Ben. If you like her, you would be mad not to let her know. Every week we come out and every week someone is all over her. One of these times she will give him a proper chance. You will kick yourself when that happens."

I'm not sure what way to play this with him. Having barely

accepted my feelings for Bex myself, I'm not ready to discuss them with anyone. Least of all Terry. He's a good guy, but secrecy is not one of his strong points. More than likely, he will start a scheme of crazy plans to get us together.

"Don't know what you're talking about, mate." I look him dead in the eye, hoping my confidence is convincing. "Bex is a friend, and she's also Kelsey's friend. I've known her for years and never thought about her in that way. Dating my ex's friends is not something I do," I continue, then add, "not that I would want to," as an afterthought. Damn, that sounded convincing in my head, but the look on Terry's face says otherwise.

The club is dark and moody. People are becoming intoxicated and losing their inhibitions fast. Bex is still on the dance floor with the blond man, her arms around his neck and his lips at her ear. They are swaying to the music now, but it's not the music's rhythm they are moving to. Their bodies are pressed up against each other, his hands firmly on her behind, holding her close to him.

Strobe lights fly across the crowd in an array of colours, and a machine sprays out smoke at intervals, giving the place a mystic feel. As much as I don't want to watch, I can't pull my eyes away from them. I can't deny it. I want to be him on the dance floor. I want to feel her body in my arms and have my lips at her neck. I don't think I've ever wanted anything more.

A bubbly brunette approaches me, all smiles and giggles, introducing herself as Abbey, an aspiring model. She immediately places her hand on my arm.

"Oh my, you do have the bluest eyes I have ever seen," she purrs in my ear. Looking me dead in the eyes, she runs her tongue over her teeth. "You have no idea how much pleasure I could give you, gorgeous." Her voice is seductive, and I feel myself harden.

Smiling, I remove her hand from my arm. "Sorry, darling, I've got to go." I dismiss her and turn back to Terry, who is staring open-mouthed at me.

Watching Bex grind on the dance floor with that prick is driving me insane. I must get out of here. Terry knowingly raises his eyebrows at me, smiles, then saves me graciously. He turns to the girl who is looking forlorn at my automatic rejection. She is beautiful, but I'm not in the right headspace.

"Sorry, honey. Yes, he is an idiot, turning down a stunner like you, but see that blonde over there?" He points blatantly at Bex, and my jaw drops. "He wants a bit of that, but he doesn't have the balls to tell her. He would rather sit here, lust, then mope in his self-pity." She giggles, and he beams at her. "Here's my number, though, if you fancy a good time." Terry stands up and marches toward the door. I follow, stunned by his boldness, not knowing whether to congratulate him or punch him.

It's Monday morning, and I head into work. My career is progressing well. Better than I could ever have expected. Being noticed during my graduate years by a professor who still works actively within the industry has boosted my career. He is an elite in my preferred specialist area of oncology. When I graduated, I phoned him, and he offered me a job. I pinch myself every day, still shocked at securing the position.

Dr Eamon Riley is a diamond to work for. I am working with the Master of Oncology. He is respected worldwide, and many doctors ask his opinion on complex cases. I'm lucky to be included in his consultancy work. He opens my mind daily to the range of illnesses and the available treatments.

My interest in oncology comes from losing both my grandparents to cancer within a year. I was in my early teens and had spent every weekend with them since I was a young child. Both my parents worked Saturdays and Sundays at our restaurant, so they had very little free time for me. The family picnics and trips to theme parks were taken with my grandparents. I spent many a happy Sunday afternoon sitting by the lake fishing with Gramps. We would spend hours talking about my week at school or just sitting in companionable silence.

Gramps went first with stomach cancer which stemmed from his oesophagus, his decades of puffing his pipe eventually catching up with him. I continued to spend the weekends with Gran until she began to feel unwell around six months later. My mother took her to an appointment with the local doctor who referred her directly to the hospital. Within weeks, the cancer was everywhere, even the end of her nose. Before the anniversary of Gramps' death, we had lost her as well. The desolation was all-consuming, but it offered me a direction in life. I wanted to help people who found themselves in the same situation: those who were given a death sentence out of the blue, needing a shoulder to lean on.

When I announced my decision to study medicine, my parents had been stunned. I was never the most academic or focused in school, mainly enjoying the social perks of being in the popular crowd, but they rallied behind me and supported me in my quest to become a doctor.

Eamon has called a team meeting in his office this morning to discuss our ongoing cases. Some are looking promising, but others I know are marking time till they take their final journey. As much as I love seeing people recover and move forward in their lives from cancer, the real joy for me is spending time with my patients on a time limit. I always thought working with a patient who is in palliative care would be a depressing experience. However, these people are often the most open and honest. They relive their memories with you. I am often humbled by the trust they place in me, gaining a little comfort from the fact I can help make their final days more enjoyable. Quite often they come as patients, but when they leave for the final time, they leave as friends.

Eamon has the whole team in his office, but there is something different about today. He's quiet and forlorn, not his usual bubbly self. This can only mean one thing: we've lost someone. He continues summarising each patient's case. We have twenty on the ward now. Most of them are complicated cases requiring specialist care. Some have lost their mobility, some their minds, and others, both. Finally, all the patients have been accounted for, but he doesn't close the meeting. I see him taking a deep breath to compose himself before he continues.

"We have an additional patient on our ward this morning," he says.

We all look at each other confused. Normally we are all advised by message before admittance.

"My wife is in room E32." His admission hangs in the air. "She began experiencing headaches a few weeks ago, and last week, she had an episode where she lost consciousness," he explains matter-of-factly. "She has an aggressive tumour on her brain. We begin treatment immediately. In all honesty, the odds are poor, but I know you will all help me to the best of your ability." His haunted eyes rise, and we all stare at him, speechless.

"I need you all to help me save my wife," he states then walks directly from the room.

We all stand in silence, taking in the monumental challenge ahead of us. Somehow, we must succeed.

Room E32 is next on my list. I have only met Melissa Riley a handful of times. Each time she has brought in cakes for the team, normally after a tragedy. She is a happy woman and immensely proud of her husband's achievements.

I chap the door softly before entering. She's a small, burly woman with a riot of grey hair piled on top of her head.

Engrossed in the book in her hands, she has reading glasses perched on the end of her nose as she sits up in bed. Warm eyes turn to meet mine. "Doctor Jones." She smiles. "Have you been sent to check up on me?" She laughs loudly and heartily. "The nurses are correct."

I look at her, confused.

"You are a handsome young man. I've only ever seen you rushing past, but now it looks as if I will have time to enjoy the view." She winks, and I laugh. This woman is a handful.

"How are you feeling?" I ask.

"Oh, bloody awful, but you will know that. These headaches are killing me, and if they don't, that bastard cancer will," she says and smiles.

My face must look stricken; she takes pity on me. "Oh, Doctor Jones, if we can't laugh, what can we do? We must take these knocks on the chin. Eamon is beside himself with worry. I know this is bad. I have not been married to an oncologist for thirty years without learning a thing or two about cancer. As I told him, if I have any chance of surviving, then this is the best team that could be looking after me. He needs to concentrate on being my husband, not my doctor."

This woman is a firecracker. She's amazing. "I believe you are correct, Mrs Riley. That is his most important task, and I will see what I can do with regards to your headaches. Perhaps I can change your medication. Call me Ben, and let me know if you need anything," I say sincerely.

"Thank you, Ben. In that case, call me Melissa."

Little did I know that this would be my first proper exchange with a woman who would become like an Aunty to me. One of my greatest supporters.

After twelve months of appointments, operations, and treatment, Melissa Riley has hope of survival. The tumour has shrunk in size, and it now feels like there is light at the end of the tunnel. Most of her year has been spent in room E32, and we have chatted for hours. Sometimes, after my shift ended, I would sit with her, and we would discuss anything or everything. She knows all about my relationship breakdown with Kelsey and my ongoing crush on Bex that doesn't seem to be going away.

According to Melissa, the fact Bex hasn't had a serious love interest in the past twelve months speaks volumes. She says that I need to grow a set of balls and tell her how I feel. What's the worst that can happen? She pesters me every time I see her, but I'm terrified at losing Bex. Even though we haven't progressed romantically, we have developed a close friendship. Spending hours together every week, I trust her implicitly, but we never discuss our love lives. It's just a subject I don't trust myself to talk about with her. Not being sure I could keep a lid on my feelings. Or if I did tell her and she rejected me? Would I be able to cope?

When she rejected Wendy's advances, I knew that hadn't gone well. It was a few months after the Halloween party at Terry's apartment. Bex had invited Wendy around for dinner as a thank you for all her support. Unfortunately, Wendy had seen this as a green light to make a move. Bex had been stunned and gently told her she didn't see her that way. From what I understand, they rarely speak now, and she makes Bex's life at work difficult.

Friday evening has arrived, and I head home for our usual takeaway and movie night. All four of us normally attend this evening but both Terry and Amy have plans tonight. I wonder if those plans could include each other, then I laugh that off as an absurd thought. To be honest, I can't even remember the excuse they each gave for not being able to come tonight. This means Bex and I have the place to ourselves. I can ask her what I want to, without listening ears or being interrupted. What if she says no?

Chapter Sixteen: Bex

Staring at the cream envelope in my hand, I look into clear blue eyes. Ben is staring at me with what I think is hope.

"I've never been to a black-tie event before," I say nervously. "I have nothing to wear."

He grins at me. "I will treat you. Have Amy take you shopping. She will love having an event to dress you for."

I nod. That is very true. Amy loves shopping, especially when she's spending someone else's money. And the fact the man I am besotted with is asking her to do it will drive her insane with excitement.

Dropping my focus back to the invitation, I feel my cheeks flush. I wonder if he knows he has this effect on me. The fact I fall to pieces around him. We have spent a lot of time together since Kelsey left, and I wonder whether he feels the same. I remind myself that someone who looks as good as he does would never be interested in me romantically.

"Ok, I will be your plus one," I say softly, and his face breaks into a huge smile. He hugs me tight.

"You are going to love Melissa," he shouts over his shoulder as he heads off to pick up our pizza.

Melissa Riley sounds like an incredible woman. She's battled cancer for twelve months while setting up a charity supporting women with the disease. This is the first annual ball of The Riley Foundation, and according to Ben, the whole medical community is going to be there. He has become extremely close with Eamon and Melissa Riley; they treat him like a son they never had. In return, he has committed a vast amount of time to help Melissa with setting up the foundation, becoming her right-hand man in all things Riley Foundation. I did have a giggle to myself earlier this week when he was worried about the floral decorations for the table centres at the ball. Those are not concerns I ever thought would leave Dr Benjamin Jones's mouth.

The ball is being held in a five-star hotel in the city centre; over three hundred people are attending. There is going to be a charity auction and a raffle to raise funds, never mind the thousands of pounds raised from ticket sales. Ben handed over his credit card, whispered me the pin, and told me to get whatever I wanted. I had one week to get prepared, and he wanted me to walk into the room feeling a million dollars. His eyes had twinkled at his last word. I smiled shyly, feeling my heart flutter, then leant forward to kiss his cheek.

After I sent Amy the lowdown of our conversation last night by email and a link to the event next weekend, she had appeared in my bedroom within ten minutes. The door swung open, and she bounced in. "What the fuck is going on?" she squeaks.

"We are going shopping now!"

She looks like a jack in the box, jumping up and down. Rubbing her hands together, she snaps, "Right! Hand it over!"

I look at her vacantly, and she holds her hand out.

"The card, you dipshit! You will never use it properly. Hand it over now. This needs an expert in charge."

I wander over to my bedside table and lift the golden card. It is shiny with black, scrolled writing on the bottom. *Dr B Jones.* Amy looks from me to the card and then back to me. Her eyes narrow in impatience, and she pinches the card from between my fingers.

"Right, you get dressed. We are leaving in ten minutes," she declares.

An hour later, we are at the shopping centre discussing

what type of look I should have on Saturday night. Amy has been googling the Grand Plaza Hotel where the ball will be held. She thinks we should go later for a drink to test it out. Once I explained three drinks would probably cost us a week's wages, she opted not to.

We have decided on a demure but sexy look. According to Amy, men want their women to look like a lady but act like a vixen, especially in the bedroom. Seemingly, it is important to hint at this erotic part of yourself in the way you dress. A stylist is booked to come to the apartment in the afternoon before the ball to do my hair and makeup. They accepted Ben's card, so it's all good. I haven't asked how much it will cost. I don't want to know.

After browsing the high-end boutiques for what feels like forever, we finally decide to go in. The assistant smiles at us coolly but asks what she can do to help. The way she looks at us tells me she thinks we are most likely looking for directions to the toilets rather than an evening gown. The shop is filled with expensive dresses, all sparkles and sequins. There are racks upon racks of them in every colour imaginable. A mannequin in the centre of the room displays a bright pink number adorned with feathers across the skirt. The top is a corset style displaying the wearer's assets to the maximum effect.

Amy's commanding voice brings me back to the here and now. "My sister here is attending a charity ball at the Grand Plaza next Saturday, and she requires an evening gown." She makes this statement and waves her hand around the shop indifferently. "Do you have anything appropriate?"

The shop assistant looks outraged by the apparent insult but composes herself. "Well, we are the largest stockist of evening wear in the city, madam. I am sure we will have something suitable."

Amy nods then gestures to me to take a seat on the sofa. "Perfect." She smiles. "Do you want to show us what you think might be suitable? As you can see, Bex is stunning, so we want something to knock everyone else out of the park. She needs to turn heads," Amy proclaims. "Well, a certain someone's head, anyway," she adds.

I grimace at her and hiss, "It's not like that, I told you."

She laughs but doesn't respond.

So far, I have tried several dresses, including a pink contraption that felt like wearing a straitjacket. Then there was a white, floaty number that looked as if I was going to walk down the aisle. The final straw was when the assistant brought out a neon-yellow jumpsuit.

"Stop!" I exclaimed. "I don't want to be noticed for the wrong reasons, and that would make me look like a traffic cone. Don't you have something a bit more understated?"

Amy huffs. "Boring, you mean."

I raise an eyebrow at her. "Perhaps something in a darker colour, and maybe with a slight sparkle?" I ask hopefully. The assistant eyes me warily then stalks off in the direction of the storeroom.

Around ten minutes later, she emerges with a long pink dress bag and hangs it from the hook outside the changing room. Slowly lowering the zip, I hold my breath. If this is another jazzy number, I'm giving up. As she lifts the dress from the bag, my jaw drops. It is a long navy gown with a hint of sparkles on the waistband and bosom. The assistant's eyes meet mine, and we both smile.

"Would you like to try this on?" she asks.

"I would love to," I reply, and I step forward to take the beautiful creation from her.

The shop has a viewing area like you see on those American wedding dress TV shows. I'm standing on the raised platform, admiring myself in the mirrors that surround me. This dress is incredible; it hugs my curves and finishes on the floor. The material is soft, feeling luxurious against my skin, and the colour is a beautiful deep navy with similar coloured crystals detailing the waistband. My breasts are on full display as the V-shaped neckline plunges low to my ribcage, and short capped sleeves display my early-summer tan. I feel incredible. Amy stands speechless as she looks at me. Then, she simply hands over the golden card.

Mission accomplished.

"I don't need sexy underwear." I scowl, my face resembling a beetroot. "No one is going to be seeing it!"

Amy shakes her head. "Are you really that stupid? You can't see this . . ." She waves her arms around. "For what it is, Bex?" She shrieks with laughter.

Her speech continues as we eat lunch. "No man, whoever he is, hands over a credit card to a woman he is not interested in." Now tears have started streaming down her face. "I can't believe you would be that dense."

Glowering at her, I continue to chew on my roll. What she says makes sense, but this is Ben. I just can't comprehend that he would like me that way.

Never having owned sexy underwear, the thought that I might sends shivers down my spine. I'm unsure whether it is from excitement or nerves. Probably both.

"What if he checks his credit card statement and sees we've been shopping there?" I panic, gesturing toward the lingerie shop across from us.

"Then he will know he's in for a good night." Amy giggles. "Oh, Bex, you're mad about this guy. Accept it and enjoy it. Come on, let's get shopping." We throw some money on the table and off we go in the direction of the shop with suspenders in the window.

Saturday finally arrives. I've had a full-on week of preparations with Amy. Ben has been busy between work and arrangements for the ball. We've agreed to meet at seven o'clock. A taxi is arranged to take us to the hotel. I woke up this morning full of nerves. I can't decide what I am most anxious about, the ball or him.

The hair and makeup artists have worked their magic. My blonde hair is curly and piled up on top of my head, except for two loose curls that drop down the sides of my face. My eye makeup is dark and smoky, highlighting the long lashes that frame my eyes. The pillar-box red lipstick is a statement. I don't even look like me. I look like a 1950s movie star.

Amy is helping me dress and adding the finishing touches. Eventually, she had managed to convince me to invest Ben's money in the sexy lace underwear, just in case. Looking at myself in the mirror as Amy pulls my dress up over my hips, I smile broadly. I look hot!

There is a knock at the door, and Ben asks if he can come in.

"No!' Amy barks. "You have to wait to see the finished article."

"Alright." He sighs. "There is a little something here for you, Bex." I listen to him walk back down the hall. Amy immediately runs to open the door, grabbing the small pink box off the floor. She quickly passes it to me.

"Well, open it!" she orders. I untie the delicate pink ribbon and lift the lid. A pair of diamanté earrings sparkle up at me. Amy's jaw drops, and she looks from the earrings to me.

"He's buying you diamonds now," she whispers, and I chuckle.

"They won't be real," I murmur and roll my eyes. "It's just a small thank you for going with him tonight."

She looks at me pointedly. "I wouldn't be so sure," she says then drops the subject.

With fifteen minutes to go, I am ready to leave. Entering the living room, I walk cautiously in my super-high heels. Ben is standing by the door in his tuxedo, looking incredibly handsome. My heart skips a beat. His bright-blue eyes roll over my body, and I see his expression change.

Surprise, maybe. Possibly awe.

He steps forward and takes my hands in his. "You look incredible, Bex." He bends slightly to kiss my cheek. "Come on. Let's get out of here."

With his hand on the base of my spine, he leads me to the front door to a night I know I won't forget.

Chapter Seventeen: Ben

The function room looks incredible; the design team has worked magic to bring my vision for the ball to life. Cream fabric hangs in swags from the centre of the ceiling, framing a massive crystal chandelier. The room is already stunning with heavy golden wallpaper and a cream-colored marble floor. Each table is laid with cream linen, and the table centre holds a silver candelabra with fresh flowers. The whole place looks opulent and expensive which, in all honesty, it was, but you cannot justify charging £1000 for a ticket without spending a lot of money.

We have booked the best band available in London within a year's notice, The Tones. They play an eclectic mix of music from formal dancing to good old knees up. I have only attended a few events like this, but from what I have seen and heard, most of the time, it goes from a posh ball to piss up rapidly as the alcohol flows. My heart is pounding in my chest. I cannot believe Melissa trusted me with this, letting me have a considerable influence in its organisation. When I see the room, the pride I feel is immense.

Bex's gaze flies around the room, absorbing our surroundings. I know she has never been anywhere like this, being more comfortable at the local bar and the places she knows well. I stand beside her quietly, waiting for her to speak, to say something. She is speechless and just smiles at me like an idiot.

"So, what do you think?" I ask softly. I have been touching her since we left the apartment, either guiding her along or holding her hand like I am now. It feels perfect, her hand in mine.

She takes another sweeping glance. "It is stunning, Ben. I can't believe you organised all this." She waves her hands at the surroundings. Then her eyes light up when she sees the table centres. "Lilies!" she squeaks. "Oh! They are my favourite!"

The excitement in her eyes is breathtakingly beautiful. I want to blurt out that I know they are; she is the reason I chose them. But not wanting to frighten her off, I just smile and squeeze her hand.

We haven't spoken much since leaving the apartment. To be honest, I couldn't speak. When she walked into the living room, I swallowed my tongue. She looked incredible, as if she had just walked off a movie set. The more time we spend together, the stronger my feelings have become. Tonight, it was as if I saw her for the first time and could appreciate her unique beauty. It took all my willpower not to jump her right there in our home, bugger the fact that Amy was watching on. All I could muster was a smile, a compliment, and a short statement that it was time to go.

Navigating the stairs in her sky-high heels had been interesting. I assume the purchase had been of Amy's suggestion. Bex very rarely wears heels, and they are never as high as the fuck-me shoes she has on tonight. Her grip on my arm was cutting my blood circulation as we walked down the stairs; she was giggling to herself in the process and swearing at the offending shoes.

The Bentley sat at the kerb, waiting for us. It was a kind gift from Melissa. She knew tonight was incredibly important to me, and not because of the ball. Her excuse was that she wanted to treat me because of all my hard work. The truth is she wanted to be involved in impressing the girl. The girl I wanted so badly.

Bex had looked up and down the street as we reached the pavement. "I thought you said the taxi was waiting?" she asked, confused.

"It is," I replied simply and then gestured to the waiting car. Her scream must have been audible back in the apartment, the shock evident in her voice. "This?" she gasped excitedly. "How? Why? Fucking Jesus!"

I laughed and wrapped my arms around her, kissing her temple. She froze briefly in my arms, clearly taken aback by my affection. Then she softened. "Thank you. This is going to be a special night," she whispered.

Now here we were at the first-ever Riley Foundation Ball. Bex's first-ever black-tie event, neither of us quite sure what is happening between us. I lead her over to the table plan; we have been allocated seats at the top table alongside Melissa and Eamon. Melissa took full charge of the menu and seating arrangements; she was able to organise all that from the comfort of her home while recovering from her last treatment. The chef even had samples of food sent directly to her door. She had kept the final menu a secret, so no one knew what was being presented, not even Eamon.

Scanning the guest list, I see that everybody who is anyone in the medical community is coming tonight. Eamon is a highly respected doctor. When Melissa was diagnosed, the whole community rallied around her. There are also a good number of celebrities and influential people such as politicians and business owners. For our first event, the guest list is far better than expected, and I am hopeful we will raise a good amount of money tonight.

Warm arms wrap around my waist from behind, and I turn to see Melissa beaming up at me.

"Ben, my boy, what an incredible job you have done with the room." Eamon is standing next to his wife, gazing at her with pride. For a woman who has been to hell and back this year, she looks fantastic. Her hair and makeup are under-stated but polished, and she is wearing an emerald-green evening gown that compliments her voluptuous figure. But her broad, beaming smile is the most attractive part of her out-fit; this woman is genuinely happy to be here.

Her eyes move from me to Bex, who is standing quietly be-side me. "You must be Bex." She smiles at her. Bex holds out her hand, and Melissa ignores it while pulling her into a huge hug. "You look beautiful, my dear," Melissa enthuses. "Ben has told us so much about you. It is wonderful to finally meet you in person."

Melissa winks at me cheekily, and I feel my cheeks flush. She takes Bex by the arm, leading her away. "Come now, my dear, you're sitting next to me." I watch her lead away my gorgeous date and feel as if I am being set up. I look to Eamon, who laughs and shrugs his shoulders. "Come, boy, let's get a drink. I think you might need it."

The room is starting to fill up with guests. I have shaken hands with more people than ever before. Eamon introduces me affectionately as his colleague and Melissa's right-hand man in The Riley Foundation. There are lots of congratula-tions and kind words regarding the ball. Bex has been no-where to be seen since disappearing with Melissa thirty minutes ago. All the guests have arrived and are sipping their welcome drinks, so we decide to go off in search of our girls.

We find them at the table, sitting and chattering away like old friends. Melissa has Bex's hands in hers as I slide into the seat on the other side of her. Bex's face is animated and full of laughter; she has been having fun.

"Where have you been?" I prod Bex gently in the ribs, bringing her attention to me.

She looks at me warmly. "Oh, just hearing all about what a wonderful man you are. Melissa thinks the sun shines out your arse. I told her you leave your socks lying fucking

126

everywhere."

I laugh, shaking my head. "I think we need to get her started on some medication again, Eamon," I shout across to him. "This one is losing her marbles." Melissa gives me an evil look, then sticks her tongue out playfully.

The Master of Ceremonies (MC) takes his place on stage to announce a start to the proceedings. He is a short, tubby man with bright eyes and a balding head. His tuxedo is a size too small and strains across his stomach. There is a chorus of dresses swishing into their seats. Then a hush falls over the crowd.

After taking a sip of his water he begins, "We are here to-day to celebrate the first-ever Riley Foundation Ball." The audience bursts into applause, and excitement buzzes around the room. "You have all paid enough to be here, so you can expect tasty food and goodies. But understand that you were only allowed to come because you have deep pockets, and we expect you to empty them before the night is out." Everyone laughs, and the MC invites everyone to drink freely while enjoying their meals.

Our table is filled with medical professionals and people integral to the creation of the foundation. A younger man in his early thirties sits across from us. He is suave and confident, chatting away to the ladies on either side of him. They are captivated by him, hanging off his every word. Melissa sees where my eyes are directed and leans over. "That's Edward Brown. He is the kind bank manager who helped with the financials. Single and quite a catch," she says conspiratorially to Bex.

I give her a dirty look, and she smiles sweetly then continues talking to Bex, completely ignoring me. "Single, as I said, but he's looking for someone special. I could introduce you later if you like?" Bex looks from Melissa to me then across to Edward, who catches her eye.

Mr Brown has been listening to this exchange and takes the opportunity to introduce himself. Standing quickly, he walks around the table and crouches down between Melissa and Bex. I can't hear what he is saying. His eyes are travelling all over Bex's body, and my anger starts to rise. He lifts Bex's hand and kisses it softly.

"Till later," he says, smiling. Then he strides back to his seat.

The evening continues uneventfully, and the conversation is pleasant around the table. Everyone is enjoying themselves. The food has been delicious; Melissa did nail it with the menu. The MC stands back up on stage to conduct the charity auction. Bex leans in, asking what is available, and I hand her the catalogue listing the available prizes. Her eyes widen as she reads down the list, absorbing the value of what is on offer. "Think I will just watch." She giggles, and I nod my head. She is so happy; it makes me want to dance with glee.

Edward "The Wanker Banker" sidles back to our side of the table, pulling a seat up between Bex and me, turning his back to me and focusing fully on her. He starts whispering in her ear. My annoyance sits just below the surface, and my eyes bore into the back of his head. What an arse; imagine hitting on someone's date so blatantly. Squaring my shoulders, I tap him on his. "Excuse me, do you mind not interfering with my date?"

He turns around in his chair. "Your date?" He looks at me, confused. "Melissa said you were both just friends, that she was here as your platonic plus one."

I blink rapidly, trying to clear the confusion in my brain. "Well," I stumble. "Yes, we are friends, but we are here together."

He looks at me as if I am an idiot. "So, you're not together then?"

I look from him to Bex. "Guess not!" I snap and stalk off

toward the bar.

Sipping my whisky, I sit on the high stool and look out over the ball; the party is in full swing. The music fills the room, and people are dancing merrily. I feel a hand on my arm, and turn to see Bex's concerned eyes looking me over and weighing up my mood. "I'm sorry," I say quietly, embarrassed by my outburst at the table.

She smiles at me sweetly and cuddles me. "It's ok, I kind of like the fact you were jealous."

Our eyes are drinking each other in, and I can't look away. We hold hands just looking at each other. She is beautiful. I have never wanted anyone more than I want this woman right now. Taking her hand, I lead her to the dance floor and into my arms. Everyone around us disappears; it is just us and the music. This feels so natural, so right. I have wanted this for over a year and now it is happening. I spot Melissa standing at the side of the room, watching us. She has a huge smile on her face, and her eyes are alight with happiness. This is turning out to be an incredible evening.

CHAPTER EIGHTEEN: BEN

What have I done?

I lie in turmoil at the situation I have created.

Closing my eyes, I hope that when I open them, I'll return to being the sorry single sod of yesterday. My sheets smell of her perfume. It's potent and enticing, and my cock twitches at the memory of last night.

Returning to the present, I glance over to the other side of the bed. No sign of her. Perhaps she woke and ran. I wouldn't blame her. What a fucked-up situation this has turned out to be. Shame washes over me as I think of Kelsey back in her childhood bedroom cuddled up somewhere between her pink sheets and stuffed toys. I am an absolute bastard; this is a new low.

Music playing grabs my attention. She's still here. My body relaxes. She's not running for the hills. I quickly pull the crumpled sheets up over myself, wrapping them around my waist. Swinging my feet out of the bed, I flex my toes before they connect with the cold laminate floor.

Scanning the room, I think it looks like a bad porno has taken place. The side table has been knocked over, leaving a bottle of wine smashed on the floor. I vaguely remember my back connecting with it as we whirled into the room, all mouths and hands. Clothes are scattered across the floor; we had ripped them off each other in our enthusiasm. I look up, and a dirty smile stretches across my face when I notice the black lace hanging from the ceiling light. How the fuck did her bra get up there?

I laugh to myself. Last night was amazing. It was the best sex I have ever experienced. My cock agrees with my mind, wakening from his slumber. Anticipation of round two courses through my veins.

Forcing myself out of bed, I pull on my boxers and head off to find the vixen from my dreams last night. Music is pumping through the house; it's happy and upbeat. I see her. Her back is to me. She is in the bathroom, removing the last remnants of her ruined makeup. Her blonde hair is heaped on top of her head, giving her a just-fucked look. She is wearing my shirt with only a little red G-string. Her pert buttocks are jiggling as she wiggles from side to side along to the music. My body responds to the sight in front of me, and I clench my jaw as my arousal surfaces. I imagine what I could do if I moved that little string to the side.

In my hiding place behind the doorframe, I peek around to enjoy the show. Visions of her riding my cock cowgirl-style flash through my mind. I have never been with a woman who takes control like her, someone who knows exactly what they want and how they want it. It was refreshing, exciting, and I bloody loved it.

Dark eyes rise to meet mine in the mirror. She gives me a sexy smile then continues to gyrate her hips across the bathroom. She drops her toothbrush on the floor and exaggerates bending over to retrieve it while giving me a full view of her sexy ass. I move forward, wrapping my hands around her from behind. We look at each other in the mirror, both lost in memories of the night before. My hands roam over her body, twisting her erect nipples beneath my shirt.

Bex turns to face me. We are at eye level with each other. Her eyes are wide and wanting. She grabs my face, kissing me hungrily. Then, without a word, she turns and leads me by the hand back to bed. Round two it is.

We sit in our post-sex fog of happiness on the lounge sofa,

wrapped around each other's bodies. This woman drives me insane. We have fucked like rabbits all night. Just when I thought things couldn't get more fulfilling, she produced a set of handcuffs from her bedside drawer. Being secured and ravished by her is officially the best fucking thing that has ever happened to me.

Amy hasn't been home, so we have the place to ourselves. Which is helpful, as Bex and I cannot keep our hands off each other. My need to touch her is constant. I can't control myself. I must be physically connected to her at all times.

"Earth to Doctor Jones," she smiles softly. I glance over to her. Shit, she was talking to me.

"Sorry, gorgeous, was in a world of my own." I grin back at her.

She raises her eyebrows, licks her lips, and whispers, "I hope you were re-running my lap dancing exhibition from last night."

My body constricts and tenses. Instantly hard. My breathing quickens, and she smiles knowingly, loving my obvious reaction to her words. She leans over, running her fingers over the front of my boxers. "There is plenty more where that came from," she purrs.

Standing, she shakes her beautiful behind in my face. It jiggles from side to side, teasing me. My mind goes wild, and I grab her pert ass. She giggles. It's the sweetest sound in the world.

"I need to fuck you now," I growl in her ear and run my teeth down her neck then bite her hard.

She struts off in the direction of her bedroom, calling over her shoulder, "You won't touch me again, boy, till you feed me!"

I laugh and shout after her, "Typical woman! Rile me up and leave me hanging. Ok, wench, go get your glad rags on. We're going for food."

Half an hour later, we are sitting in the small café down the street from our apartment. It is late morning on a Sunday, so the café is quiet. They tend to rely on weekday trade from people commuting to and from work. It is a quaint little place called Peggy's Tearoom. The front door is old, and on either side, it has traditional windows, the kind with lots of little square panes of glass. Inside, there are ten wooden tables with bench-style seating. Red and white chequered cloths cover each of them with individual bottles of salt and pepper.

We pick a table at the back of the room which is private and away from prying eyes. Sitting next to each other, our hands are constantly intertwined. We open one leather-bound menu to share. It is an old-fashioned brown binder with the word *Menu* embossed in gold across the cover. Sitting silently, we study the options, and my stomach growls hungrily.

Bex's eyes lift to mine, and she laughs. "Did I work you so hard, Doctor Jones, that you require sustenance?"

I raise my eyebrows and wink. "I am going to eat my fill of this breakfast. Then I am going to take you home and eat my fill of you." She blushes and smiles shyly as I run one finger down her cheek.

Arriving back at the apartment, we have a welcoming party waiting for us. Amy and Terry are sprawled on the sofas eating ice cream and watching a terrible American sitcom.

"Rain check on the eating you out," I whisper to her. "We may have some questions to answer. Have you told Amy about us?" She shakes her head, and I breathe a small sigh of relief. It surprises me she hasn't told her. Puzzled eyes meet mine, and I squeeze her hand. "Let's just keep this between us for now."

Her silence speaks volumes. She's hurt, but we are so new, the last thing we need is all our friends sticking their noses in our business.

Terry gets up from the couch and stretches, his podgy belly

hanging over his jogging bottoms. Last night's takeaway is decorating his t-shirt.

"Good night?" I ask, lifting an eyebrow.

"Urgh," he stammers. "I feel as if I have swallowed a porcupine." He rubs his hand over his face. He does look like shit. "Amz, what did we do last night? I can't remember anything after the local."

A slow groan starts on the other sofa and Amy shakes her head. She has a glazed look; she may be still intoxicated.

I begin laughing. "God, you both look like shit. We don't need to know what you have been up to. I'm not sure I want to know."

Amy suddenly spots Bex standing behind me. "Oh, your big night out! How did it go?" she asks.

"It was fine," Bex responds quickly, and hotfoots it into her room, closing the door behind her. Amy looks at me suspiciously but says nothing. I know she will ask her later.

Following Bex, I tap lightly on the door and go straight in. She is sitting on her bed staring into space, playing with her fingers, twisting them together one way then the other.

"Everything ok?" I ask. "I had a wonderful night last night." She turns to face me, her eyes cold and sad.

"Did you?" is her snarky reply. "So good you don't want to tell anyone about it?" She turns away. Redness is spreading up the back of her neck and around her throat. She's angry. I stand for a minute, considering what to say.

Even though I have lusted after her for the past year, this is a situation I never expected myself to be in. Bex is one of Kelsey's oldest friends. Me dating her has never been an option, and right now, it doesn't feel like it should be.

"Bex, I just want to keep this between us for now. The last thing I want is to invite everyone's opinions on us. Last night was amazing, but we are so new. Please let us just enjoy each other for now." I take a deep breath and continue, "You know that there will be people who don't agree with this. I don't want to open us up to judgement. I have been lusting after you for a year."

"A year?" she snaps. "You have been wanting me for a *year?*" Her eyes widen, and I chuckle.

"Guilty as charged. I want to keep you to myself for a bit longer, if that's ok?" I hold open my arms and invite her in.

She crawls across the bed and curls tightly against my chest.

The intense feeling running between us is immediate, and my body automatically responds. Turning her to face me, I take her face in my hands and kiss her greedily. I go to lock her door. She starts to protest, but my finger over my lips silences her. Taking her hands, I stand her in the centre of the room. Slowly, lifting her top over her head then tucking my fingers into the waistband of her jeans and pulling her gently toward me. Popping the buttons open, I fall to my knees, gradually pulling the jeans down her legs until she can step out of them.

As I look up at her in her black lace bra and panties, she is the most beautiful woman I have ever seen. Her breasts are firm and round, and her erect nipples are poking through the soft lace. Grabbing her around the hips, I pull her toward me, placing my mouth at her sex. Her arousal smells divine; my cock hardens further in anticipation. She goes to remove her bra, and I stop her with a growl.

"No, I want to fuck you with it on. You look incredible."

Moving her panties to the side, I lick her clit with short, sharp laps. Then, taking one finger, I slide it inside her. She is so wet, ready for me. Her breathing quickens as I pump her, inserting a second finger. Standing, I lean into her ear and bite hard. "I'm going to bend you over and fuck you now. Get on your hands and knees," I order.

She complies, placing herself on the edge of the bed, ass in the air. I stand behind her and rub my length over her backside. My cock is straining against my boxers, wanting to be released. Quickly, I slip them down, roll on a condom, then impale her in one swift move.

She's warm, wet, and feels velvety as I take her, one hand round her hips, the other holding her breasts and teasing her nipples. I get lost in the rhythm and her orgasm builds. She tightens around me. When I drop my hand from her breasts to massage her clit, my thrusts quicken as my orgasm rises. She's whimpering now, and I growl at her to control herself.

"Wait for me, baby."

Then it happens. She convulses around me as my cum shoots inside her. I crawl onto the bed beside her, wrapping her in my arms as we both feel the vibrations of ecstasy coursing through our bodies. Nothing has ever felt righter than this does now, but still most definitely wrong.

CHAPTER NINETEEN: BEX

M y heart is hammering in my chest as those eyes lift to meet mine. I've seen that look so many times, full of love and passion. I love the fact this look is now one hundred percent directed at me. The whole situation feels unreal. After years of lusting after him, he's mine. Now we are sitting in a romantic restaurant, drinking each other in. It is completely unnerving. I am loving it.

"So, what do you fancy?" I ask as I peruse the menu.

He glances up and smirks. "Well, your pussy was mighty fine last night," he says, deadpan.

I swallow my wine the wrong way, and it comes out through my nose. "Doctor Jones, you cannot say things like that to me and expect me to act as if you have said something dull." He winks at me, and my heart flutters. I am in love with this man. We have been sneaking around for four months since The Riley Foundation Ball. The only people who are aware of our relationship are Eamon and Melissa.

Ben is still struggling with going public. I am in touch with Kelsey on occasion, and Ben is in close contact with her dad. I have told him I don't want to sneak around forever; we are not cheating on anyone. He is adamant that we will get a lot of negativity when people find out. He keeps dodging the subject.

When it is just the two of us, things are fantastic. But when we sit apart in groups, not allowed to touch each other, my heart breaks that little bit more. I sometimes wonder if he is embarrassed about being with me. The insecure teenager in me is rearing her head, whispering in my ear. She tells me there is no way a man like that wants to be with me. He is using me for sex. I'm not beautiful enough to be seen on his arm in public.

Since the ball, we have not attended any other public events. We go to obscure restaurants such as this, or events where we will be seen as a platonic couple. I feel like a naughty schoolgirl stealing kisses from her boyfriend behind her parent's back.

The waitress approaches our table. She is an older lady with greying hair and an apron around her waist. She smiles kindly at us and glances down at our hands intertwined across the table. "What can I get you lovebirds to drink?" she asks. Her voice has a lilt that makes it sound like she is singing the words. Her face is open and warm. I can't help but smile up at her.

"Could we have a bottle of the house white please?" Ben asks. She nods and waddles off in the direction of the bar.

Blazing blue eyes meet mine across the table. "You look stunning tonight, Bex." This is one of my favourite things about Ben. He is always full of compliments that make me feel amazing, and it is not always what he says but the way he looks at me that sends my head spinning.

Our waiter returns with a bottle of wine and pours a splash into my glass. Ben gestures at me to try the wine. I look at him dumbly. "Me?" I squawk, "I wouldn't know a good wine from a bad one."

He rolls his eyes at the server with a smile. "Just taste it, Bex," he huffs.

Laughing, I lift the glass to my nose, breathing in like in the movies. I tip my head back to take a small sip, swirling the golden liquid around my mouth, trying to taste different flavours. It's sweet and sharp. Just like Ben, I think to myself. After what feels like an age, I swallow and bring my eyes back to his. "It's perfect. Just like you."

He turns to the waitress, who is watching our exchange intently. He nods at her and says, "Yes, I think the wine will do." She smiles at him and fills our glasses. "Can we have ten minutes before we order?" Ben asks. "Maybe just some bread for the table. We're in no rush." Again, our server scurries off on command.

His hands tighten their grip on mine, and his eyes hold me firm. I would love to know what he is thinking at this moment. It feels as though he is building up to say something, steeling himself. My nerves start to rise and blood rushes to my head. This, what we have, makes me so happy. I am terrified it will end.

He smiles softly, reading my mind. "There's nothing to worry about, honey. I know you want to make our relationship public. I know you are fed up sneaking around as if we are doing something wrong. I want to make you happy."

I watch him carefully, hanging on to his every word, my mind racing with what he is going to say next. My heart rate relaxes when I realise this is not the unwelcome news I have been dreading. He takes a deep breath and continues, "I want to go public, too. But we need to give people time to get used to the idea of us as a couple. I'm loving being with you, Bex. I don't want anyone to ruin it for us." His eyes plead with me to understand his position on this. "So, I was thinking we should tell Amy and Terry first, if they have not already worked it out. Then tell our parents."

It is obvious he has been planning this little speech, but judging by his face, I don't think it is coming across the way he wants it to. "How do you feel about going away for two weeks? Just us. Somewhere warm, where we can focus on each other and let everyone else get used to the idea. I don't want to be dragged from pillar to post to justify our relationship to anyone."

I stand up and walk round to his side of the table then sit on his lap, holding him tight. "I think that is a wonderful idea, my darling. A few extra weeks of summer sunshine with you sounds like a great way to end the school holidays before I go back to work. And if it gives everyone some time to process us as a couple, even better," I whisper then kiss him gently.

Last night, we spoke at length about what we should say and who we should tell about our relationship. I'm not stupid. When Ben and Kelsey broke up, their families and friends were devastated. For the past year, since it happened, many acquaintances have been tasked with the challenge of getting them back together. As far as I am aware, neither of them has made any move to rekindle their relationship.

I only speak to Kelsey on occasion. The fact Ben continued to live with Amy and me once she left is a problem for her. I am expecting to be quizzed on when our relationship started and whether I had any part to play in their demise. The truth is, I did, as Ben had started to develop a crush on me, but it took over a year for him to act on it. Even though he never cheated on Kelsey with me, when we were discussing the possible outcomes last night, I did end up feeling like the other woman.

Amy is in the living room in her usual position when not working. For a fitness instructor, she does a lot of lying around. She is sitting on the sofa in her sweatpants with a large bowl of crisps between her legs and a bottle of pop on the side table, engrossed in a celebrity dating show. They are on a tropical island wearing next to nothing and hooking up with each other. Ben and I walk into the room holding hands. She looks up from her TV show, says hello, and returns to her earlier position.

A few seconds pass, and she suddenly pauses the TV. Her focus returns to us. She stares at our knotted hands, and her jaw drops open. Ok, well, she didn't know. This doesn't really surprise me, as Amy skips through life oblivious to everything around her. Her gaze moves from our hands to our faces and back again, the cogs in her brain spinning around as she tries to process what she is looking at. I'd told her the ball didn't go well.

"How long?" Her voice is sharp, abrupt. "How long has this been going on?" Her tone surprises me, but I know she's wondering if this has something to do with Kelsey's departure.

"Four months," I reply bluntly. "We wanted to see if this would go anywhere before we told anyone." She raises an eyebrow suspiciously, then shrugs her shoulders. "Well, just don't have sex in the living room, because that would be gross."

She fake gags, and we all laugh. I don't have the heart to tell her it's too late for that; Ben had me bent over the couch last Thursday while she was at aqua aerobics. She walks over and pulls us into a hug. "I'm delighted for you both." She smiles.

My parents are not the most forthcoming when talking about our personal lives. They know my friends and the history of Ben and Kelsey. I decide the best way to tell them about my new boyfriend is to send an email. They can digest the information and respond with any questions they may have. The likelihood of them giving me an opinion on the subject is limited. So, I type out a simple message informing them Ben and I have been seeing each other for a few months, things are going well, and we are heading off on holiday. Once I'm back, we will pop up to see them.

A reply bounces back almost instantly. "That's nice, sweetie. Have a nice time." Sometimes, I wonder if they even read my emails. Like the time I told my mother I had cut myself down below shaving my pubes and needed stitches, her response was to enjoy myself.

Ben's parents were not thrilled with the news he had a new partner. He took the phone call to his mother in his room, but I could hear him trying to calm her down through the door. Amy and I were standing with our ears up against it, listening intently to the conversation while Terry sat on the sofa and ate popcorn. He had brought the popcorn for this event, as he said it would be better entertainment than watching a soap opera.

Ben's mum loves Kelsey like the daughter she never had. They still go for coffee every week and speak daily on the phone. Every time Ben talks to his mum, she asks him to make amends, telling him Kelsey wants him back. They were so good together, soul mates, she says. Repeatedly.

Hearing his footsteps walking toward the door, Amy and I dart over to the sofa and sit down. He appears from his room looking forlorn. "They want us to go and see them," he says. "They want to meet you."

I look at him blankly. "They already know me," I reply, confused.

He pinches between his brows and talks to his feet, "She says she can't remember you."

My jaw drops open in shock. "I ate in their damn restaurant every week!" Then a trail of expletives leaves my mouth. "When?"

He shifts awkwardly from foot to foot. "Now, if possible?"

I roll my eyes; we leave for our holiday tomorrow, and now I have to spend the evening brown-nosing his parents to keep them happy. Just fucking great.

Caroline and Gregor Jones live in a small bungalow beside their restaurant. The restaurant is more of an American-style diner. It's open every day, all hours of the day, serving anything cooked in grease. The house has seen better days and could do with being refreshed from top to bottom. The restaurant hasn't been doing as well lately. Ben has helped them out a couple of times financially. But Mr and Mrs Jones are proud people, business owners who don't take handouts easily.

We walk up the front path. There are two small steps at the front door, and the tiles are broken and falling off. Ben places his hand on the base of my back. He's nervous. He rings the bell. The trilling sound echoes through the house, and I hear the yapping of a small dog. Caroline opens the door, holding the offending animal, which continues to growl and bark.

"Come on, Larry," Ben laughs and removes the dog, which is more like a rat, from his mother's arms. I follow them into the house, her eyes sizing me up. She is a stout woman with dyed black hair styled into a tight perm. Her features are sharp with eyes the same piercing blue as her son's. She is wearing the tabard for the restaurant which hangs loose; she has lost weight recently.

I smile brightly at her and thank her for the invitation to visit, she grunts at me, non-committal.

The procession continues into the front room. Larry has now calmed down in Ben's arms, and he places him back on the floor. The little rat runs up to me, and I feel myself stiffen. I'm not keen on dogs of any size—they smell fear, though I force myself to be brave.

Mr Jones is sitting in a single armchair in the corner of the room. His legs are raised, there is a newspaper on his lap, and he is puffing away on a pipe. The wallpaper is yellowed with age and nicotine, and I doubt the room has been decorated in twenty years. The walls are covered with a mishmash of photos and memorabilia. Family wedding photos, holiday snaps, and newspaper cut-outs about the restaurant. They seem to run in a timeline around the room, showing the key historical events of the Jones family in order.

Then I see them, the more recent photos, dozens of them, of Ben and Kelsey at family days out and special occasions displayed proudly. My heart constricts slightly, and it dawns on me that they really do want them to get back together. As far as Ben's parents are concerned, I am the interloper.

"Sit down, the two of you," his mother orders. "Do you want a cup of tea?"

I accept a plain tea gracefully, glad I have something to hold onto to try to steady my shaking hands.

Gregor Jones continues to puff on his pipe while watching us. Ben sits beside me on the sofa not quite touching me. I will him to put his arm around me. The evening is slow and painful; there is an overwhelming sense of sadness in the room, like a person has died or something. We have danced around the topics of my job, my hobbies, and my general outlook on life. But overall, nothing untoward happens until we are preparing to leave.

Caroline puffs out her chest and prepares a question in her head. "Ben, have you told Kelsey about this?"

His cool eyes meet his mother's identical ones. "This," he gestures to me, "is my girlfriend, and her name is Bex."

His mother eyes him thoughtfully, knowing she's hit a nerve. "Yes, but Kelsey was your partner for years. I think she deserves to know you are fooling around with one of her so-called friends."

The comment hits me square in the stomach. Fooling around? So-called friend? That's what they think of me. I am just someone Ben is passing time with until he goes back to her. I try to keep the pain off my face so he doesn't see it, but he can.

Ben composes himself before he speaks. "Mother, not that it is any concern of yours, but I will tell Kelsey. However, we separated more than a year ago. My relationship with Bex had no part in that."

With that final statement, we bid them farewell and leave.

The car journey back to the city is quiet. We don't speak. I knew his parents would not be happy about our relationship, but open hostility and the lack of respect was unexpected. My hands sit on my knees. I'm dying to reach across and touch him, share my warmth with him, but Ben is miles away in a world of his own. Our visit to his parents had clearly not gone well in his eyes. His phone starts to buzz uncontrollably, and the name Kelsey flashes up on the screen. Rejecting the call, he says nothing. Then the phone starts to ring again.

When he doesn't answer a second time, a voice message pops onto the screen. He pulls over and places the phone at his ear to listen.

"Fucking bitch!" he yells and hits the steering wheel.

"What is it?" I stammer, reaching over to him.

"My bitch of a mother told her before I had the chance. She told her we are fucking. That's her calling to see if it's true."

My jaw drops, and tears prick my eyes. His phone continues to buzz and beep all the way home. We pull up outside the apartment.

"You go on up, Bex, I won't be long. I'll give her a call and explain the situation."

The situation. My heart sinks. He hugs me tight. I walk miserably through the door as my boyfriend walks in the opposite direction to phone his ex-girlfriend.

CHAPTER TWENTY: BEX

I am so relieved to be standing in the departure lounge of Gatwick Airport. Ben had spent an hour on the phone with Kelsey. It took him forever to calm her down, but he assured me it would be alright. She would accept us eventually.

At three o'clock this morning, I couldn't sleep, the drama of earlier still playing on my mind. London is beautiful in the dead of night, so peaceful in stark contrast to the busy hours of the day. When I looked outside, Kelsey was standing on the pavement staring up at the flat. If she saw me, she never let on. I haven't told Ben. She's hurt, and I don't want to make things more complicated or cause drama when it's not required. Two weeks away with him will be the perfect tonic. We can come home refreshed and ready to face any issues together.

Our escape is a complete mystery to me; he won't tell me anything. All I know is I was to pack a bikini, and we would not be on the plane for more than three hours. At this point in time I am so excited, I could burst. We are sitting in the airport lounge, sipping our overpriced coffee and sharing a huge chocolate muffin. Ben looks relaxed and happy—he was stressed this morning—but as we travelled further from the apartment, the stress drifted away.

His eyes hold mine across the melamine table, and I feel my cheeks heat. The look he's giving me is making my panties damp.

"Stop looking at me like that," I say playfully, swiping at his cheek and glancing away from the predator in front of me.

He laughs under his breath, but I hear it catch in his throat. His eyes stayed fixed on my face; I can feel it.

"Like what?" His voice is cool and commanding. "I'm just looking at my girl like I do every day." He starts stroking the back of my hand. "Like I want to rip her clothes off and fuck her over this table." My nipples harden instantly at the vision he has just created in my head.

I'm bent over the table, skirt around my waist and panties at my knees. He is behind me with his hard length, teasing my opening and then thrusting in. The area between my legs goes from damp to wet. My breathing quickens. He smiles at me innocently and removes his hand from mine. The shit knows exactly what he has just done to me.

"I will tell you something, honey. I am going to thoroughly enjoy this holiday with you. If that is the reaction a few words get, imagine what will happen when I touch you." He winks then wanders off toward the gate as they start calling our flight.

The pilot announces we will be landing at Alicante Airport in ten minutes. He promises thirty degrees and blue skies; looking out the window confirms this prognosis. I know we are staying in Spain. Ben says the accommodation is no more than an hour's drive away. Having never been to Spain or anywhere abroad, excitement is bursting out of me. I have lusted after the warm sand and blue sea for years; it is going to be incredible sharing this first time with him.

We bundle all our bags into the pale-blue hatchback provided by the hire company. I had to take my jacket off walking down the plane stairs; the heat hit me with a force that took my breath away. The sun beat down on my face as we made the short walk to the terminal, triggering a huge smile across it.

Ben digs out the hotel confirmation from his bag and plugs the postcode in the sat-nav. He slides his acoustic pop music

CD into the player, and we set off on our forty-five-minute journey. We speed along the three-lane carriageway on what is the wrong side of the road for us. We have mountains bordering one side of the road with a huge expanse of ocean on the other. The scenery surprises me. I expected a vastness of desert and brown tones, but there is green interspersed with the beige hues surrounding us. Old buildings that look like farms of days gone by are scattered around the countryside.

After half an hour, we take a left turn heading up into the mountains away from the ocean. The roads are narrow, twisting and turning through the sheer-faced rocks. In front of us, there are groups of cyclists we must navigate past. It feels like we are on an episode of the world's most dangerous roads. Why anyone would cycle up these mountains perplexes me, but Ben tells me that lots of tourists come to Costa Blanca for cycling because of the steep roads. No thank you.

Every so often, we pass a small restaurant on the roadside. Old, rickety tables set up under shade are full of elderly Spaniards, enjoying their lunch in the mid-afternoon sunshine. It only takes fifteen minutes more to arrive at our hotel, but the journey has felt like travelling to another world.

We pull up to large black gates, the type with little golden arrowheads on the top. The property is surrounded by high walls, so you can't see in. The gates have been painted a soft pink colour. This place screams opulent and private. Ben gets out of the car, walking up to a small black box on the wall. He keys in a code, and a flap opens. He extracts what I assume must be a key from it, then walks back to the car. A strange hotel, I muse. He presses a button on the key fob in his hand, and the two gates start to open. Then the car slowly starts to move forward onto the white pebble drive.

The white stones lead up a long, straight driveway bordered by palm trees. At the end stands a tall white house. With pillars along the front terrace, it screams grandeur.

There are four towers—one on each corner—and huge expanses of glass. We crawl slowly up the driveway, both silent and in awe of the mansion in front of us. Parking at the base of the steps, we both climb out. I look at Ben in confusion. "I thought we were staying in a hotel?"

His bright eyes meet mine, and he smiles shyly. "Well, I decided you deserved the best. This is all ours for two weeks. We can do whatever we want and have complete privacy." He winks cheekily at me, and I burst out laughing. "Shall we go and explore our new home? Well, for two weeks, anyway," he suggests, and I nod enthusiastically, running up the front steps.

"Think you might need the key? What's it worth?" he calls from behind me, and I swing around to face him. I throw myself into his arms, he drops our bags to catch me. My hands are in his hair, my lips taking his forcefully and my tongue claiming his mouth.

"That will do for now," he whispers and dangles the key before dropping it into my palm.

I slot the key into the tall black door decorated with frosted glass and golden furniture. A plaque across the front declares, "Welcome to Paradise." The door glides open silently, and a huge modern foyer comes into view. It is decorated in shades of white and silver highlighted with chrome. There are two velvet sofas that look as if they could sit about ten people each, and on the walls, there are vast paintings of beautiful women in various stages of undress. At the back of the room, a white marble staircase leads to the upstairs overlooked by tall stained-glass windows. Sunlight streams through them, reflecting a patchwork of colours on the tiles.

"Will we go and find the bedroom?" Ben sneaks up on me, whispering in my ear.

I smile and kiss his cheek. "Why are you whispering?"

He chuckles. "That's right, we have this whole place to

ourselves. I can make you scream as loud as your lungs can manage. That will happen, I promise you."

He grabs my hand and drags me toward the stairs. We take them two at a time, both of us beyond excited to see what else this beautiful home has to offer.

At the end of the upstairs corridor, two tall white doors mark the entrance to the master suite. We walk into the room, and my jaw drops; our whole apartment would fit in this space. Unlike the rest of the house, this room is decorated in rich colours. The focal point of the room is a huge four-poster bed displayed on a platform with a tall velvet headboard. The sheets are made of silk, luxurious in tones of red and gold. A chandelier hangs in the centre of the room with thousands of diamonds hanging from it. They reflect the light, sending sparkles across the ceiling and walls. On a low table snuggled between two deep red sofas, there is an ice bucket holding a chilled bottle of champagne surrounded by chocolate-dipped strawberries.

My stomach growls, and Ben winks at me. "Fancy a bite, honey? Of a strawberry, that is." He strides over and lifts the bottle of fizz from the bucket, popping the cork in one swift move. He returns to me with two glasses of fizz and a strawberry between his teeth. He leans forward as if to kiss me, and I take the strawberry in my mouth, making sure our lips connect before I bite down to retrieve my half of the sweet delight.

On the far side of the room, there is a wall of sliding doors. We walk over hand in hand, and he pushes them open. Outside is a large balcony; it houses a table set for two and a Jacuzzi. But the most incredible part is an infinity pool that has a glass wall overlooking the ocean view. When we had headed into the mountains, I assumed we wouldn't be able to see the ocean, but there it is in all its glory.

My eyes fill with tears as I take in everything before me,

and strong arms wrap around me. "Are you happy, honey?" Ben whispers in my ear, and all I can do is sob quietly while he holds me tight. I don't think I have ever felt so complete. These two weeks are going to be the best of my life. I just know it.

The sun is going down on the most incredible day. We spent our evening wrapped around each other on the four-poster bed. We made love then talked for hours about everything and anything. I have never felt so at ease with anyone. This man worships me for who I am. He loves every part of my body fully and thoroughly. After my fifth orgasm of the evening ripped through me, I had grabbed his head from between my legs and demanded food. We had raided the cupboards for a takeaway menu, and we are currently sitting on our balcony eating pizza, watching the evening sun disappear.

The perfect end to a perfect day.

Our first three days pass in a haze of sex and food. I'm impressed that Ben had been forward-thinking enough to have shopping delivered prior to our arrival. I have only been dressed in my skimpy gold bikini or my birthday suit the entire time we have been here. Ben has been naked the whole time; I love watching my man strutting around the house on full display.

I know when he is relaxed and soft, but also when he is aroused and needs me. We swam in the infinity pool and made love against the wall while overlooking the ocean. Ben has displayed his limited culinary skills, but he decided to wear an apron after a near-miss with his crown jewels and some oil. The rule of complete nakedness could be relaxed in these circumstances, as damage to his member would drastically reduce our extracurricular activities.

Day four has now arrived, and Ben announced we were

going to venture out. As much as I wanted to protest and attempt to convince him to stay in our naked paradise, I'm curious, ready to explore this beautiful country with him.

Armed with a beach bag filled with sun cream, a picnic, hats, and fly swatters, we head off in search of the beach. I'm wearing my most demure bikini; it is a soft blue and covers all necessary areas while accentuating my cleavage. Over the top, I have a white summer lace dress that my bikini peeks through. I feel free, sexy, and so bloody in love.

Ben is relaxed and happy. It makes him even more beautiful. He is wearing long denim shorts which finish just above his knees and a loose-fitting white shirt that is open at the neck and hints at the athletic body below. He looks magnificent in his aviator shades as he walks toward the car, a man confident and in control.

As we cruise back toward the coast down the winding roads, the ocean comes into view again. We enter a whitewashed town perched on the rocks above the water. The roofs are a mixture of red and blue, highlighting the Mediterranean feel of the area. Parking the car on a small side street, we climb out and wander hand in hand through the small town. It is busy with people enjoying the sunshine and socialising with friends.

Investigating the maze of streets, we come across a staircase leading down the side of the rocks next to the sea. Ben winks at me then leads me down the stairs. They are old and worn, but we step out into the most amazing private cove. There is a sandy beach, and the water gently laps against the sand. The tall rocks feel like a cocoon around us. The area is deserted apart from a single gentleman sunbathing a few hundred metres further down.

I lay out our towels the way I have seen it done in holiday brochures and movies; Ben watches me quietly.

"I've never done this before," I admit. "This is my first time abroad."

He looks at me, stunned. "Why didn't you say? I would have arranged something special." He smiles a wide beaming smile. "Oh, wait. I have. A high-class mansion and private beach." He winks, and I chuckle. "Well, ok, the beach was just luck," he admits grudgingly.

I pull him down to me, we lie on the sand tangled in each other's arms, and he kisses the top of my head. I love the feeling of the sand between my toes. Time passes, but I am unaware. We eat our picnic and paddle in the sea. Ben has got me in as far as my knees, but I am frightened to go any further. I have never swum in the sea; the currents have a life of their own. The lack of control is unnerving.

Finally, I agree to *put my brave girl pants on* and go deeper with the agreement he won't let me go. We wade out into the blue ocean, hand in hand. Then he takes me in his arms, and I wrap my legs around him. My arms cradle his neck, and he holds me as close as our bodies allow. The beach is still quiet with only a few people sunbathing. I guess not many make the trip down the old stairs.

Ben nuzzles my earlobe, his lips starting to trail small kisses from my ear to the base of my neck. My nipples stiffen underneath my bikini, and a strong hand starts to twist them through the thin material. "I want to fuck you here," he murmurs, and my body responds with vibration between my legs. I don't know if it's the sun, the sea, or the wine, but I am open and willing to do anything this man asks of me.

He walks us out further from the beach and behind a small stack of rocks protruding from the water. I am pressed up against them, the hard surface against my back, his cock, hard and firm against my pussy, ready and waiting to take me. His lips hold mine, invading my mouth, while his hands roam over my backside. In one move, he pulls my bottoms to the side and spears me with his hard length, pumping hard and fast. My orgasm builds as he works faster. The pain in my back from the rock is intense, but fuck, this is so good. Ben bites my neck hard, and I convulse around him, coming fast and hard. He responds with his own orgasm, and we stand pressed against each other in our sweet ecstasy.

On our final evening, we head out to a small beachfront restaurant. It is quaint and romantic with fairy lights hung around the terrace. The music playing is the sound of lapping waves. Ben has been quiet today. He's feeling nervous about our return home. I am wearing his favourite white lace dress with no underwear; he was shocked when I ran his hand up the inside of my thigh in the taxi here. A hint to what was in store for him when we got home tonight.

We sit directly across the small table from each other. A single candle burns in a green bottle, and the wax dribbles down the side. The meal has been an exquisite display of seafood. A lady selling single red roses approaches. Ben buys one and presents it to me like it's a diamond ring. I laugh and accept it willingly. He holds my face in his hands and kisses me softly, his kiss is gentle but full of possession.

"I adore you, Bex," he murmurs. "You complete me."

Tears prick my eyes. I kiss him back hard and greedy. "I love you, Doctor Jones." We hold each other for what seems like forever. He kisses me softly on the lips, and I fall further. The look in his eyes tell me he feels it, too. We have found our soul mate.

A quiet cough from behind us breaks the moment, and we look up into the embarrassed eyes of our server. He offers us a drink to finish our meal, and we both accept happily. Sitting with the man I love, full and satisfied after a delicious meal in the most beautiful place really is the most wonderful feeling.

My mind wanders to what may be waiting for us at home. Everyone will have had time to consider our relationship. My

stomach somersaults with nerves as I wonder what their conclusions will be.

Chapter Twenty-one: Ben

The voice messages started bombarding my phone forty-eight hours ago. They were desperate and hysterical.

I need you!

Please call me!

I'm not sure I can survive this!

Where are you? I'm getting an abroad dial tone. Call me.

I'd dismissed the recordings as Kelsey's usual dramatics, but when my mother called me last night, I realised something life-changing was happening.

Ben, this is your mother. A disaster is unfolding in your partner of a decade's life. It's time to stop pissing around and remember where your loyalties lie.

Not wanting to ruin the mood or the fantastic holiday Bex and I had shared, I hadn't told her about the contact. For that, I feel guilty, but she looks so happy with her smiling face, full of joy, the last thing I wanted to do was destroy that. She asked me why I was subdued, and I lied that I was just enjoying the moment. This seemed to placate her. She continued to hold my hand and kiss my lips as we lounged around the villa or wandered the local streets.

We really have had the most amazing two weeks together. Making love in the sea, wandering naked around the villa, and spending our nights in each other's arms. Then, last night, she took my breath away by telling me she loves me. It was unexpected and beautiful. The perfect end to a perfect holiday.

The plane touches down on the runway, and I look out the

window at the grey London sky which, at this moment, is like my mood. Glancing at Bex makes my heart lift. Her skin is sun-kissed, and her hair has brightened in the Spanish sunshine. She looks relaxed and happy with her nose stuck in a book. Judging by the half-naked man on the cover, a romance novel. I could tell when she was reading a naughty part as her breathing hitches ever so slightly, the way it does when I run my fingers up the inside of her thigh unexpectedly. Soft eyes meet mine, and I try a smile.

She frowns slightly as she takes in my expression, then leans forward, kissing the side of my mouth. "I love you," she murmurs.

Unable to say it back, I feel my heart constrict, the sinking feeling in my stomach growing at an alarming rate.

Arriving back at our apartment, the taxi pulls up to the front door. The weather hasn't improved between the airport and home, and neither has my mood. Bex skips to the communal entrance, her short summer dress bouncing as she does so. It's bright pink, scattered with white daisies finishing just below her butt cheeks. When she bends over, I'm treated to a view of her plump behind. Her ass and I have become well acquainted over the past two weeks. Sex has never been so intense, losing myself in her night after night. I will never get bored with this woman.

My phone vibrates to alert me that yet another call is incoming. I'd switched it onto silent hours ago. Part of me wants to just ignore it, but I know if I don't respond, another attempt will soon follow. I resolve to call her back ASAP. I plan to let her hear the venom in my voice, but she won't notice. My mother is an expert at ignoring other people's feelings and projecting her views onto everyone. I wander toward home behind my girl, feeling hollow. Tonight is going to be a rough night.

The cases are packed away and Bex is getting settled for the night. The drama on my phone won't go away unless I deal with it.

"I just need to nip into the hospital for a few hours," I say, aiming for casual and relaxed, but my tone doesn't convey that. Bex looks up from her book. She is spread along the sofa, wearing a silky nightdress in a deep red. The neckline is low, and her long, elegant legs are on display. Her eyes question me without saying a word. "I won't be long, honey. There are just a few things I need to check on," I lie as smoothly as I can. She shrugs her shoulders, accepting my reasoning.

My conscience is screaming at me to stop lying to her. This is not the way to manage this situation. Our relationship is too new, too fresh, even though we have known each other for years. We are only now truly getting to know each other.

Grabbing my long black coat, I head out the door with a huge sense of guilt hanging over me. I have just lied to the woman who confessed to loving me. A woman I have spent two weeks with continuously and loved every second of. But how do I explain that I must go?

Rain is pelting down, filling the roads with water. I step in a puddle as I climb into my car, and it does nothing to improve my self-loathing. Now I am in a foul mood with wet feet. The night is only just beginning.

As I pull up outside my parents' home, a feeling of desolation overwhelms me. The fact Kelsey is here with my parents is alarming. She is my ex-partner, and my parents still treat her as if she is their future daughter-in-law. We were never engaged.

My feet feel heavy as I walk up the old stone path. My father opens the door with a grim line across his face. "You're here, finally," he barks. "Where were you?"

I shrug my shoulders, knowing better than to answer. I follow him into the living room, wanting to walk straight back out the door with each step.

She's sitting on the single chair by the window. Her head is lowered, her focus on her feet. She is clutching a mug on her lap. Soft brown curls have fallen forward over her face, and she's crying softly. My mother is crouched in front of her, one hand on her knee, the other stroking her back. They have been in this position for a while, as my mother is moving from foot to foot, spreading her weight.

Both look up as I enter the room, and I get a full view of Kelsey's tear-stained face. My mother takes the mug from her. Kelsey rises, swiftly running into my arms. I instinctively wrap them around her as she breaks into huge sobs, her head on my chest and arms around my waist. It feels so wrong but so familiar at the same time. The feeling is unsettling.

We stand like that for what feels like an eternity. Then I manoeuvre her to the sofa and sit down beside her. She is holding my hands with an iron grip, as though terrified if she lets go, I will disappear. I'm still at a total loss as to what has happened. I look to my parents for answers. Stone faces stare at me in response.

"Kels, what's the matter? What's happened?" I keep my voice quiet and soft. After years at her side, I know cajoling is the best offence.

Her sad eyes meet mine. "He's dead," she simply says. I look from Kelsey to my parents, and my heart sinks. Her father is dead. This, I was not expecting. I pull her into my arms and kiss the top of her head. She falls to pieces. I hold on as tight as I can to her.

Kelsey's father had been driving to his allotment only five minutes from his house. We had arranged to buy the piece of land as a birthday present for him after his wife had died. It had become a focus for him in those terrible first few years. He hadn't seen the van pulling out in front of him from a side street and had driven straight into the side of it. The shock of the accident had sent him into cardiac arrest. He was dead before the ambulance got to the scene. His trusty little dog Benji was on the passenger seat still in his harness. He was now curled up in front of the fire in my parents' front room.

The police had called Kelsey at work, taking her into the patient consulting room to break the news. When my parents had arrived to collect her an hour later, she was still crumpled on the floor, sobbing her heart out. They had brought her back to the house, and she hadn't left since.

The angry eyes of my mother are burning into me. I carry Kelsey to bed and tuck her in, kissing her forehead as she drifts off. She has no one now, just us. A sudden feeling of responsibility overwhelms me. She needs me.

Back in my parent's living room, the three of us sit sombrely, watching the seconds on the clock tick by. No one has said a word for thirty minutes since I sat down. Their disapproval emanates from them.

"Why didn't you tell me what had happened? I would have caught a flight home." I look to them both for answers.

"Kelsey asked us not to tell you. She said you had moved on, and she didn't want to be a burden. She didn't tell us she had contacted you herself until I called you." My mother's words are cold and direct. Guilt is creeping up my spine as she continues, "Ben, you spent a decade of your life with this girl. You know how vulnerable she is. I am so angry with you for not taking her seriously. Judging by the number of calls she made to you, did you not think the situation was important? I saw her phone; you blatantly ignored her pleas for help."

I take a deep breath and consider my response, but whatever I say, I am going to sound like a bastard. "The thing is, Kelsey has always been dramatic. And we have been separated for a year. If I had known, I would have come home to help." My voice is sad and pathetic.

My mother rolls her eyes and *tsks* through her teeth. "Too

busy with your latest fuck, you mean!" she snaps, stomping off in the direction of the kitchen.

Bex. Shit, I completely forgot about her waiting at home for me. My phone has been on silent since I arrived. Pulling it from my pocket, I see I have three missed calls with voicemails. More guilt layers on top of the last lot.

Darling, I'm waiting for you.

Assume you're busy, babe. Don't leave me hanging too long. May have to take matters into my own hands.

Wake me when you get home. Love you. Xxx

Glancing at the clock, I see it's three in the morning. I've been here for hours. She hasn't called me since midnight. Hopefully, she's sleeping.

I feel my father's eyes watching me. He is assessing the situation in front of him. My ex-partner is asleep in his spare room and has no family to rely on now, so she came here. I ignored her calls for help because I was too busy with my new girlfriend.

He sighs softly, then starts to speak, "Son, what you do next is going to affect the rest of your life." I look at him blankly, and he continues, "Kelsey is vulnerable, she always has been. Without you this last year, she has been completely lost. If you choose to support her now, you will need to be here for her for a while. You need to consider how that affects your current relationship."

He's right. I am not going to be able to do both. My partner of ten years is falling to bits in my parents' spare room, while the woman I am crazy for is waiting for me in sexy lingerie at my apartment. Could the situation be any more fucked up? Walking out into my parents' garden, I call her phone, and to my relief it diverts to voicemail. I leave a message.

Honey, the situation here is complicated. Just going to stay here tonight. Will be back tomorrow and explain. I Miss You."

Strictly speaking, this is not a lie, but it's certainly not the truth. I really don't want to get into a discussion about where

I am currently. Calling my boss, who I know is on duty, I arrange the day off work due to a family emergency, resolving to sort things in the morning.

I wander upstairs and pop my head in the spare room. Kelsey is awake, staring up at the ceiling. Fresh tears run down her face. Going to her, I sit down on the bed and hold her hand.

"Lie with me," she whispers. Kicking off my shoes, I lie down on top of the covers, and she snuggles into me. We both drift off to sleep. I wake an hour or so later feeling chilled. Kelsey is sleeping soundly, so I get up and take off my clothes, then slide under the duvet with her. She's warm in my arms. We automatically move into our normal position to sleep on our sides with me wrapped around behind her.

Sunlight pours in through the window, and I wake with a rock-hard cock. Kelsey is facing me, propped up on one elbow, watching me sleep. She has a wicked smile on her face.

"Well, someone is pleased to see me," she purrs. My eyes widen as I realise her hand is wrapped around me, stroking my length deliberately.

"Kels, don't do this. Not now. This is not why I'm here. I am here to support you, not sleep with you," I whisper, and she smiles, pulling the duvet down to expose her naked body. My heart skips, and my cock hardens further in response. She leans forward to kiss me, but I move away.

"Kels, I'm not doing this now with you. You're grieving. I'm not being that man who takes advantage," I tell her.

"It's not taking advantage, if I ask for it," she says sexily. I jump out of the bed and wrap the cover around my waist. She laughs, then bursts into tears. This woman is a mess; how can I leave her?

Today has been difficult. As far as Bex is concerned, I'm at work. We had a simple conversation this morning, but the guilt is eating me alive. She will be back at work now, still enjoying her post-holiday glow. I will see her tonight, but I have no idea what I am going to say. Right now, I have no idea what I am going to do.

Kelsey and I both went to her father's house today — well, I say her father's house, but Kelsey lives there, too — since she said she couldn't face going back alone. I agreed to go with her. His morning paper and empty coffee cup were still sitting on the kitchen table, which caused her to break down in tears. She sat in the kitchen staring at the walls while I gave the house a general tidy up, moving all the obvious personal items of her father's into his room. At least this way she can deal with those when she is ready. I had helped her start to sort through paperwork to make plans for the funeral. It had been heart-wrenching to watch her break down at points during the day. All I could do was hold her and let her sob into my chest. She was so fragile. Broken.

We arrived back at my parents' house around six in the evening. A lot of the funeral preparation is complete. Kelsey's father didn't have a lot of friends since distancing himself from everyone after his wife's death. After her mother's unexpected passing, Kelsey and I had been her father's main source of social contact. She has assumed the role of wife. I could see from her demeanour she was going to be completely lost without someone to care for. I had asked her if there was anyone special in her life I could contact. A friend, perhaps? She had simply shaken her head and said, "There is only you and your family. I want no one else."

After a long discussion with my parents and Kelsey regarding arrangements moving forward, I called Bex telling her I would catch up with her after work tomorrow. Even replaying the conversation in my head, it sounded dismissive and cold. She hadn't responded, but only listened and mumbled. I worried about what she was thinking. However, my decision was made. Now, I had to see it through.

CHAPTER TWENTY-TWO: BEX

Forty-eight hours ago, I was the happiest I had ever been in my adult life. As a child, I was happy up to the age of thirteen. The years where you are young enough to be strange had been a blast. Making mud pies and counting rocks with my friends. Pretending to be a species from another planet and wearing whatever made you happy. But hitting my teenage years, I had struggled immensely with fitting in, never knowing what to say, who to be friends with, or how to be cool. I had always gravitated to the outsiders or them to me. I was never sure which way round it worked.

These past few weeks with Ben had been perfect. He had made me feel like the only woman in the world. I had worshipped him in response. The two weeks in Spain had cemented my love for this beautiful man.

I had always found him attractive since we were teenagers, but never once thought he could be interested in me. The fact he put up with me as a friend had shocked me, not being the kind of girl people like him were seen with. In the beginning, I had assumed it was a practical joke, but the punchline never came.

Kelsey and Ben were my friends. The familiar guilt when I think of Kelsey rises in my throat. What kind of person am I to start a relationship with my friend's ex-partner? But that man is also my friend. And I love him.

That is the one thing I am sure of: Dr Benjamin Jones has my heart.

I cannot imagine my life without him.

The lack of contact since we returned from Spain is making me uneasy. It has been two days since I saw him. He called me an hour ago to say he would be back by eight o'clock. It's now 7:30 p.m. He was working today, and I know he keeps spare clothes at the hospital. It is perfectly plausible that he has been there this whole time, but I have a dreadful sensation filling my belly, and it's doing nothing to ease my worries. The television is on, but I'm not watching it.

His key in the door signals he is home; it opens and closes with a click. He kicks off his shoes the same way he does every night. His sock-clad feet pad slowly along the hallway, and he appears in the living room. He looks nothing like the man I kissed goodbye two days ago. Haunted eyes meet mine. Suddenly, I really don't want to have this conversation.

"Amy isn't home yet," I stutter, not knowing what else to say. I want to ask where he has been, but I am frightened to know the answer.

"No, I asked her to stay away until I had spoken to you." His response is calm but distant, as if this has been rehearsed in his head. "Bex, we need to talk."

My heart feels as though it has been ripped out and is lying on the table in front of me. I look at Ben in complete shock. He's leaving me. We haven't even got started, and he is leaving me. It is strange how sometimes you have a premonition that something is going to happen. It is even more alarming when it comes true. Once it became apparent what the outcome of this conversation was going to be, I stopped listening. I didn't want to hear anymore.

Ben had continued with his monologue for what felt like hours, but when I look at the clock, it is only 8:30 p.m., so he could only have been talking for a maximum of thirty minutes. I watch in slow motion as he holds his arms out. Then I realise he is speaking to me, expecting an answer. His voice is calm and controlled. "Do you understand what I am saying, Bex? I am going to pack a bag now and leave. Are you going to be alright? I asked Amy to come home to be with you; she will be here in ten minutes."

I nod once and blink back the tears in my eyes. He looks at me warily as if he's expecting me to explode, but everything he said made sense. Our relationship is new.

She needs him.

Ben had explained that he was moving in with Kelsey at her father's house to help her sort her financial affairs, support her in her grief, and ensure she looked after herself. Kelsey didn't have anyone to look after her, and he felt that it was his duty to be that person. Ben understood Kelsey. He was there when her mother died. He had been there when she was lost in her own anguish and struggling to put one foot in front of the other. She would need that level of support again.

He had gone on to explain they were not getting back together. He would be sleeping in the spare room. But as our relationship was so young, he felt it was too much to ask me to accept that. So he had decided that we must end things for the time being, until he was sure that Kelsey was well and could move forward in her life. Maybe, once time had passed, we could try again.

I know neither of us believed that. I looked at this beautiful man through vacant eyes. I could see him hurting. This decision was based on a decade of loyalty to this woman. He had seen her at her worst, and he couldn't live with himself if he let her go through that again on her own.

Walking silently from the living room to my bedroom, he collected the few belongings he had left there. A book, some earbuds, and a razor. I followed him like a lost sheep as he wandered around the apartment picking things up and putting them back down again, trying to decide what was important to take now and what could be collected later.

I watched on, saying nothing. I wanted to scream at him. What about us?

What about me?

Do I mean nothing?

But he had covered that earlier, telling me how beautiful and clever I was, a strong career woman whom he admired and how I didn't need him.

But I do need him. I have never been so strong and confident as when we were a team. I thought he was my right-hand man. Now, I am back to navigating this world on my own.

Amy arrives home, and I can tell by her face she is up to speed on what is happening. Her eyes search for me, and I can sense her pity from here. Ben throws the black holdall over his shoulder, his eyes looking from one of us to the other. It crosses my mind that he hasn't even touched me since he came back. Maybe he couldn't bear to. Then again, if he had loved me at all, would he hurt me this way?

A man in love doesn't walk away from that woman for his ex-partner. He's never told me he loves me, I realise. It stings.

Amy is struggling to hold her temper. She is such a happy-go-lucky person under normal circumstances. However, when she gets angry, it can be like an atomic bomb exploding in your vicinity.

Finally, she blows.

"Ben, just leave!" Her voice is harsh. "Let me know when you're coming to get the rest of your stuff, and I will be here to let you in. Give me your key."

He nods, then removes an envelope from his coat pocket. Without another word, he lays the envelope and his keys on the coffee table and exits the apartment without so much as a backwards glance.

I stand looking at the closed door and feel arms surround me. "Bex, honey, say something." Amy's eyes hold mine. "Bex, it's going to be alright. I'm here. He's an idiot."

Walking over, I pick up the envelope. Simple black writing on it says *4 months' rent share – £2000*.

I open it up and pull the notes out. There's nothing else. No message, no card, no punchline. Picking up the bundle of keys, I thumb the keyring absent-mindedly. It's a Spanish flag; we bought it only last week.

He really is walking away from us. It hurts. I have been dismissed.

There is no more *us*.

The blinding autumn sunshine pours through the window, I feel as though I am waking from a bad dream. Last night, Amy and I sank multiple bottles of wine and put the world to rights. We are officially, *completely*, off men. Men are bastards. Apart from Terry, who had come round to the apartment to help us drown my sorrows. He had agreed with the assumption that all men should be castrated at birth, apart from him, of course. Staring at the digital clock, I read 8:05 a.m. Shit! I need to be at work in forty minutes, and I currently smell like a brewery. I grab my phone to check if he had called me – desolation strikes again. No calls or messages. He really has left me.

The bonus of this week is the children only started back after the holidays on a Thursday. This means I only faced two days of work with pupils in attendance to survive until the weekend. Terry and Amy have promised me a weekend full of alcohol and drunken shenanigans. *Operation Move On* is underway.

Tonight is *Night One*, and we are going out. I am sitting at my dressing table, applying yet another coat of mascara. War paint. You can never have too much makeup, especially when attempting to recover from a broken heart. Ben had come by at some point during the day to collect the rest of his things. I hadn't seen him, with being at work. In all honesty, I couldn't cope with seeing him.

We head out on the town. The three of us walk arm in arm down the road, getting dirty looks from people having to navigate around us. Amy has implemented three rules for this evening:

1. Get pissed.
2. Hook up with someone.
3. Don't mention the Bastard's name.

I have promised to do my best to stick to the rules as far as possible. The punishment for not complying is a shot of tequila. We are four hours into our night out, and I am six shots of tequila down. The not mentioning Ben rule is not going well. Everything seems to remind me of him, and with each memory, it brings a wave of tears. My mascara is now streaking down my face, and my lipstick is nowhere to be seen.

Terry has gotten fed up with my blubbering and currently has his tongue down a young brunette's throat. He looks like he's old enough to be her dad, and it is totally creeping me out. Amy is on the dance floor with a hot blond guy. She is dry humping him, much to his enjoyment. Squinting, I am pretty sure it's the same guy she has fucked a few times, but with Amy, a lot of her conquests look the same. She has a clear type.

Perched on my stool at the bar, I drunkenly survey the crowd. People are all over each other, and it's really starting to piss me off.

How fucking dare they throw their happy love lives in my face?

Staggering off the stool, I hurl myself at a couple currently sucking each other's faces off, shouting expletives and calling them every name I can think of. Shocked faces turn to me, laugh, and give me the finger. The next thing I know, two hands are under my arms, and I'm being escorted out of the club followed by being dumped unceremoniously on the pavement outside. I lamely tell the bouncer that my jacket is still in the cloakroom. He shrugs and tells me to come to get it when I'm sober.

I totter down the dark street. My feet are killing me in these heels, so I take them off and walk barefoot down the cold pavement. Finding a bench to sit on, I pull my mobile from my bag to call a taxi. As I scroll through my contact list, Ben's number sits on my screen.

Feeling naughty, I hit the call button. It rings out then diverts to voicemail. So, I try again and again. Eventually, the calls go automatically to voicemail. The bastard has switched it off. Fine. I will leave a message.

"Ben, it's me. Well, by me, I mean Bex. Just so you know, I'm fine. You hear me? Fine. I don't need you. I don't miss you. I hope you and Kelsey are very happy together. It was fun while it lasted, but it wasn't love. Crazy to pretend it was. Meaningless sex. Have a nice life."

I hang up and pat myself on the back for telling him straight.

Then, everything goes black.

The sound of beeping machines wakes me from my slumber. Then I hear raised voices.

"Get the fuck out of here." Amy's voice is shrill and angry.

A man's voice responds in hushed tones, "She left me a strange voicemail. I was worried about her, so I called Terry, he said she was here. Amy, please just let me see her."

It's Ben, he's here.

"No, this is all your damn fault, leaving her like that. She fell for you, Ben, and you fucked off. Get out!" Amy yells.

Then it all goes dark again.

Amy is sitting by my bedside when I come around. Maybe

it was a dream.

"Ben?" I ask groggily.

Amy smiles sadly. "No, it's just me, Bex. How are you feeling? You gave us one hell of a fright." I look at Amy and see Terry standing behind her. His hand is resting on her shoulder. Something about the gesture is intimate, but I dismiss the thought.

"What happened?" I ask, confused. Amy's concerned eyes look at me, unsure what to say. "Tell me the truth, Amz, please." She rolls her eyes but concludes that I need to know.

"Well," she says, "you were chucked out of the club and collapsed on the street. They had to pump your stomach, as you were having some sort of fit." I look at her blankly. I remember nothing.

"Was he here?" I whisper.

She nods and gives me another sad smile. "Yes, but he has gone now. He knows you're ok. But Bex, you can't phone him again. He asked me to tell you to leave him alone. You have been phoning every night, leaving messages. Life's complicated enough for him just now, and you need to move on without him."

Shame fills me. It's true. Every night since he left, I have been drinking myself senseless and phoning him. After the first night, he stopped answering and diverted my calls to voicemail. I really have lost it. My chance of happiness is gone.

Chapter Twenty-three: Kelsey

Six months have passed since my dad died. The black hole swallowed me up again, just like when mum passed away. Without Ben, I would have been lost, but he came back to me. I'm not stupid. He is here because of loyalty, not love. But I will have him any way I can.

There have been dark moments these past months, like the time a woman turned up on my doorstep claiming to be my father's partner. She was tall and blonde, nothing like my mother.

"My father's partner?" I asked, stunned.

"Yes, my name is Jackie. Your father and I had been seeing each other for a few months. I loved him very much. I want you to know . . . ."

I'd cut her off then, slamming the door in her face. The last thing I wanted to hear was about some cheap harlot my father had been having good times with. The cheek of her calling herself his partner. The only partner my father ever had was my mother. Ben had calmed me down and went to speak to the woman outside. She never returned, and I never asked him what was said. She was of no interest to me.

We have gotten into a routine of living together, taking turns with the housework, splitting the bills, and spending the weekends watching movies. His hours are long, but they always have been. Still being signed off work from depression after my father's death, I use my time at home to create a safe space for him with home-cooked meals and relaxed conversation. Together, we work like a well-oiled machine with years of experience under its belt. He watches me closely, judging my mood each evening, but the dark days are becoming less frequent. I'm smiling more, and it's because of him.

This weekend, the weather forecast is glorious, so I am going to treat us to a picnic in the countryside. It's something we used to do when we were together. I would create a delicious spread of sandwiches, cakes, and goodies. We would find a secluded spot somewhere and lay out our old chequered blanket and sit for hours, savouring the food and each other.

Sometimes, I think of her and what happened between them. But he chose me, so I don't hold any grudges. I do miss my London friends. I hope one day we can reconcile and spend time together again.

Saturday morning rolls around, and all Ben knows is to be ready to go by ten o'clock. He appears in the living room wearing an open-necked white shirt with khaki cargo shorts. His hair is tousled, and his shades are propped on top of his head. Those bright-blue eyes give me the once over, and he smiles. "You look lovely today, Kels."

My heart skips a beat. I wore my white lace summer dress he loves. My hair is in soft curls down my back, and I am wearing minimal makeup, just a touch of lip gloss and bronzer. I want to glow. A blush fills my cheeks at his compliment. I hope today turns out the way I am praying it will.

Thirty minutes later, we are past the edge of the city and out into the green fields of the English countryside. I have plugged a location into the sat-nav that, after much internet research, has promised to be private with beautiful views. Turning up a quiet lane, Ben looks at me suspiciously. "Should I be checking the picnic hamper for a knife?" He raises an eyebrow, and I laugh.

"You have nothing to worry about, darling. If I was going to kill you, I would have done it months ago," I purr and blow him a kiss. He doesn't recoil or dismiss me, so I take this as a positive step forward.

We stop at a clearing that opens onto a small lake. "This is it!" I squeal. "Isn't it beautiful?" Jumping out of the car, I run up to the water's edge, taking in my surroundings.

The lake is surrounded by trees and shrubs, and there are lily pads floating in the water and the sound of birds singing in the trees. I hear the boot open and turn to see Ben lifting the big old-fashioned picnic basket out of the car. With the hamper in one hand and our blanket in the other, he walks down toward me.

"It's stunning, Kels." He smiles. "And I love seeing you so happy." He begins to lay out the blanket, smoothing the edges. Then he starts to bring out the picnic. I set up the boombox and pop in a classical CD. The music floats around us as we sit opposite each other, just enjoying the moment.

I'm not sure how much time has passed, but the picnic is eaten. We lie, side by side, with the summer sun beating down on our faces.

"Ben," I whisper, "doesn't this feel just like old times?"

He doesn't respond, but I hear his breathing hitch slightly. Taking this as a positive sign, I reach across and intertwine my fingers with his. We lie in silence, holding hands for a while. Then he props himself up on his elbow and looks me in the eye.

"Thank you," I say softly. "Without you, I don't know how I would have survived."

He leans forward slowly and kisses me; it is sensual and meaningful. The afternoon has turned out to be everything I hoped for.

"Let's go home," he says, and we start to pack up.

Sharing a bed with Dr Benjamin Jones is a familiar but new experience. He is more sexual, more adventurous than when we were last together. His preference is more dominant now; he likes me in positions where he has control of my body. I wonder idly where he learnt this from, and my mind immediately goes to her.

We have never discussed his relationship with Bex, but we have both agreed that the time has come when we attempt to rebuild bridges with our friends. To do that, we must also have contact with her. I am nervous because, in truth, I don't know how serious their relationship was. It lasted for a matter of months, possibly only weeks. They had a holiday romance just before he came back to me. But Ben has never said any more, just that he knew I needed him and that the fairest thing for everyone was to break it off.

It turns out that not much has changed in the past six months. Bex and Amy are still living together in our apartment. Terry moved into Ben's old room, but I'm not convinced he contributes much, as yet again, he is out of work.

The five of us meet at a small coffee shop not far from the apartment. We all sit around the table looking at the floor. No one is quite sure what to say.

Finally, Terry breaks the ice. "So, how're things, you two? Long time no see." It's not a very imaginative line, but I'm thankful he has started the ball rolling. The chatter is quiet and skirts around the usual topics: work, family, and extracurricular activities.

Bex sits quietly in the corner as far from us as she can get without sitting at the next table. It's clear she really does not want to be here. Her eyes are bloodshot, she's lost a lot of weight, and generally, she is looking unwell. When I hugged her on arrival, I could swear I smelled alcohol on her breath, but then again, I may just be imagining it.

Ben and Terry are deep in conversation about work, but I notice Ben's eyes glancing at Bex regularly. My insecurity surfaces for a moment, but I squash it down. *He chose me, remember.* Amy is her usual bubbly self; she looks incredible. I notice she has a hold of Bex's hand under the table as if giving her moral support.

Pity for her should fill my chest; this must be a hellish situation to be in, sitting opposite your ex with his girlfriend he chose over you. I can feel the smile playing on my lips. *That's karma, bitch.* The afternoon draws to a close, and we all start to wish each other farewell, promising to keep in touch.

Ben is talking to Bex quietly so no one else can hear. Her eyes watch him cautiously, taking in what he is saying. She is shaking her head, and I can see him getting more frustrated by her response. He leans into her and whispers something in her ear. She recoils as if he has slapped her.

Her eyes blaze angrily and fill with tears. "As if you care," she snaps and marches out the door. It's then I notice she is limping slightly as she walks away. Amy kisses me quickly and excuses herself to run after her.

Terry shrugs his shoulders. "It's just how it is, mate. She is determined to self-destruct. She seems to hold it together at work, but everything else is a shit show." He's talking to Ben, not me, but I am listening intently. "She has started hiding the bottles. Amy found one in the bathroom cabinet last week. Then she found a bottle of lemonade filled with vodka in the fridge."

My eyes widen when I realise what he is talking about. Ben rolls his eyes. "If there is anything I can do, you know where I am. I have a colleague who can help with alcohol dependency." His voice is detached and clinical, as if he is talking about someone he doesn't know, not a woman he was sleeping with only months ago. Terry nods and shakes his hand, walking the same direction the two girls left before.

The drive back to our house is quiet; we don't talk much. I know we are both thinking about the events that unfurled in the café. "How long?" I ask. "How long have you known about Bex's drinking problem?"

He glances over at me, and I can tell he is unsure how much

to say.

"Only since last week," he responds with his tone measured. "Terry called to warn me when this meeting was arranged. Seemingly it's been getting gradually worse since I . . ." He pauses. "Since I left her."

I can hear the regret in his voice.

"It's not your fault," I tell him. "Don't ever think that. She never knew when to stop. She's been broken since we were teenagers. Alcohol has always been her nemesis or her Band-Aid for a bad day."

He smiles at me and squeezes my hand. "I know, sweetie, I know."

Chapter Twenty-four: Bex

Sitting on the old, worn sofa, I stare at the pink and white envelope in front of me. I know what's in it. Amy warned me. She and Terry received their invitation today as well.

Being a couple now, they get lots of joint invitations. I am thoroughly the lemon of our little threesome. Living with a couple is depressing; they don't mean to be hard to live with, but it is becoming increasingly impossible to stand being around them. All the touching and kissing is sweet, but after day 145, it's very irritating.

My focus falls back to the envelope, challenging me to open it. To confirm what I already know.

The expensive white paper is decorated with hand-drawn pink flowers winding along the edges, and my name is written in fine black calligraphy across the centre. I slide my finger under the flap, and it pops open. I extract three pieces of thick white card: the invite, the menu, and the reply form. There is also a self-addressed envelope with a stamp to make replying as simple as possible. More pink flowers decorate every section of the invite. I mean, who the hell has time to draw all that?

Mr & Mrs G Jones
Request the pleasure of your company at the wedding of their son
Dr Benjamin Jones to Miss Kelsey McMillan
on the 4th of May, 2000.
We hope you will be able to join us for their special day.
RSVP by March 1st, and please include your meal choice.
No gifts. Donations will be collected for the local cancer centre.

Tears fill my eyes as I read the words again. He's getting married. I knew they were engaged. Being linked with them through friends kind of makes it inevitable that you find these things out. And, just for my benefit, someone had phoned Amy within minutes of *happy* event to tell her.

I listened to how Ben had gone down on one knee in front of a restaurant full of people and declared his undying love for her. He promised to care for her forever and produced an exquisite diamond ring. There had been a round of applause and congratulations after she had said yes. The image I created of them smiling and cuddling is ingrained in my mind.

I throw the invitation to the side.

I will deal with it later.

Since our reconciliation a year ago as a group, we have kept in touch and have tried to socialise every month. We normally meet at the local pub, and the five of us have a few drinks and a catch-up. I am careful not to drink too much on these occasions because I really cannot trust myself around Ben. I deleted his number from my phone to remove the temptation of making embarrassing drunken phone calls. We keep our distance from each other but steal glances whenever we can.

I know by the way his body responds to mine on our brief greetings and goodbyes that he still finds me attractive. My feelings have never gone away. If anything, they have become stronger. He is the one in my dreams.

Since I heard of their engagement, I have a recurring dream of walking down the aisle to him, only to be exchanged with her at the bottom. Then, I'm being made to watch them complete the ceremony as an onlooker in the crowd, still wearing my wedding dress. Each night I wake up soaked to the skin with tears staining my cheeks.

Amy and I have discussed all the pros and cons of me attending the wedding. But at the end of the day, they are my friends, and it's my responsibility to show my support. Well, so Amy says. My relationship with Ben was a long time ago, I need to shake it off and move on. I'm not sure what she thinks I have been trying to do, but getting over Dr Benjamin Jones is not that easy. The man is a permanent resident in my head.

I tick, *I will attend* on the reply form and post it before I can change my mind.

When I asked Max to accompany me, he gave me a flat no. He hates Ben for leaving me and breaking my heart.

"But Max," I wailed. "They've been my friends for years, if I don't go isn't it more obvious?"

"Do you honestly think I'm stupid enough to agree to go to that asshole's wedding with you? The day will be a disaster. For you. I'm telling you now, Bex, this is not a good idea. What Amy thinks is irrelevant. This is about your needs and your inability to get over that prick."

"Some friend you are!" I shout. "You're nothing but a jealous bastard."

"Bex, I'm done. Contact me when you get a grip of yourself and need a real friend." Without another word he storms out the door not looking back. He thinks I should have cut all ties years ago, but I don't want to be the destroyer of our friendship group. That's not who I am. Max can go to hell.

Sitting on the rock-hard wooden pew surrounded by people *dressed to impress* in a church is one of the most uncomfortable places I have ever been. Every colour, style, and adornment are on show today. Weddings bring out the peacock in everyone. People primp, preen, and practically prune themselves into perfection. Or so-called perfection. Their perceived perfection.

I giggle under my breath. Jesus, what do half of them look like?

I stretch my arms in front of me, wiggling my bright-pink

fingers. What the hell am I doing here? It certainly isn't through choice. Bloody Amy. My sister is a fucking bridesmaid. Someone dropped out at the last minute, and Amy fit in the dress.

I have been left to fly solo.

Mrs Lewis, a kindly old woman, leans forward and whispers in my ear. "Isn't it beautiful, dear? The flowers, the music, the church."

I swipe her huge orange feather that is dangling from her boat-sized hat away from my ear. *Just breathe, Bex. You can do this.* I smile but choose not to respond. My current choice of words running through my head is probably not appropriate in the Lord's House.

Whether I believe or not.

A hush falls over the congregation, and the organ starts its droning tune. Ben stands tall at the front of the church with his best man, Terry, on his right arm. He looks so handsome. Tall and dark, his muscular shoulders are prominent through his dress coat.

Ice-blue eyes meet mine, and I smile shyly. I deliberately tried to position myself at the back of the hall out of sight. That didn't work. He snaps his eyes away from me, returning to talk to the minister, only turning again when everyone stands for the entrance of the bride.

Kelsey enters the church with her uncle by her side. Her poor father and mother didn't live long enough to see their daughter marry the love of her life. The love of *my* life, I think bitterly. I am not sure why I came. Maybe because it would look a lot worse if I didn't.

But it bloody hurts.

I chose my outfit carefully, deliberating and changing umpteen times before settling on my choice. A sleek fitted black dress with silver buttons finishing just above my knee. My blonde hair is up and glossy. My lips are painted red, and my eyes are dark. To be honest, I look as if I am going to a funeral, but I look hot. I needed armour today. A protective cover to contain me while I watch the man I love marry one of my oldest friends.

Her dress is lace, and she is fully covered. She has that sexy but classy look all women want to pull off on their wedding day. And bloody hell, she pulls it off.

I grind my teeth as my last hope that this isn't going to happen disappears. Fuck's sake, *I* would marry her. She looks so damn good. My eyes flick to look at Ben, and his eyes are wide. Excited. A soft smile is spreading across his face. I can see him undressing her from here.

Bile bubbles in my stomach as my panic kicks in. This is happening. I'm going to be alone forever. The universe is officially pissing on me and making me watch.

She makes it to the front of the church. Her uncle cuddles her warmly, and she kisses the old man's cheek. Tears are bubbling under the surface, an uncle handing his niece over. An absent father. An absent mother. She turns to her future husband. They take each other's hands. I swear I see electricity pulse between them. My stomach drops to my toes, I hang my head, and I listen to the exchange that is like someone repeatedly punching me in the stomach.

The vows are beautiful, and of course, they wrote them themselves. Everything is perfect. Screams of joy echo around the room as they are pronounced husband and wife. Ben kisses her passionately as he punches his fist in the air to celebrate, then leads his new wife back up the aisle hand in hand.

Tears fill my eyes as I watch them, and I quickly put my sunglasses on to hide, then hang at the back as the guests start to file out behind the happy couple. Amy told me that the wedding party would be leaving to get professional photos; both she and Terry are involved, so I was to drive to the reception and wait for them. I was not to get drunk or snog anyone before she gets there. Her words circle around my head. This is what I have become in the eyes of my sister. A drunken whore.

The hotel is stunning, as I expected, sitting in acres of gardens planted with rose bushes and oak trees. Of course, the sun is shining as requested, too. There is a long driveway up to the Victorian mansion. In front of the property is a roundabout with a fountain bubbling away. I park the car around the back and walk up the steps into the foyer. A dashing young man carrying a tray of champagne offers me a glass, which I accept gladly. The bar is filling up with people chattering excitedly about the ceremony.

Everyone is gushing about what a lovely couple Ben and Kelsey are. I stand in the corner and sip my champagne, watching the interaction. No one here is familiar, and I make no effort to speak. I just want to get through the day.

When Amy and Terry arrive, she hugs me fiercely. "Are you ok?" she whispers. I give her a tight smile, and she nods, ordering Terry to get us all a glass of fizz. He scuttles off in the direction of the bar.

Amy has him so tight around her finger, I'm sure he worships at her feet every morning and night. Terry might be a loser professionally, but he adores my sister. He makes her happy.

An announcement that we should take our seats for dinner echoes around the room. A small lean man with a dinner suit on is directing people toward the ballroom. Looking for my name, I see I have been put on a table in the far corner of the room as far away from the top table as possible. Our table is called Twister. I'm not sure why, but each table is named after a board game. I do hope we are not all expected to play the games later in the evening. I can barely walk, never mind twist, in this dress.

Looking around at my table companions, I can see why we

have been stuck together on the outskirts. We are *the people they felt they had to invite but didn't want to come* table. Made up of parents' friends, forgotten school pals, old teachers, and, well, me.

The meal was delicious, and the speeches were done, so the band starts to play for the first dance. The lead singer announces, "I would like to invite Dr and Mrs Jones to the floor for their first dance as husband and wife." Ben stands and holds his hand out to Kelsey; she accepts it, and he leads her up to the floor. The music starts; it's a classic love song, but I can't quite place it, as the wine has started to cloud my brain. They move to the slow beat, and I realise it is a practised routine. The dance finishes with him lifting her in the air. They both laugh, and the crowd bursts into applause.

The knife twists in my chest, letting the blood run from my body.

I sit at my table of ten, but I'm the only one still there. The reception ended hours ago. I'm still hanging with good old cava. Cava and I are old friends. We keep each other company when times are tough. My sexy black dress is ruined. I believe the wet stain down the front was the bottle of red I decided to neck unsuccessfully.

Amy begged me to go back to my room after the band finished playing, but I refused. Tonight was the night from hell, but I made it to the end. It wasn't until the band announced the bride and groom were leaving and wished them a wonderful honeymoon that I fell apart.

Watching from the safety of my chair, I saw them hugged and kissed repeatedly. Told to get a move on and make some babies. Ben's eyes had met mine a few times over the day, but he had never approached me. He kept his distance and looked at me with a coolness. He has probably heard all about my bad behaviour recently and is disgusted.

Monday to Friday, I am a professional English teacher

working my way up the ladder, but on the weekend, I lose myself in alcohol and men. Amy has asked me to stop bringing men to the house after one of my one-night stands stole Terry's tablet.

PART 3

London
August 2006

CHAPTER TWENTY-FIVE: BEX

Relief runs through me as I reread the letter that dropped through my post box this morning. I consider pouring myself a glass of fizz to celebrate. It's ten o'clock in the morning. It was my drunken behaviour that got me into this mess. Well, my drunken behaviour and my lack of willpower when it comes to Dr Benjamin Jones.

Dear Miss Corrigan,

I am writing to inform you that the outcome of the investigation into your behaviour outside Hilltop Manor Academy has been concluded. Having liaised with the parents' association and your fellow staff members, it has been agreed you may return to your post as Director of English.

We accept your admission of having issues regarding alcohol and have arranged ten weeks of support to help you accomplish your goal of being able to stop drinking permanently.

Please note, although you have been reinstated in your role, this is for a probationary period of six months. There will be an evaluation at the end of this period to finalise any future steps required.

I look forward to seeing you back at Hilltop Manor Academy when school restarts in September.

Kind Regards,

John Fraser

Principal of Hilltop Manor Academy

When I was suspended for my behaviour at The Smoking Goat, I really did think it was the end of my career. My whole life seems to have spiralled out of control these past years, but my job was something I was confident about. I am a good teacher. I get the best from my students. I have deserved every promotion I have been given.

Now, I know I must cut all ties with Ben and Kelsey. It was ridiculous to think we could be friends, after all the drama that has gone on between us over the years. I had never intended to be the mistress of a married man; it was never in my life plan. The affair between Ben and me wasn't constant. We didn't arrange to meet, and no hotel rooms were booked or secret weekends away planned. Since he married, we had slept together three times, and it was always the result of a drunken night out. Kelsey, having young children, would often go home early, leaving the rest of us to party on.

The first time it happened was about two years after their wedding. There was a school reunion taking place for our age group, and we all decided to go along. Amy and Terry were still going strong. She was excited to show him off to her arch enemies from her teen years. Terry had finally got his act together, holding down a regular job at the local theatre. They were living together in a one-bedroom apartment near me. Life seemed to be falling into place for them. Constant whispers were flying around that he was going to pop the question.

Ben and Kelsey had been two years married with a beautiful daughter already. In true teenage dream fashion, she had fallen pregnant on her honeymoon. Savannah was now eighteen months old and a bubbly blonde-headed little cherub. Anytime I saw the three of them together, I felt my heart ache for the family I would never have. When the man you fall in love with walks away and starts a family with another woman, it is a soul-destroying experience.

I've never had a fulfilling relationship since. My body still yearns for Dr Benjamin Jones. I'm a glutton for punishment, and any contact with him was better than none. So I continued to socialise in the group. Lust after him from afar. Sometimes, I would feel his eyes watching me, and I would wonder if he missed me at all.

The night of the reunion had been a lot of fun. The drinks were flowing and people were swapping stories of failed jobs and marriages. We all arrived together but have split up over the course of the evening. Suddenly, a tap on my shoulder grabs my attention. I spin around to stare into deep green eyes. The man who owns them is tall and dark. He has a warm complexion, Max. He smiles warmly at me then pulls me into a huge bear hug.

"Bex Corrigan, you look mighty fine!" he shouts and gives me a cheeky wink. I laugh and cuddle him again. It's so good to see a friendly face. "It's been too long, gorgeous."

"Max, how are you? Life treating you well?" He is a good-looking man, and my body responds in recognition of this. We chat idly about our lives these past years, where we live, and our families. Turns out we are both still single, stuck in a group of friends who are all in couples. Max has a very normal life; he is a teacher like me. He travels a lot. In some ways, it sounds as if he has never really grown up. His life is full of beaches and cocktails.

We swap numbers and agree to meet up later for a drink. "Not a bad night," I giggle to myself as I go off in search of the others.

Kelsey is sitting on a plastic chair near the door. She looks exhausted, which is to be expected. She has a young child to care for while working as a nurse. Her eyes are heavy, and it looks as though she has been crying.

Ben is standing at the bar with Terry. They have a pint of beer each and are chatting between themselves. I sit down next to Kelsey. "You alright?" I ask. Our relationship is civil, but I tend to keep my distance. Today, she looked like she needed a friend. I felt I should try.

She looks at me stonily. "Yes, fine, I'm just ready for home." She glares and points at Ben. "He has organised a taxi for me."

She stands, marching toward the exit of the hall, and Ben scurries out after her. Ten minutes later, he returns with a huge smile across his face. "Time to party," he shouts to Terry, and the two of them walk off in the direction of the bar.

I roll my eyes and laugh at their childish behaviour.

Amy has been standing next to me, watching the proceedings unfold. I turn to her. "What's this all about?"

She eyes me warily as if weighing up what to say.

"Amy, is everything alright?" She clearly considers lying, but decides to tell me the truth.

"They had a fight," she says simply, not offering anything further.

I raise an eyebrow, silently asking for more information.

"They had a fight about you."

My eyes widen at the admission. "Me?" I squawk. "What about me?"

She sighs, shrugging her shoulders, obviously deciding that it would make her life easier just to tell me. "About the way Ben watches you."

I look at her, perplexed. "The way he watches me?" I repeat back.

"Yes, Bex," she snaps. "Don't tell me you don't notice the way his eyes follow you around the room. The obvious jealousy when he sees you talking to another man. The fact you are his ex-girlfriend, and he still has feelings for you."

I laugh, not believing a word she is saying. "He left me, Amy." I open my arms wide to exaggerate my point. "I am a single loser at my high school reunion with two couples. He walked away and never looked back."

She shakes her head. "If that's what you see, Bex, you're

more stupid than I thought." Then she turns on her heel and storms off in the direction I saw the boys walk in.

I look up, and Ben is there watching me. How long has he been standing there? His face tells me he heard the whole exchange.

"Is it true?" I stammer.

He lifts an eyebrow. "Is what true?" he responds smoothly. "The fact I fought with my wife? Or the fact I still have feelings for you?"

My heart stops. Did he just say that? Out loud? I can tell by his mannerisms he is well-oiled. His eyes are slightly out of focus, and he has that confidence people acquire by having too much to drink. I am not exactly sober, I remind myself. Who am I to judge?

"Well, any of it?" I answer sharply, more sharply than needed.

His cool eyes survey me as if considering what to say next. The time of the night has arrived when peoples' inhibitions are lowered. Bodies are writhing against each other, hands investigating places they shouldn't. There is sex in the air. He walks forward so our bodies are pressed up against each other, and I feel his hard length on my stomach.

"What do you think, Bex?" he whispers in my ear softly.

We walk hand in hand from the gym hall and dart down the corridor, giggling as if we are skipping school. Old lockers still line the walls, and we escape through the familiar blue door into the storeroom. Amy and I used to hide in here to skip PE class, which is ironic with her job now. The room is filled with boxes of supplies, and there are books and fitness equipment piled everywhere.

Ben takes my face in his hands and kisses me fiercely; tears start to run down my face. I have missed him so much. My heart has been broken time and again, watching him move on without me.

I am wearing a white satin blouse with a short black skirt. He runs his hand up my inner thigh and hisses as he feels the top of my lace stockings.

"Easy access," he growls in my ear, and my insides somersault in approval.

Suddenly, his need is urgent. He rips open my blouse and roughly pulls at my bra to expose my breasts. His teeth bite my nipples firmly, and I squeal in appreciation. "I am going to fuck you hard, Bex." His voice commanding.

Even if I wanted to, I don't think I could stop him. What the hell am I doing? He's married, for Christ's sake. But his touch feels so right. My body is craving it. I need this. I've wanted to have him for so long. I miss him. Just once. It will only happen once. As if on cue, my body is responding to him; the area between my legs is wet with need as he slides two fingers inside.

"That's my girl." He smiles on my mouth as he kisses me.

I start to pull at his trousers, but he grabs my hands, pinning them above my head against the wall. He releases himself from the bindings of his boxers, and my eyes drift to his rock-hard cock.

"You want this, honey?"

I nod silently and bite my lip.

"Don't bite your lip. That's my department," he reprimands. Then he is inside me, lifting me and penetrating me in one swift movement. His hands are on my backside, and he fucks me hard against the wall.

We are not making love; this is fucking, our needs overtaking our wants. He comes quickly and urgently, emptying himself inside me. I liquefy in his arms, completely spent from the unexpected arousal. We look at each other, and I smile at him shyly.

A look of shock is etched on his face as if surprised that I am real. His shirt is open and pulled off his shoulders. That's when I see the tattoo wrapping around his arm, waves of black ink spelling out her name.

Kelsey.

He sees what I'm looking at and answers my unspoken question. "On honeymoon. To prove she was the one."

Pain surges through me. He's been branded. He's hers. If being married didn't make it clear enough for me, the tattoo made it real.

Without saying another word, he stands me back on the ground and readjusts his clothes. We return to the party and don't mention the incident in the storeroom.

After our escapade, we didn't see each other for months, and when we did, it was as if it had never happened. Life continued. We skirted around each other for the benefit of our friends.

The second time we ended up in bed — or fucking is probably a better way to describe it — it happened the same as the first time. Kelsey and Ben argued, she went home, he got angry, and I was willing. Then we carried on as if nothing had ever happened. I could feel his eyes watching me when we were in the same room. I stalked his social media and berated myself at every opportunity about my behaviour.

Over the years, I became more desperate and promiscuous while relying more and more on alcohol to build my confidence and drown my sorrows. Being the other woman had never been on my agenda, but here I am, in love with a married father of two, soon to be three, children. I need to draw a line in the sand and move on from this.

I need to forget Dr Benjamin Jones and accept what could have been for us never will be.

Chapter Twenty-Six: Bex

Finally, the day arrives. Back to school.

I am dressed and ready for work by seven o'clock sharp. I cannot wait to get back in front of my blackboard where I belong. In the weeks I have been suspended, I have used the time to create an action plan for myself.

Stage one is cutting alcohol completely from my life.

Stage two is removing myself from my friendship group.

Stage three is to take up a hobby.

Since that fateful weekend four months ago, I haven't had any contact with Ben or Kelsey. I heard from Amy that she had given birth to a baby boy, Oliver Jones. Both mum and baby were doing well. Ben had removed his account from Facebook immediately after our night together or he blocked me; I am not sure which, but I haven't seen anything from him.

Arriving at school, I take in large gulps of air to steady my nerves. I have spoken to Max about returning to the school, and he assures me all the teaching staff are happy about my return. Well, everyone except Wendy.

It turns out it was Wendy who highlighted my behaviour to Principal Fraser. She had gone to great lengths to have me removed from the school, tracking down the CCTV of my indiscretions at the back of the pub and adding fuel to the fire by ensuring the rumour mill was well stocked.

The demise of my friendship with Wendy saddens me. I used to consider her a close friend and colleague. I loved her like a sister. It was because of her investment in me that I had become the confident teacher I was today. Even after I rejected her romantic advances, we remained on good terms at work.

The real issues started when I climbed the ladder quicker than she did. Being older than me, she always expected to be my superior, but after moving to Hilltop Manor Academy together, then my promotion to Director of English, our relationship had deteriorated quickly. I was naïve to think colleagues will be happy for each other no matter the circumstances.

Unfortunately, we had both applied for the position and were the final two for the interview. I was offered the job the next day. She spat on my shoes when I told her. "You must have sucked the principal's dick for it," she hissed. Her low opinion of me had started a war of words. I said things I am not proud of. We never recovered from that.

Max told me she's changed schools, back into the public sector. When she heard I had been reinstated, she accepted the new position. In all honesty, I'm relieved. Facing her today would have made this more difficult.

But today is the first day in my new life, and I'm determined to make it a good one. I'm relieved to find my classroom exactly as I left it. No one has automatically assumed my position. A class of thirteen-year-olds file into the room and take their seats. I expect an assortment of questions regarding where I have been and what I have been doing. Knowing the children at this school, there will be plenty of tall tales flying around the playground, but my classes pass quietly and without incident. There are no awkward questions. It is as if I have never been away.

I am happy to survive until lunchtime. A knock at my door signals Max's arrival. He promised to come and walk me to the staff room.

"I'm not having you walking in there yourself. I've got your back, gorgeous."

I smile at the memory of his phone call last night. My cheerleader is ready to catch me if I fall over in the next few days. Thinking of how I've treated him at times, I'm lucky he sticks around. We've had spells of distance, but always rekindle our friendship. The bell tolls for the end of the day, and I breathe a welcome sigh of relief. I did it. I got back out there.

Three weeks go by, and I resume my routine. Work, gym, and home. I have been spending my evenings researching healthy recipes and honing my cooking skills. Amy drops by a few times a week to check on me. Secretly, I know she's making sure I'm staying off the booze.

But, in all honesty, I have not been feeling so well lately. Each morning I wake with a sore head, and I feel nauseous. Dismissing it as stress, I carry on, determined to embrace a healthy lifestyle. Everything will fall into place, I tell myself.

It's Friday night, and this marks twelve weeks sober. Amy has come to celebrate with me. She has non-alcoholic fizz and Chinese takeaway in her hands as I swing open the door to greet her.

"Congratulations!" she sings and dumps her goodies on the table before hugging me tight. "I am so proud of you, sis!"

I feel tears prick my eyes, and I squeeze her, too. "Thank you," is all I can say before sobbing tears of joy.

The meal has been eaten, and we are lounging on my sofas, watching a terrible film featuring Amy's latest man crush. It has been a lovely evening, and we have chatted animatedly, Amy filling me in on all of Terry's misdemeanours. I am still amazed they are together even after all this time, but it works, and my sister is happy.

Her face looks at me, horrified, as I explain how I've been unwell for a few weeks, the morning nausea and sore heads. "I am not sure what is wrong with me," I say. "Maybe I need a vitamin or something. Why are you looking at me like that?"

Her eyes are wide. "Bex, don't freak out, but when did you

have your last period?" Her voice is calm but direct.

My mind starts to race. So much has happened in the past few months, I can't recall the exact date. "Um . . ." I stammer. "I'm not sure. A few weeks ago, I think. I don't really keep track. No boyfriend, you see." I flash her a smile, but a sense of unease is filling me.

"Bex," she continues firmly, "did you use protection with Ben? Have you slept with anyone else? Have you had a period since you slept with him?"

Amy and I are now in the supermarket, scanning the aisles like a pair of errant schoolgirls. I'm thirty-three years old, and I'm having to sneak to the shop to buy a pregnancy test because I cannot remember if the guy wore a condom.

How embarrassing!

My ears are still ringing from Amy's rant after I confirmed that I didn't know if we used protection. But I hadn't had sex with anyone else recently. If I'm completely honest, Ben is the only man I have had sex with this year. Not that anyone would believe me if I told them. After he got engaged, I did have a lot of one-night stands, but since the wedding, I tried hard to rein in my behaviour.

Finally, we find the sexual health section of the medical supplies. The shelves are filled with brightly coloured bottles of lube promising amazing sensations. There are more sizes and flavours of condoms than I knew existed, ribbed, large, apple or chocolate. The choice is endless, I think absently.

Amy had to spell the situation out for me. "You had unprotected sex over three months ago. You can't remember having a period since. You could be pregnant," she had stated plainly.

I laughed then ran to the bathroom to be sick.

So, here we were, staring at the selection of pregnancy tests available at eleven o'clock on a Friday night.

"You do know this is a complete overreaction," I snarl,

trying to convince myself. Deciding to purchase a pack of three tests, I approach the counter meekly, not looking the salesperson, an older lady maybe in her fifties, in the eye. She smiles at me kindly, scanning my tests through.

"Fifteen pounds and thirty pence please." Her voice is kind, and I can't help smiling softly as I hand over my card. "Thank you, dear," she responds. "I hope you get the result you're hoping for," she murmurs as she slips the tests in a carrier bag.

Amy and I leave the shop, almost running. I need to get home to pee on these sticks.

The result I am hoping for. The salesperson's words swirl around my brain and confuse me. I am not sure what I am hoping for. What will I do if I am pregnant with a married man's baby?

I peed on all the sticks ten minutes ago. We sat them at the other side of the bathroom, next to the sink, so we couldn't keep looking at them. Amy is sitting next to me on the edge of the bath. "Whatever happens, I am here for you," she whispers and cuddles into my shoulder.

I smile at her loyalty, but I am so disappointed I have gotten myself into this position. And even more disgusted that part of me is hoping the result is a positive one. But if I am pregnant with his baby, it means part of him will be with me forever, and my heart softens at the thought.

We stare down at the six blue lines, two on each test.

"Yep," Amy says softly, "You are definitely up the duff." She bursts into tears then starts jumping around the bathroom, chanting that she is going to be an auntie. I look at her, dumbstruck, but I can't help the smile spreading across my face.

Children were something I had written off as impossible because of my age and relationship status. But here I am, according to these little white sticks, pregnant with the child of the man I love. Now, I appreciate the complication is the fact he is already married with children, but I am not letting that small fact dampen my mood.

The months passed, and the time was never right to tell Ben. I could never bring myself to upset his perfect family.

I know via Amy, who knows via Terry, that Kelsey had known about our indiscretions, but they have discussed it and decided to try again as a family.

The only contact Terry has now with Ben is the odd text message. Terry doesn't know who the father of my baby is, and I begged Amy not to tell him. I know Terry, and he's loyal to Ben; he could never keep his mouth shut.

So, here I am, nine months pregnant with a baby boy and ready to pop. My work has been incredibly supportive, and I have a job to go back to when I am ready. Nursery placements are sorted, and for once in my life, I have my shit together.

My apartment has been cleaned and decorated; the broody phase rubbed off on me. Poor Terry has acted like a surrogate husband, lifting, painting, and moving whatever is required for an easy life. Two weeks ago, he asked Amy to marry him, so now we have two life-changing events to look forward to.

Even though I am going to be a single parent, I am confident I can do this. I can bring this little boy into the world and love him completely. He is going to be my focus in life and have my heart.

I'm lying in my bed, one week overdue, and pains start to crease my stomach. I pull myself out of bed and waddle to the bathroom. Another wave of pain washes through me, and I lift my phone to text my sister.

Baby Corrigan is go.

I text, and I laugh at my own humour before doubling in two with another wave of pain. Throwing on my dressing gown, I grab my overnight bag as Amy and Terry burst through the door.

They really do live way too close.

We all traipse to the hospital, squashed together in the back of a black cab we flagged down. I'm admitted to the maternity ward. Exactly five hours, thirty-two minutes, and fifteen seconds later, after more pain than I ever thought I could have handled, my son, Liam Benjamin Corrigan, makes his entrance into the world. His lungs filled with air, and his screams echoed around the delivery room. The nurse hands me a little bundle covered in blood and gunge.

I look down into the brightest blue eyes with a shock of black hair and see Dr Benjamin Jones has forever stamped his mark on me.

CHAPTER TWENTY-SEVEN: BEN

5 years later . . .
September 2011

Never in a million years did I expect to become a single father. Co-parenting with Kelsey has been one of the toughest challenges of my life, especially with my workload and three active children to look after, but I wouldn't have it any other way.

Oliver was only eight months old when she decided she was leaving me, packing her case and walking out.

I was left staring at the closed door with three small children at my feet. We had been arguing again. I can't even remember what our fight was about, but I know it was insignificant. Perhaps my dirty socks were left next to the washing basket or she hadn't tidied the children's toys. Possibly I had stood on a stray building block, I muse, wincing at the memory I have of standing on those little cubes of torture. The pain is worse than getting kicked in the balls.

For the first two years of our new routine, it had been difficult, to say the least. We agreed she wouldn't return to work until Ollie turned three and was eligible to attend nursery. Our home was our sanctuary, so we continued to live together but separately. This allowed us to share the responsibility of the home and care of the children. Our three babies grew up surrounded by love, but I must admit, it was an awkward situation. In public, we kept up the pretence that we were together.

Although my personal life seemed to be disintegrating before my eyes, my career was moving from strength to strength. Having the two years to plan a future as a separated family meant I was able to put strategies in place to be successful both in my work and as a father.

My credibility as an oncology consultant continued to grow, and I was offered more opportunities than I ever dreamed of. Positions abroad were presented, and I was invited to make addresses at professional conferences.

With Eamon's support, I was able to negotiate a position at a private hospital nearer to our home. The shifts were fixed with a mixture of days and evenings. I was able to drop the children at school some days and collect them on others. Kelsey then returned to her much-loved job as a nurse, and I moved into an apartment not far from the house.

Somehow, we made it work for us. The children have a stable home environment, albeit split between two locations. Both homes are financially secure. As parents, we communicate openly. I still love Kelsey, but not in the way I used to. I see now our relationship was the teenage dream, not only of us but of our families. We never developed beyond that and struggled when life got real.

So here I am, pushing forty, a single father of three. Our apartment is modern, sleek, and situated in a good area. There are three bedrooms, which is a relief, as it means only the two girls need to share a room when they stay, which is multiple nights per week.

The children are my world. Every moment I get with them is precious.

"Good morning, Jones." Eamon's booming voice carries across the ward with a huge beaming smile attached to it.

It's Wednesday morning, so I take the day shift. Kelsey drops the children off at school, and I will collect them later. Eamon followed me to Larson's Private Hospital when I moved. Said he was "too old" to be learning to work with other idiots. I suspect he and his wife, Melissa, were worried about me and about losing touch with my children. They treat them like the grandchildren they never had.

He hands me a takeaway cup filled with a steaming-hot latte. This is our routine; he buys the morning coffee, and I get the lunchtime cake. Then we set off on our rounds of the ward to see how our patients are holding up.

I find working at the private hospital a walk in the park compared to the public sector. Rooms are never oversubscribed, the store cupboards are full of supplies, and working hours are kept to a fixed number. If we are asked to do overtime, we get paid for it. I have never felt more in control or as secure as I do now. Because of the better pay and lower demand on my time, I have been able to support Kelsey with the children emotionally as well as financially during the separation phase of our marriage.

Our first patient of the day is a lovely lady called Peggy. She is well into her eighties and has stage four breast cancer. There is nothing we can do for her, but she is kept comfortable with pain medication. Her only son lives in Australia and is making his way to London this week. I just hope he arrives in time to say goodbye to his mum.

"Morning, Peggy. How are you feeling today?" My voice is light and breezy, but this woman is not stupid. She is fully aware of the seriousness of her situation. She smiles up at me. The nurses have her propped up so she can see both the television and the door clearly.

"Doctor Jones, aren't you looking handsome this morning? Give an old lady like me a heart attack before this bastard cancer gets me." She laughs at herself, amused by her own joke.

I lean down and kiss her cheek. "It's always a pleasure to be in the company of a fine woman such as yourself, Peggy," I tease her playfully. "Is there anything I can do for you today?"

She drums her fingers on her lips as she pretends to consider my question, and her lips curl into a cheeky smile. "Well, any lady would be crazy not to take that offer, Doctor Jones, and I'm sure I could come up with a few things, but I suspect you wouldn't be allowed to do what I ask of you."

I roll my eyes at her bravado. I bet this woman was a handful when she was younger. I've seen photos of her with her much-loved husband, Bernard, who she lost while still in her fifties. From the stories she has told me, her life has been lived to the fullest, and she has enjoyed every moment.

The rest of my workday goes smoothly. I don't have any bad news to distribute, which is a blessing. As much as I love my job, when you must break the news to someone that their time is limited, it becomes incredibly difficult. I hear quick, heavy footsteps behind me and turn to see Eamon running to catch me up as I head out the main entrance.

"Time for a quick one, Jones?" He yells so loud that people in the waiting area lift their heads in surprise. "What time do you pick up my little pumpkins?"

His love for my children is heart-warming; they just adore each other.

"Not for a couple of hours. Savannah and Rose have after-school dance, so Ollie stays in for the club," I respond, laughing at the fact my kids have a better social life than me.

"Excellent," he shouts, rubbing his hands together and licking his lips exaggeratedly. "This way. We are going for a refreshment." I watch his burly figure stride off in the direction of the local tavern and almost have to run to keep up with him.

We sit at one of the old wooden tables marked from years of pint glasses and the days when you could smoke inside. A pretty young woman approaches our table. She is around her mid-twenties, and her blonde hair is pulled into a high ponytail. Her ample bosom is on display in the low neckline of her fitted black dress. She smiles at me with perfect rows of bright white teeth behind plump ruby-red lips. Eamon is sitting opposite me and waggles his eyebrows. We each order a pint of lager. I notice as she walks away that her hips swing from side to side, and her abundant bottom bounces seductively on the top of sexily shaped legs. It's been a long time, I tell myself, but she is way too young for me.

As if reading my mind, Eamon pipes up, "It's time you got yourself some action. No point sitting around the house while the kids are at Kelsey's. You need to get back out there. You're too young and too damn handsome to be on the shelf." He looks pointedly at me then continues, "She's dating, you know."

"Who?" I demand.

"Kelsey, who do you think? According to Mel, tonight is her third date with a bloke called George, a firefighter from outside the city. He has a dog called Meg and no additional baggage."

I laugh. "Fuck's sake, Eamon! You sound as if you have been reading profiles off a dating website."

He pulls a face at me but is undeterred by my rebuke. "No, Jones, I am just telling it like it is. Kelsey is moving on, and you're allowed to as well." His eyes are locked on me.

I have heard this little speech plenty of times before. About how a woman would do me good, something fun, nothing serious. I have tuned him out, but he is still talking.

"Ben!" he snaps. "Bloody listen to me. You deserve some fun, some happiness away from the children. You're a youngish man with red blood running through your veins. Are you telling me you don't need sex?"

I glare at him. "Eamon, not that it is any of your fucking business, you don't know who I have in my bed."

He gives me a look, telling me he knows I am lying but I

charge on.

"Anyway, sex doesn't require a woman. A dirty magazine and my right hand are more than sufficient."

Colour floods my face as I realise what I have revealed to him, and we both burst out laughing.

Things settle back down, and he leans over like a father would. "You can't take a porn magazine to a restaurant. Please just consider trying again. You have so much to offer to someone special."

Two hours goes quickly with Eamon; we are never short of conversation topics. Working in the same field, our blended families and my unruly children give us plenty to chew over.

Savannah had received her first detention last week; Kelsey had been beside herself with embarrassment. We had been called into the Headteacher's Office to discuss an incident. When I had asked what the incident was, I was told they would rather talk to both of us in person. I was surprised to find that when a child's parents don't live together, the school sends identical correspondence to both. It gave me some relief in the beginning that all information would be passed onto me directly.

Kelsey and I arranged a time convenient with the school when neither of us was working. I think about the text message conversation we had to arrange it. The words were so normal. There was no venom, no nastiness, we just talked about what was required.

I consider myself lucky. My colleague had split with his wife five years ago, and he still has blazing arguments with her about the kids. Once, I remember him telling me his wife had driven the distance between their houses and calculated an exact halfway point for drop off and pick up. My mind boggles at the idea I would grudge my children an extra mile of fuel or a minute of my time.

As I pulled up into the school car park, Kelsey was sitting

on a bench in front of the entrance. Her hair was down and loose on her shoulders, and she was wearing a simple pink dress with small heels. It hugged her body, accentuating her figure. Thinking back, I did notice she was wearing more makeup than usual, her lips a bright pink in the sunshine. Eamon's words come back to me about her seeing someone. It didn't even cross my mind at the time, but yes, she did have a glow about her last week.

The secretary had shown us to the Headteacher's Office. Mrs Pringle is like a caricature of a schoolteacher. She has dark-brown hair pulled up into a severe bun, her eyes are sharp, and huge glasses with a neck strap are perched on the end of her long nose.

She gestured for us to take a seat and plonked herself in a large green chair. Her considerable tweed-clad backside made the wood creak underneath it. This woman sees the school as her domain, and I am sure she rules it with an iron fist.

Mrs Pringle cleared her throat loudly. "Mr and Mrs Jones," she began.

Kelsey's voice cut in, taking me by surprise, "Actually, Mrs Pringle, I'm returning to using my maiden name, McMillan."

She looked to me and back to the headteacher. I opened my mouth to say something, but nothing came out. Talk about a curveball.

The tyrant in front of us took no notice. "Very well." She started again. "Mr Jones and Ms McMillan. I am concerned about the recent behaviour of your daughter, Savannah. Yesterday, she struck one of the other children." She paused, letting that sink in. "Now, as this is her first warning, no action beyond detention will be taken. But if it happens again, there will be a suspension period."

Kelsey and I looked at each other in disbelief. She struggles to deal with conflict, so I decided to take up the reins in the conversation. Using my most professional voice, I asked, "Which child did she strike? And what was the situation that caused the incident?"

The woman shook her head, "I'm sorry, Mr Jones, but I can't divulge that information."

I narrowed my eyes at her.

"This isn't MI5, Mrs Pringle. It's a school. You have accused our daughter of being violent, and I want to know what led her to be so. Savannah is a good girl and has not caused any issues in the past. Don't you think this requires a bit more investigation?"

She shrugged her shoulders, not interested, and I stood.

"I will be speaking to Savannah this evening, and I will contact you with what I find out. Come on, Kels, let's go. And, Mrs Pringle, in the future, please use my correct title. It's Doctor Jones." We left the office and headed to the front door.

Kelsey's eyes were wary. "Do you want to grab a coffee?" she asked, her voice quiet. I nodded and followed her to the small grubby coffee shop across the street. The sun was shining, so we could sit outside.

"Ben," she ventured. "I want a divorce."

I sat, stunned, as she put a hand on mine.

"You and I both know this is over. Neither of us wants to go back. It's time we moved on. I am going to start using my maiden name."

I nodded in assent but kept my lips squeezed tightly closed.

There was nothing more to say.

Now, talking with Eamon, the school meeting and her request for a divorce all make sense. She's met someone else.

"So, what about Savannah?" Eamon whacks my arm, reminding me what we are talking about. A huge grin splits my face. I am so proud of my little girl.

"Well, it turns out, the little shit Raymond in her class had been picking on one of the younger children during break. Savannah had been watching from a distance but went over when the little one had hit the ground. She had proceeded to tell Raymond to stop being so nasty, and when he didn't, she clobbered him."

Eamon's eyes go wide, and he starts laughing heartily. "The wee devil!" he shouts. "That's my girl!" He lifts his hand for a high five.

I walk over to the bar to pay the bill, and the pretty bartender shoots me a smile. She hands me back my change along with her number. "Call me," she mouths, and I give her a wink. You know, I just might.

After-school pick up is always a bit of a mission. Savannah and Rose leave through the door to the west while the small children exit via the rear gate. Parents all stand around and watch through the bars as the children play.

I can see Ollie playing with a little boy I have never seen before, but he's his double. They run around playing planes, shouting with their arms outstretched. Both their little faces have red cheeks and huge smiles, and I feel my heart melt, watching my son with his friend.

Ollie loves school. He's the oldest in his class, as we kept him back a year due to his speech development being poor. I think it was the best decision we made for him. His confidence is growing day by day.

The bell rings, and I walk forward to the gate to collect Ollie. We wander back to the car to meet the girls, hand in hand. He is skipping along beside me, singing a nursery rhyme; I can't quite make out the words.

"Who was that you were playing planes with, Ollie?" I ask.

He beams at me. "Oh, Dad! That's my new friend, Liam. Today was his first day."

Then we all climb into the car and head home for pizza.

Chapter Twenty-eight: Kelsey

Cutting the call, I feel relief flood my body. The lawyer says it will be straightforward as long as we both agree. I know Ben will want to make this process as painless as possible. He always puts our children first.

Divorce had never crossed my mind until I met George. I always assumed Ben and I would remain married but separated. It seemed simpler that way instead of dragging us all through courts and debates over money.

I had been making toast and cheese under the grill in the kitchen. It was a simple enough task, but my phone had rung, distracting me. When I returned, the flames were flicking the ceiling. Luckily, the children were with their father, so I ran out of the house and dialled 999.

It felt like an overreaction as the fire engine blared into our street, blue lights flashing and sirens wailing. Nosey neighbours peered out their windows. Three brawny firemen had jumped out the truck and ran into my house to control the blaze. I stood in my pink fluffy dressing gown and slippers, watching on as if it was a TV show.

"Not much damage, Mrs," the yellow giant had announced when he approached me. "Are you alright? Is there someone I can call to come help you? Your husband, perhaps?" He removed his helmet, and the most stunning green eyes met mine. They were kind and concerned as he looked at me.

"No, sir. I live by myself, well, while the children are at their father's, anyway. Thank you so much for coming." Unexpectedly, I find myself batting my eyelashes at him.

What the hell are you doing?

He smiled and nodded. "Let me take you inside and make you a cuppa then. I want to make sure you're settled before I leave. My name is George."

He led me up the path and back in the house on his arm. Making my drink and then searching the cupboards for biscuits, he chatted randomly about the day's events. How the fire station dog had escaped again and how his last call had been a pet cat up a tree.

I just sat and listened, mesmerised by this beautiful man. His hair was short, almost a buzz cut. He looked older than me, probably nearer fifty than forty. He had a strong jaw with designer stubble that was greying. I found myself imagining what it would feel like to have him kiss me. When it was time for him to leave, I felt a sense of sadness, knowing I would never see him again. Something about him captivated me.

The next morning, I opened my front door to a dozen roses on the doorstep. I looked around but couldn't see who had delivered them.

Wrong house, but aren't they lovely. I could keep them. Who would know?

The card was nestled amongst the greenery, and I picked it out to see if I could work out who they were meant for. It read:

To The Toast Incinerator,
I couldn't help but return to see you.
Am I right in assuming you are single?
Would you do me the honour of having dinner with me?
From Your Fireman x

I step out onto my front porch and look up the street. Clutching the card between my fingers, I can feel the huge grin spreading across my face. "Yes, I bloody will," I mutter to myself. But how the hell do I contact him?

Then I see him leaning up against a lamp post. He looks completely relaxed, dressed in a checked shirt and fitted jeans. I wave at him shyly, and he walks toward me. His stride is long and purposeful. I feel as though within three steps he is in front of me.

"Hi." He smiles and sticks out his hand. "I'm George, and I was so awestruck by you while saving you from the burning toast, I had to come back and ask you out."

I giggle nervously. "Well, George the fireman, I would love to accept your offer of dinner." We swapped numbers, and he pecked me on the cheek.

"See you later, gorgeous," he said, and my heart jumped out of my chest.

George is picking me up in half an hour, and I am terrified. I've changed my outfit ten times. What does a woman pushing forty wear on a date with a hot fireman? Standing looking in my wardrobe, I flick through the rows of mumsy dresses. Finally, I settled on a fitted blue dress with scoop neckline, demure and classy. I will pair it with kitten heels and pearl earrings. Perfect.

When Ben and I separated, dating was the last thing on my mind. Over the past five years, I have been on two dates — blind dates set up by well-meaning friends — and they were both disasters. I hope George will be different.

Deciding to leave my husband when Ollie was only eight months old had been a tough decision. I walked away from the man that, for all his faults, had supported me faithfully for the best part of twenty years, stepping up when times were hard and sacrificing his own wants to ensure I was safe. Our teen romance and fairy tale relationship had finally bowed to the pressure. I am relieved neither of my parents lived to see this, their daughter, the divorcée.

Neither of us was happy in our marriage. We loved each other, but we were completely incompatible. I sometimes wonder if my mother hadn't died all those years ago when we were still so young, would we actually have stayed together? Or would our teen romance have fizzled out like so many others do?

I couldn't pretend with Ben any longer. Every time he touched me, I wished he wouldn't, and every time I rejected him, I felt guilty. He tried to love me, but I came to the realisation I didn't want his love anymore. He was my security blanket. We both needed out. Our relationship became a friendship rather than lovers, which is sad because Ben is a man who can love completely. I hope he finds that with someone.

My mind wanders to Bex. We don't see her now after the last fiasco when I was pregnant with Ollie. She is a complex girl, clever, but she couldn't seem to get her act together. She spent her life pining over a man she couldn't have. It was a proper tragic love story where she was the victim. I wonder where she is now, if she's got herself sorted or is she still pissing up the walls every weekend.

The sound of a horn signals my date has arrived. With renewed vigour, I strut out my front door and down to the waiting car, ready to see what life has in store for me.

CHAPTER TWENTY-NINE: BEN

Within weeks, the divorce proceedings are underway. As it turns out, we agree about finances and the childcare situation; this should speed the process along. Kelsey told me about her new love interest. She didn't use the word boyfriend; seemingly it is too soon for that.

The word boyfriend just sounds wrong when talking about a grown man, but who am I to judge? When she told me she was dating, I was sad, but surprisingly, not jealous. Even though I don't want Kelsey, I always assumed I would hate anyone who did.

The night after we filed the paperwork, I called the pretty bartender who had given me her number. We arranged to meet on Friday evening for a drink.

Her name is Felicity, and she is only twenty-four years old. She is bright and bubbly, turned out to perfection with a skin-tight red dress and fuck me now eyes. I knew she wasn't looking for anything serious and was brazen about what she wanted from me. After hearing all about her three previous sex parties with a variety of men and women, she invited me along to the next one.

As free and exciting as it sounded, and even though my cock was in full agreement of taking advantage of the situation, I declined the invite politely and scuttled off home to bed. Perhaps I had missed the time in my life to be sexually free, explore what is out there. Her offer had little appeal. I've always been a romantic at heart, and fleeting relationships with no connection don't do it for me. When I'm with a woman, I want to be consumed by her. The thought of performing in front of multiple partners sent chills down my spine. But Felicity was refreshing, and the way she kissed me when she left reawakened something long dead as the blood rushed through my veins.

I realised I wanted to try again.

Ollie will not stop talking about his friend, Liam. They are joined at the hip in school and play constantly together. When I go to collect Ollie each afternoon, I can't get over how alike they are. Baby-blue eyes and jet-black hair. Their teacher tells me it's as if they are old souls that have known each other forever. I ponder idly that I should try to introduce myself to his family. I have never seen him collected, so I don't know who his parents are. Ollie tells me that Liam only has a mummy, and she looks like Barbie.

I hide at the back of the group of parents waiting for their children at the gate, listening to some idle chitchat about the price of milk or what hair salon they use. When the mums discovered I was separated, there was a six-month period of being cornered at every school pick up. Being single and a doctor in your late thirties has its advantages when it comes to women. I enjoyed the attention, but the advances became too blatant. I had to stop turning up so early.

Spring is well underway, and most of the women are wearing some sort of dress, legs on show. The last few days have been lovely, warmer-than-normal spring days. The cloud of winter has disappeared along with the cold weather.

A tall redhead called Kelly Winston approaches me. She lost her husband in a car accident a few years ago. Left with two kids and spiralling debt, she has been on the hunt for a replacement for a while. It's a position I have no intention of filling.

"Ben," her voice purrs, and I freeze in position. It's best to only respond with noises, not words, the best line of defence.

"Kelsey tells me you're getting divorced now. Her new man seems like a keeper."

The information she possesses surprises me, and I blink at her, lost for a second.

"Maybe now you will take me for that drink?" she whispers in my ear. "We would be so good together. I bet I could make you scream in ecstasy."

Not being able to say anything, I walk to the other side of the group of parents standing around. She huffs angrily in the background.

"Not a snowball's chance in hell," I mutter under my breath.

It's then I notice the small black-haired boy, Liam, running toward a woman standing by the fence. Her back is to me. She's tall and wearing fitted black fitness leggings with a long t-shirt that finishes at her butt. Platinum-blonde hair is pulled into a ponytail and slid through a black baseball cap. She looks as if she's been running or at the gym.

Liam runs to her, and she kneels to scoop him up, her arms wrapped around his tiny body, his nose in her neck. The show of affection is beautiful to watch. Then, she turns, and I see her in profile.

Recognition hits me hard. Fuck, it's her.

"Bex," I call before I can stop myself. I feel the other mothers' eyes on me, watching the exchange. "Bex, it's me."

She turns, and her face drops at the sight of me. Ollie spots me from the gate and runs up to join our little group. The boys start to play a game they have obviously been playing on and off all day, falling into character easily.

Bex's face looks as if she has seen a ghost; there is horror there. Her eyes dart to the little black-haired boy playing with my son.

"How are you?" I ask carefully. "It has been a long time. Six or seven years?"

She nods, but no words come forth.

"Have you just moved here? Terry never said anything, and I only spoke to him last week."

Her eyes are moving from my face to the children and back again. She looks as if she is getting ready to run.

"The boys have made friends. For weeks, all Ollie has talked about is Liam this, Liam that."

Finally, she opens her mouth to speak. "Yes," she smiles. "Liam is quite infatuated with Oliver, too."

My eyes hold hers. "So, what brings you here? Is he your friend's? Are you helping on the school run?"

She looks at me blankly. "Liam?" she asks.

I nod, expecting her to say the little boy is her friend's son, but she sighs deeply and takes the little boy by the hand. "No, Ben, he's mine." She snaps her eyes away from mine. "Come on, honey, time to go home. See you tomorrow, Ollie." They both walk off in the direction of town without a backwards glance.

Sitting in my living room with the children in bed is probably the loneliest time of the day. This is the point in the day where I would love to have a partner to chew the day over with, moan about the crap times, and celebrate the good ones. The bedtime routine is tiring on your own. I think back to seeing Bex, and I wonder if her husband helps her. I wonder if he is in the picture at all.

Exhaustion overwhelms me, and I decide to go to bed. My dreams are filled with old images of past lovers and little black-haired boys with bright-blue eyes.

There is a nervous sensation in my belly that won't go away, and I wake in the early hours, sweat pouring off my brow. I start to calculate the years. Liam is in the same class as Ollie, but depending on his birthday, they could be up to twelve months apart in age.

When was the last time I saw Bex?

You slept with her the last time you saw her, you idiot. Then you ran out in the morning, blaming her. But when was that?

Kels was pregnant with Ollie, I think. My brain hurts from trying to retrieve the information I need. Yes, I am sure Kelsey was pregnant.

Liam is around the same age with blue eyes and black hair. Shit, could he be mine? But surely Terry would have told me? Then again, if Bex had asked him not to or just never admitted who the boy's father was, maybe he wouldn't.

We've never discussed Bex. I know he was angry with both of us for the affairs we had. I need to find out. I consider calling Terry now, but the clock is blinking three in the morning. Settling back on my pillow, I tell myself I will ask her tomorrow.

Directly. No third-party interference.

The next morning, I arrive at the school and drop Ollie off ten minutes early. I sit and watch everyone else arrive. Children are being herded by harassed parents from cars, bundled into jackets, and pushed through the school doors. The tiny people carry bags the same size as them, bags that are filled with books and pencils.

I'm watching a large lady with four small children. She's extracting them from her car and lining them up military-style before distributing their equipment for the day when I spot Liam. But it's not his mother walking him to school, it's Amy, and I feel my anger start to fizz.

She kisses him on the cheek goodbye and turns back the way she came. I run after her, catching her up within seconds.

She is shocked by my sudden appearance. "What the hell, Ben? Are you trying to give me a heart attack?"

I laugh sarcastically as I feel my anger rise. "Amy, why didn't you tell me about Liam?"

She looks away, guilty. "It was none of your business." She lifts her head and sticks her chin out defiantly. "Last time I checked, you were married."

My eyes flare, and I glare at her. "When was he born?"

She ignores the question and keeps walking.

"Is he mine?"

She stops and turns to face me then takes a step forward, standing on her tiptoes so we are nose to nose. "No, Ben, he's not yours. He's not anyone's. He doesn't have a father. He's Bex's son, and she is an incredible mother. Leave her alone!" Her voice is shrill and angry.

Amy stalks off in the direction of a white 4x4 parked by the kerb, flinging open the driver's door as she jumps in. I yank open the passenger door and climb in next to her.

"You fucking know what I mean," I growl at her. "Is he mine, Amy? He's my spitting image. He looks like Ollie's brother."

She's sitting on her seat, hands in her lap with tears running down her face.

"It's not my place to say." Her eyes are an angry red. "Please, Ben. Just leave it. You don't want to open this can of worms. Think of Kelsey and your children."

I throw open the car door, almost knocking a man off his bike in the process.

He starts shouting at me.

Amy takes her chance to bolt, leaning over to close the car door and driving off.

Chapter Thirty: Bex

"Shit! Shit! Shit!"

Amy flies through my front door in a panic. She is screaming at the top of her lungs.

In a rush to get to her, I trip over Liam's toy truck. I fly through the air and land in the middle of my hallway, splayed out like a starfish.

"Fuck! That hurt!" I snap. "What the hell are you shouting about?"

I try to push myself up into a seated position, but I can't put any weight on my hand. Bloody hell, my wrist hurts. Eventually, I manoeuvre myself up to sit and wait for her to provide any more information on her outburst.

She's standing in front of me, breathing heavily with her hands on her knees.

"Ben," she gasps. "He's worked out that Liam is his."

I look at her, horrified, but not surprised. It wouldn't take Einstein to look at the two of them and conclude they are related. Being a doctor, I am also sure Ben is quite capable of doing the maths.

A feeling of panic starts to flood my body. "What did he say, Amz?" I try to keep my voice level, but I feel the complete opposite inside.

She tells me about him accosting her outside the school and sitting in the car, demanding answers. I feel terrible for the poor cyclist who was nearly taken out by his tantrum exiting the car. Ben was always hot-headed when people didn't tell him what he wanted to know. His alpha-male persona is something I still find attractive.

"I will need to talk to him," I mutter.

I'm not looking forward to that conversation.

Calling Terry to ask for Ben's number was the last thing I wanted to do. After falling pregnant, I deleted Ben's and tried to wipe him from my mind. Terry was the only one of us who had kept in touch with him, and that was sporadically.

Even though I have never confirmed to Terry that Ben was Liam's dad, he always knew he was. When I was pregnant, there had never been anyone else mentioned as a possibility of being the father. Terry had told me I'd want to talk to him — the father — one day, and told me not to delete all traces of him from my life, but I ignored him. At that point, I couldn't have loved or hated Dr Benjamin Jones more than I did.

After what felt like hours of lecturing from Terry about what I should or shouldn't do and what to confirm or deny, I managed to escape with Ben's number typed in my phone.

There had been no sign of Ben when I collected Liam from school. I did notice a woman who looked like Kelsey, but she was standing with a man I didn't recognise. Their arms were linked affectionately. It must not be her. She's married.

I breathed a sigh of relief and headed home. At least I could approach Ben on my terms, rather than him jumping me outside school. Now I was sitting on my bed, looking at the number on my screen, wondering what the hell to do.

Do I call him?

Do I text him?

The little voice in my head is telling me, "You wouldn't be in this position if you had bloody told him as you should have. Liam is his son; he deserves to know. Liam deserves to know his dad."

But Ben has a wife and three kids, I argue. A happy life. Can I really upset his perfect existence with this bombshell? Am I willing for my son to be the catalyst to war in someone's home?

An hour later and fifteen typed, deleted, and retyped messages written, I still haven't sent any. Finally, I hit the call button, and he answers after one ring, taking me by surprise.

"Doctor Jones speaking." His voice is professional; he thinks this is a work call. I stay on the line, silent. Suddenly, the confidence I've been building for the past hour has disappeared.

"Hello, Doctor Jones speaking." He raises his voice. It's got a sharpness that indicates the type of boss he is, calm and in control. He takes no prisoners. I feel my insides liquefy. Even after all these years, his voice affects me.

He's obviously getting pissed off by my lack of response. "Who is it?" he snaps then mutters to himself. The words are not audible, but I sense he is going to hang up.

"It's me," I whisper. "I need to talk to you."

There is silence on the line, but I can hear him breathing. "I need to talk to you about Liam. Your son."

Tears prick my eyes, and I can hear my breathing escalate. He stays on the line, completely silent. It feels terrifying to admit that out loud.

"Can we meet and talk about this? I know it's a shock." My words start to fall out rapidly. "Bring Kelsey. We can discuss it all together."

I continue to blabber on about being a blended family and reciting the parenting blogs I've been reading since I bumped into him at school. How to get along with your child's father. How to co-parent successfully.

"Why would I bring Kelsey?" he asks. "This is only between us. I can't believe you never told me. How could you not tell me?" His voice is confused and hurt.

"But Kelsey is your wife. This affects her, too," I respond.

His next words stun me into silence, and my head explodes with the information. "Kels and I are getting a divorce. It didn't work out, Bex."

Not knowing what to say, I mumble something about being sorry to hear that, and we decide to meet to discuss moving forward.

I hang up and immediately grab my bag, storming out my front door; it rattles on its hinges as it slams shut. I'm halfway through storming to Amy and Terry's when I remember, Liam is asleep upstairs in his room. Major mum guilt hits me. I hotfoot it back toward home, pulling my phone from my bag and scrolling to Terry's number.

After hitting the call button, I hear the phone ring out and then go to voicemail. I try again but get the same result. As I'm climbing the stairs to my apartment, the name *Terry* flashes up on the screen.

"Did you fucking know?" I spit down the phone. "He's getting a divorce! Did you not think that information was kind of important?"

I can hear Terry trying to contain his laughter at the end of the line. He gets himself under control before speaking.

"I am sure your words, Bex, were, well let me get this right." He pauses for effect, and I snort angrily so he knows just how bloody annoyed I am. Then he continues, "Your exact words were *Ben is Liam's dad, but it has nothing to do with me. I'm not interested in his personal life.*"

I cringe as I remember my little speech in response to Terry's lecture when I asked for Ben's number. It is true. I did say that.

We meet in the café across the road from the school. It's raining miserably. Moving to part-time hours has allowed me to be there to collect Liam most days.

We have two hours until the boys are due to be collected. I arrive ten minutes early because I want to be here first. I position myself at a table with a good view of the door. Today, I don't want to be caught off guard.

The waiter approaches, and I order a strong black coffee. Not my normal choice, but I need all the help I can get. My nerves are dancing in my belly, and they have been since I woke up, which wasn't long after I got to sleep at five this morning. I am wearing a soft wool dress with black knee-high boots. My hair is down, and my makeup is natural. I wanted to be classy but not try too hard. Hopefully, I nailed it.

Looking up from my coffee, I see the doorway filled with Dr Benjamin Jones. He's scanning the room. His eyes come to rest their gaze on me. His stance straightens, and I know it's the professional Dr Jones who is here, not the sweet Ben I love so dearly. *Loved so dearly*, I tell myself. Past tense.

He makes his way through the mess of tables and chairs. The café has filled up with ladies who lunch and tradesmen who'd knocked off work early. Pulling out a chair, he sits down opposite me, and his azure eyes stare directly into mine. The waiter runs over, and Ben orders a green tea. He looks incredible, dressed sharply in a plain white t-shirt and jeans, his hair messed up in a just-fucked look. The look he is giving me is dangerous; he is beyond pissed off.

"Thanks for coming to meet me," I say timidly.

His blazing eyes turn to me. "Didn't have much fucking choice, did I?" he snarls. "You turn up almost seven years since I last saw you, with my six-year-old son."

He rubs his hand across his forehead, trying to calm himself down.

"Bex, is he mine? I must ask."

I look at him, dumbfounded. My anger erupts. I want to jump across the table and punch him. "Are you fucking serious?" I hiss. "Of course he is yours. Have you seen him? He is your bloody double." My face flushes red, and I scrunch my hands into fists. Calming myself down, I try to speak calmly. "Ben, I know this is a shock, but Liam is your son. You are his father. No one else."

I stand abruptly. I need to get out of here. This was a bad idea.

Ben stands, sensing my instinct to run, and he places a hand on my arm. "I'm sorry. I didn't mean to offend you. But how can you be sure he's mine, Bex? We both know you weren't in a good place back then. Let's talk. For Liam's sake. If he is my son, Bex, I want to be in his life."

Still standing, I walk around the table until I am facing him. Tears fill my eyes. "Ben, I know he is yours because you are the only person I slept with at that time. And there has been no one since." He stares at me, surprised by my admission. We return to our seats.

My heart rate starts to slow, and we discuss how Liam will meet him and how often. Ben needs time with his son and Liam with his father. I worry for my little boy. There has only ever been him and me. Now he will have a father, two sisters, and a brother. I pray his little mind can cope with this.

Chapter Thirty-one: Ben

Twelve months have passed since Liam landed in my life. If you had told me that I would have another child, I would have laughed in your face. But Liam has fit in like a missing puzzle piece. Co-parenting with two mothers has its challenges, but I think we have created a routine between us.

Bex and Kelsey don't speak directly to each other; all communication goes through me. I feel like I am mediating an ongoing family argument, and in some ways, I am. But the whole situation is my fault. The children split their time between me and their mothers. We also ensure that the four children get time together which, between dance clubs, football, and after-school club, can be tricky to navigate.

My apartment is buzzing and filled with laughter almost every day of the week. I rarely get a day on my own, but I am happier than I have been in years. Bex is coming over to drop Liam off tonight. I find my heart beats faster when it's her at the door. To me, she looks her best dressed in her running gear with her hair up on her head, makeup-free, and relaxed. Our interactions are brief but civil. Today, I want to try to move our friendship forward, if a friendship is what it is.

The door buzzes, and I almost run to go let them in. She is standing on the doorstep of my apartment. She has her hair loose, and she is wearing her jeans with a low-cut t-shirt. Liam is holding her hand, looking up at his mummy. He turns to me. "Daddy!" he shouts and jumps into my arms.

Holding him close, I look over his shoulder at Bex, who is watching the interaction intently. Her cheeks are wet with a few tears as she watches us, father and son.

I smile softly at her. "Do you want to come in for a coffee?" The question sounds simple enough, but it is monumental for me. I hope she accepts.

"Ok, I will stay for one." She is wary, but we all walk into the apartment together.

My kitchen is open plan onto my living area, and I wander over and flick the silver switch on the kettle. It springs to life as I hear the buzz of the element heating up. Bex sits on the sofa, and Liam begins to bring out his toys from his bedroom to show her.

"Can I show Mummy my bedroom, Daddy?" he asks hopefully.

"Of course," I reply, smiling. I watch as he leads his mum by the hand down the corridor toward the room he shares with Ollie. Luckily, both boys have dinosaurs on the brain, so it was easy to redecorate the room for them both. I can hear Bex, her voice excited, as Liam explains his room and what parts are his. They both reappear, and my boy has a huge smile on his face as his mum tells him how wonderful his and his brother's room is.

Watching Bex interact with our son is rousing feelings that I thought were long gone. She's so sweet and attentive to him, no matter how much being here must be strange for her. I can't fool myself that this is easy to accept. She has been Liam's only parent for the first years of his life and now she has all of us to compete with. He spends time away from her with me and his siblings doing exciting things. She must sit and listen to him gush about it all in detail when he gets home.

In the beginning of our shared parenting, I had tried too hard to gain Liam's affection. The first six months were filled with exciting trips out and gifts, my guilt for being absent for the first part of his life on my mind. I was angry with Bex for not telling me she was pregnant. She had cheated me out of years in my son's life. It stung. I wanted him to love me more than her. Part of me wanted to turn him against her. But Liam is a kind and loving little boy, and he has accepted his extended family as a blessing. He loves the bones of his mum. Now, I'm glad I saw sense and never succeeded with my plan.

Liam had spent the weekend with me. I had picked him up from school on Friday afternoon and was dropping him back to his mum's on Sunday. It had just been the two of us, and our relationship was developing well. I had packed our days full of trips out. We had been to the zoo and the cinema, and we had topped it off with a hot chocolate on the way home. He was exhausted, falling asleep in the car on the way home.

When I carried him up the three flights of stairs to Bex's apartment, she was waiting at the top for me with the door open. She was already dressed for bed with her hair plaited down her back, wearing cotton pink pyjamas. I could see her nipples peeking through the material. Arousal ran through my body as I looked at her. She had a small frown on her lips. I could tell something was bothering her.

"Can we talk?" she asked quietly, trying not to wake Liam. I nodded and followed her into the apartment. We tucked Liam into bed and then returned to the hallway. I gestured for her to speak.

"The thing is," she paused, obviously unsure about how to say what she wanted to. "The thing is, I am glad you and Liam are getting on so well, but I can't keep up with the money you spend on him."

I look at her, shocked.

She carried on. "You don't need to make every weekend a big adventure, Ben. He is beginning to expect it. Just spend time with him. That's all he needs. I know you are trying to make up for lost time. I am sorry I never told you. But please don't make me out to be the poor parent."

Feeling my temper rise, I'm about to explode. I look up,

and she's crying. I hold my tongue.

"I'll think about it," I snap then turn for the door. "I will pick him up from school on Tuesday." Not looking back, I march out the front door and down the stairs at top speed.

That night, I lie in bed thinking about what Bex said. Have I been trying too hard? In all honesty, I have, and it's not fair. She has been doing this solo for years. The least I can do is not make her life harder.

Picking up my phone, I swipe through the photos of all my kids. I am so lucky to have them all and to have two women who are excellent mothers. Their faces are all happy and smiling with their arms wrapped around each other. I know Bex was concerned that the others would not accept Liam, but they have with open arms.

Ollie and Liam are inseparable at home and at school. The teacher has had to split them up to stop them from talking. I laugh to myself as I remember the conversation when Ollie told me that Mrs Read had said they needed to concentrate, so he could not sit with Liam anymore. Liam had proceeded to tell her the rules suck and stuck his tongue out. This time, Bex and I were called into Mrs Pringle's office. It was time to stop being so selfish and work together as a team.

So, another six months on, here we are. I am attempting to hold out olive branches so I can start repairing the relationship between us. As much as Bex is attractive, I know she would never consider another romantic relationship with me. I was an absolute bastard; *I* wouldn't give me another chance.

She looks perfect in my living room, playing with our son on the floor. My heart breaks for what could have been. This is the woman I have yearned for, for all these years. When I left her after our holiday in Spain, I was heartbroken. Going back to Kelsey felt the right thing to do. When Bex disappeared from my life after our last night together, I was relieved. I tried to focus on being a good husband and father, but all this time she was raising my child. The irony is palpable.

I stare at the two mugs in front of me declaring me *The World's Greatest Dad* and *Best Doctor Ever*. I don't feel like either.

"Is that coffee ever coming?" Her voice startles me out of my thoughts.

"Yes sorry, in another world," I call back.

In another world with you.

Before sitting on the sofa opposite her, I place the mug down next to her. She smells of fresh flowers and peppermint, and I breathe in deeply. Right now, all I want to do is fold her in my arms and not let go. Having her here in my home with our son just feels right. This was how life was meant to turn out until I ballsed it up.

She stays for an hour. We chat about Liam; our conversation tends to always remain on him.

What else is there to talk about?

She finishes her coffee and walks over to place it in the sink. There is something so natural about the way she does it. My heart twists again. She leaves after confirming when our boy will be returned to her. Everything becomes a darker shade of grey when she goes.

Due to workforce shortages and other political drama, the local hospitals in our area are struggling for staff. A small charity approached my private hospital and asked if any of us could volunteer some time, mainly speaking and supporting people with a terminal illness.

Today, I'm at the Cancer Centre in Guy's Hospital supporting the team. This is my third session, so I am becoming more familiar with both the staff and patients. We congregate in small groups of one doctor to six patients, then out come the coffee and biscuits. The discussion is open about what they can expect from the treatment, personal prognosis, and end-of-life care. Most people who attend the sessions are the patients themselves, but occasionally, a caregiver will come in an attempt to make sense of the crazy situation they have found themselves in.

My noon session draws to a close, and I go in search of Eamon. It's lunchtime, and we always avoid the hospital cafeteria. My first experience of their soup put me off for life. Vegetable broth which was clearly home to some sort of meat was alarming, but when the garlic bread came with chunks of garlic propped on top, I swore to never come back. My stomach heaves at the memory, and I continue my search for my old friend.

Eamon is standing at the hospital entrance, chatting with three nurses. They are young and obviously in training. They laugh at his jokes and flutter their eyelashes at him. Even though Eamon is older and not the most attractive man, he is an incredible doctor, and his reputation precedes him. I have found him often in this situation, nurses lapping up his chat, and he enjoys every minute of it.

Then, I see her. She has her back to me, but her platinum-blonde hair is falling straight down her back. She is wearing her running clothes that I love, twisting her hands in front of her as the receptionist looks up something on her computer. The woman hands her a slip of paper, an appointment slip, and Bex walks off through the doors toward the Cancer Centre.

CHAPTER THIRTY-TWO: BEX

I walk through the large white swinging doors; they are pinned back against the wall. Clutching the appointment card in my hand, I read the sign that reads *Cancer Centre* in bold letters.

My heart is hammering in my chest. I haven't told anyone about the lump I found four weeks ago. It has been playing on my mind every day.

I'd been in the shower going through my usual routine. I'd run my hands under my breast, and there on my left breast below my nipple was a small bump. At first, I didn't think anything of it. Hormones. Everything is down to hormones, I thought. But after a week, it was becoming more pronounced. I decided I should get it checked. Now, here I am, waiting for the results of the biopsy the doctor had requested.

The waiting room is filled with people of all ages. Most are here with a companion. Sometimes, it's obvious who the patient is, and other times, it is hard to tell. Lots of doctors and nurses are striding around the place looking very important, rushing from room to room. I approach the desk, and a kindly looking woman is sitting on the other side. She is probably in her mid-forties but is so short I notice she has two cushions on her seat to help her gain a bit of height.

Smiling, she takes my name and introduces herself as Sandra. She's the patient coordinator for the centre and is here to answer any questions. I take a seat, waiting for my name to be called. Scrolling aimlessly through my phone, looking at pictures of Liam, I can't help but tear up. He's my world and, if this is serious, I have no idea how we will cope. Part of me is relieved that Ben, his father, has come into his life, but another part of me is grudging any time with Liam he steals from me.

"Rebecca Corrigan," the doctor calls. It takes me a minute to realise it is me he's looking for. No one calls me Rebecca except my parents, and since Liam was born, our contact is limited. They believed I should not have brought him into the world as a single parent or I should have given him to a normal family. We have never truly got past those conversations; I just can't forgive them for wishing my son away. I stand and follow the doctor into the room, my heart racing in my chest.

He's an older gentleman, probably in his sixties, with a grey moustache and receding hairline. His face is round, his cheeks are rosy, and his smile is warm. He immediately puts me at ease.

"Please take a seat, Mrs Corrigan," he says and gestures to a black leather sofa.

I nod. "It's Miss, actually. I'm not married."

I've no idea why I corrected him. This happens all the time, and it never bothers me. My name has become more important recently. Ben has asked me to consider adding his name to Liam's birth certificate. Liam Corrigan Jones. I am not sure how I feel about that.

The doctor introduces himself as Doctor Roy. He wasn't who I met previously, but seemingly, he has been assigned my case file.

"Do you live on your own?" he asks, fishing for information. I shake my head, and he relaxes.

"No, I have a son. He is seven."

The doctor's mouth turns to a grim line but loosens almost automatically as if he caught himself making a face he didn't want to. I see him steel himself. Then, he starts to speak.

"I'm sorry to tell you, Miss Corrigan, that the lump on your breast is cancerous. As far as we can tell, it has not spread further, but you will require treatment and an operation soon."

He pauses, giving me time to absorb his words. Even though I knew this was a possibility, the shock is evident in my face.

He leans forward and squeezes my hand. "We will do everything we can to beat this." His voice is strong as he speaks. "We have caught this in time. You must fight from now on."

The dam breaks, and I burst into sobs in front of him. He stands and goes to press a buzzer. Two nurses appear at the door.

"Can you please support Miss Corrigan? Give her a cup of tea. I will come back in half an hour to go through the treatment plan with her." The nurses both nod, and Doctor Roy leaves, away to distribute more terrible news to someone else, no doubt.

Leaving the hospital, I have a new wave of determination. I look for the new car I treated myself to a few weeks ago. It's a bright-red Mini, something I wanted for years. Now that Ben is contributing to Liam's life, I have a bit more cash to spend. My teacher's salary is adequate, and we have a comfortable life, but it has been a benefit to have a bit more disposable income. I was able to buy him new trainers the other week, designer ones, something I would never have been able to splash out on before.

Popping the trunk, I throw my bag in the boot of the car then climb into the driver's seat. The past hour has been incredibly real, discussing my treatment, all the possible outcomes, good and bad. I am terrified. Terrified of death. Terrified of leaving Liam motherless so young.

I decide to block it all out by turning up the radio full blast and opening the windows, cruising through the traffic toward home with music filling the streets and the wind whipping my hair around my face.

I feel alive, but for how long?

At my next appointment, I am given my date for surgery to remove the lump from my breast. Afterwards, I must attend the clinic every day for a week for further treatment. The operation can be done with only one overnight stay which means I can arrange for Ben to have Liam, and no one needs to know. I can just stay out of everyone's way while I recover. Telling my friends and family just doesn't seem like an option at the moment. I want to keep this to myself.

It's a Monday morning, and I was told to be at the clinic by eight. Ben has Liam for the next few days. I lied, saying there was a training course for work. The waiting room is empty except for one woman sitting reading a book.

She's wearing thick dark glasses and is lost in the words on the page. I sit across from her, and she looks up. She's in her forties, curvy with a mass of curly blonde hair. Her huge eyes look me over, and she smiles with bright-red lips.

"That bastard C got you, too, huh?" She winks. "What bit of you are they cutting off?"

I laugh at the unexpected statement and start to relax immediately.

Katie Clark is an erotic romance author, childless, and divorced. This is her third rumble with cancer, so she is casual about the whole situation. We chat about ourselves for a while. She is extremely easy to talk to, and I find myself starting to feel better. The nurse comes and calls her name, and she toddles off behind them in her tall dark heels, calling over her shoulder, "See you on the other side, Bex."

Then it is my turn to be called, and I walk off in the direction of the unknown.

I wake drowsy from the operation but relieved to be breathing. Relief courses through my body, and I smile.

"You took your time waking up," a sharp voice startles me,

and I open my eyes to find Katie Clark sitting, watching me. "You had me going for a while. You've been asleep for twenty hours," she says through mouthfuls of cheese and onion crisps.

The smell wafts over to me, and my stomach heaves.

"Urgh, can you take them away? They stink." I gag.

She laughs but continues chewing merrily.

"What are you doing here?" I ask, feeling as though I am in the twilight zone.

"Shared room, what do you think? This ain't the Ritz. You want your own room, go private." I go to sit up but my head spins. "Slow down, let me call the nurse," she barks.

Picking up the remote at the side of my bed, she presses the button with the picture of a woman on it, and a red light above my bed flicks on.

Around five minutes later, a nurse wanders in, obviously in no rush.

"She's awake," Katie states, waving her hands at me.

The nurse ignores her and smiles at me. "How are you feeling, dear?"

I have no idea how old she is, but she looks far too young to be calling me dear. Leaning forward, she helps me sit up and supports me by stuffing what feels like one hundred pillows around me.

"I'm ok. My head feels fuzzy though. Where's my phone?" I panic. I haven't spoken to Liam.

The nurse opens a drawer on the bedside cabinet and pulls out my mobile. There are three missed calls from Ben and a good night message from Liam. I feel so guilty. I quickly type a message saying I hadn't had access to my phone and hit send.

My head feels like a drummer has been hammering on it. I have never had a great reaction to anaesthesia. The nurse excuses herself and says she will return with some tea and toast which, at this moment, sounds amazing. My stomach rumbles loudly in agreement, and Katie laughs. "Welcome to the C World." She smirks.

From the outside, there is nothing that says I've spent forty-eight hours in the hospital. If I don't try to move quickly, I look perfectly normal. Ben is dropping Liam back around six, so he can have his dinner then bed. I only got home an hour ago, and they are due any minute. I cannot wait to see them. My mind corrects me: *you can't wait to see Liam.* But I must admit, seeing Ben makes my heart race.

Before we left the hospital, Katie and I exchanged numbers. We have been texting constantly. During our short friendship, I seem to have told her everything about myself. We're on the same schedule of treatment, so will be seeing each other regularly. Her conversation has been a saviour these past few days, and I can see us becoming good friends.

She has a wicked personality, calling a spade a spade. Her motto is *speak truly, speak freely, kick ass.* I think I may adopt it as my own.

We discussed my relationship with Ben from the beginning, and she thinks it sounds like a cliché romance. Star-crossed lovers, torn apart by love and loyalty. I'd laughed so hard when she described our relationship in those terms that I'd coughed my coffee all over the bedsheets. The nurse was not too pleased with having to change them for me.

The doorbell buzzes, and I walk as quickly as my broken body will allow, pressing the enter button enthusiastically. Within minutes, his little arms are wrapped around me, and I'm holding my boy as close to me as I can.

"Oh, I've missed you. I love you so much, sweetheart," I whisper into his hair, and a tear runs down my cheek.

He giggles. "Don't be a silly sausage, Mummy. I haven't been away long, and I have been with Daddy." I look up to see Ben watching me intently.

"What have you boys been up to?" I smile. "Enjoying the good weather?"

"Daddy and I have been walking in the woods. We tried to find a Gruffalo, but we couldn't. Then we went to the pond and caught tadpoles; they are starting to grow legs!" His voice is animated with childish excitement as he tells me about his time with his father. My heart swells, and my eyes return to the man standing opposite me.

"Did you enjoy your course?" he asks. "Where did you say it was again?" His eyes are soft but concerned. He knows something is wrong, but I don't know if I'm ready to tell him.

CHAPTER THIRTY-THREE: BEN

Knowing the mother of your son has cancer but pretending you don't is the hardest thing I have ever had to do. She's six months into her treatment and has still been completely silent on the issue.

I only know because I am abusing my position at the cancer clinic to keep an eye on her case. Eamon has been my informant, as Bex is attending his colleagues' support groups. He says she is quiet but never misses one. She comes with another woman called Katie, who Bex has never mentioned.

Katie is brash and bold, a long-time cancer sufferer. He says Bex hangs off her every word, and it's evident they're very close friends. It gives me some relief that she has someone sharing the journey with her.

I just wish it was me.

Over the past few weeks, she has been asking me to look after Liam more often. The chemotherapy drugs must be starting to take their toll. When I dropped Liam home last night, she was already in bed with a migraine. It grates on me that I can't support her more. If I tell her I know, then she will realise I have been spying on her. Regardless of the fact she has cancer, that will not go down well.

Our relationship is improving slowly. There are more coffees at drop off or pick up. We attend parent meetings together alongside Kelsey, as the boys are in the same class.

Today is my shift at the Cancer Centre. I spend my time here with my eyes on stalks, praying we don't bump into each other by accident. Eamon keeps a note of her treatment and appointment schedule so we know when to expect her, but this isn't always foolproof, as appointments change regularly.

My group is due to start in ten minutes. I'm chatting with the receptionist while reading the list of names attending. I am pleased to see Anita on the list. She hasn't been for a few weeks, after she received a poor prognosis. Her case is terminal, and further treatment is limited. When I spoke to her consultant, he said he'd advised she should expect no more than twelve months. From memory, her daughter is due a baby soon, so she will be here to welcome her new grandchild, but the child will never know her.

My mood nosedives at the depressing thought; this is the part of being a doctor I hate. At times like this, I can understand why many of my colleagues don't become emotionally involved. They keep the relationship between doctor and patient at a distance, just another number on the list. But I feel being a doctor is so much more than that. It's about the people, not the illness.

A loud booming female voice sounds through the department. Looking up, I see a voluptuous woman with blonde curls strutting into the room. She is talking to her friend, who I in horror realise is Bex.

Feeling the need to make myself disappear, I dive behind the reception desk and crouch beneath the legs of the poor woman on duty. She startles.

"Doctor, what are you doing?" Her voice sounds irritated at my poor manners.

I point up with my finger. "That woman can't see me." Then, I lay a finger across my lips in a sign to say, *keep your trap shut*. I hear the loud blonde approach the desk.

"Katie Clark and Rebecca Corrigan reporting for chemo." I can imagine her saluting the receptionist and must stop myself from laughing.

My eyes move to the set of legs I am currently hiding

between. She is an older woman, but I notice she is wearing stockings with a suspender belt under her skirt. The angle I have perched myself at under the desk means when I look up it's directly into her crotch.

Not being sure whether to laugh or cry, I almost lose my balance. Rocking backwards, I grab whatever there is to hold onto, which is, unfortunately, the set of legs in front of me.

"Oh!" the receptionist shouts above me, steadying herself, then continuing with her work as if nothing happened.

I hear another set of heels approach the desk. "Is Doctor Jones here yet? I need to speak to him in private."

I recognise the voice as Anita. She came; I'm glad. The receptionist tells her I'm here somewhere, to head into the meeting room, and she will book her ten minutes with me at the end. That is why my schedule changes every hour, I think, this bloody woman messing it around.

Bex's voice grabs my attention. "Doctor Jones?" she asks.

"Yes. Doctor Jones. He's one of the oncology consultants," the receptionist answers.

Bex murmurs something, then the two women head off to their chemotherapy session.

The receptionist taps me on the head. "You can come out now." She sighs.

I stand to the surprised faces of an elderly gentleman and his wife. They look between the receptionist and me. I wink at them cheekily. Then, lean forward and whisper loudly in her ear, "Loving the stockings." She flushes bright red, and I walk off in the direction of my meeting room.

I send a quick message to Eamon, updating him on the situation, and he takes it upon himself to investigate where Bex's treatment is taking place and how long for. Her chemotherapy is intravenous and requires her to sit for hours at a time to receive the necessary drugs. Apparently, Katie and Bex attend every appointment together. They sit and chat throughout the process. According to the chemotherapy nursing team, they treat their chemo as a day out rather than life-saving treatment; *enjoying every moment* is what the nurse told Eamon.

My phone pings. Eamon has sent me a message.

"Lunch at two. Need to talk."

I send back a thumbs up, wondering what he needs to speak to me about in private and so urgently. Two o'clock is only a few hours away, and I know I'll ponder the possible cause between now and then.

We meet at our usual place at two o'clock sharp. Eamon is sitting at the table waiting, already gnawing on a chunk of bread. His wife, Melissa, is next to him, her face sullen. A bottle of white is ready in an ice bucket with three glasses waiting to be poured. I walk over and Melissa grabs me into a bear hug. Eamon stands to shake my hand even though we saw each other only a few hours ago.

"What's wrong?" I ask them, concerned. "Why are you here, Mel? Are you alright?"

Eamon gestures to me to pour the wine and clears his throat. "You won't be going back to work today. I've already called them," he states.

I look at them, perplexed. Eamon ignores my confused expression and continues, "I caught up with Bex's consultant today, and things are not good. It's stage three, Ben, and it's spreading. Her chances now are about fifty-fifty, but he's concerned."

My stomach falls to the floor, and I see stars. Then I place my head in my hands, elbows on the table. Eamon places his hand on my back, and we just sit there for a while, letting the reality of what he said sink in.

"Do you want a glass of wine?" he asks.

I nod and start chewing on my own bread.

Our lunch becomes a four-hour affair as Eamon talks me

through the current stage of Bex's cancer and her treatment programme. The drugs are aggressive; they are blasting the tumour with everything they can to stop it from spreading. Melissa holds my hand across the table, and her worried eyes never leave me. She has hardly said a word, tears rolling down her cheeks as more facts are brought into the open.

Another thing I hate about being a doctor is the fact that treatment results cannot be guaranteed. One person can respond well while another doesn't respond at all. It seems Bex's response has not been as good as was hoped. Her body is starting to feel the side effects of the treatment, like her migraine the other evening. It's noted on her file she is also experiencing the early stages of hair loss. I think back to last Sunday when she collected Liam. She was wearing her hood up, which is unlike her.

We say our goodbyes before leaving for home. All the children are with their mothers tonight, so I have plenty of time to stew on the information I have.

As we leave, Melissa turns to me. It's obvious she's considering saying something but thinking better of it.

"Just say whatever you want to say." I sigh.

Eamon nods to his wife in encouragement.

"I was just thinking how short and unpredictable life is. It would be a waste not to take a risk before it is too late." Then she takes her husband's hand, and they walk away in the direction of their car, leaving me standing on the pavement, watching their burly backs waddle away.

Sitting at home alone in my apartment, I feel completely at sea. My head is telling me to continue along the path I am on, being the father Liam needs. Bex will tell me when she wants me to know. When I need to know. However, the situation is bad. How long is she going to wait before she bloody tells me? My heart is telling me to throw caution to the wind and take a risk, to put my heart on the line and tell her how I feel.

Another bottle of wine down, and my head is spinning with possibilities, so I head to bed, drunk and confused.

I am startled awake by my dreams. Terrifying movies of Bex in a coffin or sitting at home alone ill with no one to support her. Before I can change my mind, I jump out of bed and start throwing things into a bag.

I cannot cope with this.

I need to go.

Pulling on yesterday's clothes and shoes, I head out the door and jump into my car. Then, I set off to take a leap of faith.

Pulling up outside her apartment block, I look at my watch. It's one o'clock in the morning. I really didn't think this through. A madman appearing at her door in the middle of the night. Go home. I go to start my car again, but glance up at her apartment. The lights are on, and she is standing in the window, looking down at my car.

You can't leave now, she's seen you.

So I grab my bag and drag myself out of the car. I may as well go and grasp the nettle, as they say.

Climbing the three flights of stairs to the apartment is taking longer than usual. I don't know if it's because I am exhausted or terrified, but my feet are not moving as fast as they normally do. When I arrive at the front door, it's still closed; I wonder if she never actually saw me.

Turning to go, I hear the key turn in the lock. She opens the door and is staring at me as if I'm a figment of her imagination. Her skin is paler than I've ever seen it, her blonde locks pulled back into a ponytail. She is wearing fleece pyjamas with socks and gloves, totally in contrast with the warm summer nights. Tonight, she looks like a woman who is gravely ill. She goes to speak, but I lift my hand to stop her.

"Bex, I know about the cancer. I know about your treatment. I know about your prognosis. I still love you. Please let me support you. Let me be the man I should have been for

245

you all those years ago," I beg. I'm nervous, terrified of her response.

Soft brown eyes hold mine, and all I can do is hope she says yes.

CHAPTER THIRTY-FOUR: BEX

Unable to decide whether I am dreaming or not, I stare at Ben standing on my doorstep.

It's the middle of the night, but the summer heat hangs in the air. I still feel cold, though. It doesn't matter how much the sun shines. I'm always cold.

He has just made a beautiful speech about knowing I have cancer and wanting to be the man he should have been years ago. It's Ben, but it doesn't look like him. His eyes are blood-shot, his hair is a mess, and the t-shirt he is wearing has what looks like a coffee stain down the front. But the strangest thing is, when I look down, he's wearing mismatched shoes.

"Do you realise you have two different shoes on?" I ask, giggling.

He looks down at his feet then back up to me and winks. "Call it trendsetting." He snorts.

I move to the side so he can walk past me into my home. He's carrying an overnight bag, and my mind starts racing at the possibilities. Why would he turn up at my house in the middle of the night with a bag? Does he think I am some sort of bloody booty call?

My hackles rise at the thought, but I ignore it, deciding to hear him out.

We stand and stare at each other for a while. He goes to speak, and I signal to remind him Liam is asleep, so talk quietly. He gives me a slow, sexy smile, and I feel my insides tighten; how can this man still do that to me?

This round of chemotherapy has affected me far worse

than any of the others. The headaches, the hair loss, and the mouth ulcers are almost unbearable. The struggle to sleep. Katie keeps me going. She's in remission, thankfully. I wouldn't blame her if she never wanted to step foot in that bloody hospital again. But every round of chemo and every support group, she's there with me, one hundred percent by my side.

Afterwards, she must go home to her own life and her own battle.

It's then I feel completely alone.

I must look like an absolute spectacle in my fleece pyjamas with scraped-back hair. My appearance is not at the top of my priority list now. I focus on surviving each day, keeping my job, and maintaining a normal life for my son. It's getting harder, though. My body is struggling.

Ben steps forward and takes my hands in his. He smells divine—he always does—all male and full of testosterone.

"I mean what I said," he whispers. My eyes lift to meet his, then drop away shy. He is willing me to speak, to say something, but I just can't form the words. I have dreamed of this moment for years, and now it is here. I'm not sure I believe it's even real.

Gathering my composure, I try to collect my thoughts into a coherent format.

"Ben, it's one in the morning. What do you mean you know about my cancer? How?"

The anger that should appear doesn't. It's relief I feel. Telling him has been playing on my mind.

He looks sheepish but responds, "I volunteer at the Cancer Centre supporting patients."

How long has he known? I was concerned when a doctor named Jones was mentioned the other day, but it's such a common name. I put it out of my mind.

"The group you attend is run by my colleague, one who

reports to Doctor Eamon Riley."

The pieces of the jigsaw all fall into place. Dr Riley. I had seen him at the centre but kept out of his way. I was sure he hadn't seen me. How on earth did I think he wouldn't know?

"Months ago, I saw you at the centre. I couldn't ask you about it because things have been going so well with us and for Liam. I didn't want to risk upsetting you. But I would ask for updates on your case." He has the good sense to seem embarrassed by this admission, and I scowl at him.

"Perk of the job," he says, shrugging his shoulders.

My brain misfires as I realise he is probably more aware of my position even than I am. My heart sinks, and I look at him with tear-filled eyes. "It's not good news, Ben. I'm scared."

He rushes forward and folds me in his arms. His warmth surrounds me. We stand like that for I've no idea how long. It could've been minutes or even hours; his heat soaks through my body. It's my first time feeling warm in months. I'm exhausted, lonely, and incredibly afraid. His chest is broad and strong, and I cuddle in as close as possible. He drops a soft kiss on my forehead.

"You're not on your own now," he whispers, and I break down into uncontrollable sobs. "We will deal with this together. We will beat it."

By the time we finish talking, the clock shows 3 a.m. Intertwined with him on the sofa. I can't let him go. My legs are thrown over his, and he is running one hand up and down my back while I grip the other one.

We have discussed everything in detail. Our past, his marriage, my cancer. It's been difficult, and there have been a lot of tears from both of us. Going over old ground is always a tough experience, especially when you must face parts you're not proud of, but if we want this to work moving forward, we must embrace each other, warts and all.

He had made love to me then. Beautifully. Completely.

It had been nothing like our stolen and erotic moments from years before. My body had been worshipped by him. Lifting me from the sofa, he carried me to my bedroom. Laying me on the bed, he undressed me with care, slipping off my pyjamas silently. He ran his hands all over my body as if to reacquaint himself with it, taking in all my lumps and curves.

I felt self-conscious. I was not the same young, fit woman he knew from previous encounters. My body was scarred through childbearing and cancer treatment. He didn't seem to notice my blemishes.

Soft lips had trailed kisses from my neck down my chest and over my scars. He took me slowly and calmly, raising himself up on his arms above me. I could tell he was frightened he would hurt me. Every movement was careful and precise. It felt perfect. Having him inside me was like being put back together again. I finally felt whole for the first time in years. We both drifted off into a peaceful doze in each other's arms.

The alarm clock in my bedroom starts to play the morning news as a signal another day is beginning, and Ben laughs. "You wake up to the news?" he asks. "Is that not a bit depressing?"

With a pointed look, I snap, "I like to keep informed," and he kisses me softly on the lips. My breathing becomes more rapid, and he smiles against my mouth. Then he kisses me again, full of love and longing. Lying in my bed—our bed, I correct myself—we are wrapped around each other. He feels safe and strong beside me.

I laugh, and he raises an eyebrow in question.

"I was just thinking. Some things don't change."

He looks completely confused by my statement; I elaborate.

"When we were together, I mean, properly together, like in Spain . . ."

His brow creases, unsure where I'm going with this.

"You used to steal all the covers. And here I am, lying here with a tiny square of the duvet! Give me some more!" I shout smiling broadly at him.

Visibly relaxing, he lifts his ass off the bed to release more duvet for me, then gently places it over me. His arms surround me, and we lie there in silence, just enjoying this moment together.

The sound of little feet coming down the hallway echoes along the corridor, and Liam wanders into the bedroom, looking confused.

"Mummy," he calls. "Mummy, where are you? The lights are off."

Every morning, he climbs into bed with me for half an hour while I listen to the news. I leave the hall light on when the mornings are dark. Liam isn't particularly keen on change; he gets upset when things are different to what he expects them to be. His easy acceptance of Ben and his siblings was a shock. I really thought we would have more issues.

Liam loves them all.

"I'm here, darling," I call to him, and he appears around the front of the bed. He surveys the scene in front of him, and Ben immediately sits up.

"Morning, buddy." He smiles, holding his arms out for a hug.

Liam walks forward into his arms, and I feel my heart melt. He's still half asleep. I don't know if he realises that his father is actually here. Then, his eyes widen, and he shouts, "Daddy! You're here! But why are you here and not at your house? Did you get lost?"

Ben laughs and kisses his forehead. "I had to come and speak to Mummy," my beautiful man explains to our son. "I had to tell her that I love her and want to be a family with you both. You're right, I have been lost for a long time, but now I know where I need to be." Ben turns to me, and I smile at him.

Liam, not understanding his father's words, just smiles and jumps into bed with us. Squeezing in between us, he wriggles to create more room for himself. Freezing-cold toes connect with my legs, and I move away quickly as if stung.

"Liam, what did I tell you about not wearing your slippers? You're freezing!" I scold him. He shrugs his shoulders, ignoring my comment and turns to his father.

"Daddy, do you live with us now? Will you be staying? Never leave?"

His words are hopeful, my heart breaks. Ben hugs him fiercely. "Yes, son, I'm here, I'm here for you always."

For the first time in months, I feel happy and relaxed. I have hope. It's the first time since my diagnosis I truly have hope, that life is not just going to get continually worse. The dread and fear are still there, but it is not engulfing me like before.

The three of us lie in bed, holding each other, until a little voice asks, "What's for breakfast?" Ben and I chuckle.

I swing my legs out of bed and slide my feet into cosy slippers. Then I head to the kitchen to prepare a slap-up meal for my finally complete family.

CHAPTER THIRTY-FIVE: BEN
The Epilogue

4 years later . . .
August 2017

The late afternoon sun is beating down on my face. I'm lying back on the grass, eyes closed, listening to the kids playing football nearby. Bex is snuggled up beside me. She hasn't been so well this last week, but she was determined to come along to our family picnic before school restarts.

Time has passed so quickly; I'm still in shock that Ollie and Liam are going to high school this year. They have both grown considerably over the summer and need full wardrobes of new clothes again. Ollie is slightly taller than his brother, but they remain unnervingly similar in looks. It's hard to believe they have different mothers.

The best thing is they are inseparable as friends. I've been called to see their headmaster multiple times regarding them tag-teaming bullies on the playground, having explained to him, I'm extremely proud of my boys for standing up for what they believe in. I suggested that they should start reprimanding the bullies, not just the vigilantes, for inappropriate conduct.

Bex is mumbling in her sleep; she drifted off a while ago. Whenever or wherever she sleeps, I'm grateful for it. Her treatment is severe now, and she suffers from headaches most days.

Eamon took over her case file as soon as we got back

together. He was the only doctor I trusted with her care. The focus is now on pain management. There is no cure for Bex's disease, and time is limited and running out faster than we hoped. That's the sad reality of the situation we are in. We don't know how much time we have left together. It feels like a cruel joke after years apart, but I thank my lucky stars for the past four years. We have fought this awful disease together.

All the children dote on her. My children with Kelsey treat her like a second mother. Bex has forged fantastic relationships with both my daughters, taking interest in their hobbies and pursuits. At first, they were all cautious of each other, but we persevered, and the payoff has been incredible. It's not unusual for me to find the three of them locked in the girls' room, trying on random outfits or painting each other's nails. The days they announce they are going shopping, my credit card screams in pain. Normally, I can't get in the front door because of the mountain of boxes and bags.

Ollie and Liam both play for the local football club, which means most Saturdays are spent at the side of a pitch. Rain, hail, or shine, my boys play football. Watching them in their royal-blue stripes on the field together makes my heart swell.

Liam is going to lose his mum. He will lose her much earlier in life than he should. It seems so unfair. His relationship with Ollie mildly comforts me. He will be there for his brother on the toughest days.

Even on her worst days, Bex forces herself to get out of bed for the children. She's in a wheelchair now, but every week, she is present, shouting them on from the side of the pitch.

I'm so incredibly proud of them all.

Her eyes flutter open. "Hey, darling." I smile down at her.

She's wearing a light summer dress with thin straps. It's soft against her skin, as she is very sensitive to certain materials now. The hair on her body is gone. She jokes that she spent all those years going through the pain of waxing when she could have saved herself a fortune as cancer has removed the fluff for her. A bright scarf is constantly wrapped around her head to hide her missing platinum hair; it improves her mood on bad days.

Her smile is shy. "Oh, did I fall asleep? I'm sorry. What did I miss?" She tries to sit up, and I quickly help support her as she does.

"You've missed nothing, darling." I hold her tight. "You looked so peaceful. I didn't want to disturb you."

"I love you," she murmurs.

She leans forward and kisses my mouth softly; all our interaction is gentle now. Gone are the days of explosive sex and swinging from chandeliers. But when she feels in the mood, we make love, always in the same position, so I can ensure she's comfortable. She knows how to signal to me that she feels all right to try.

When we lie in bed and she runs her fingers over my stomach and down my happy trail, then I know she wants to feel me inside her. I spend as long as necessary, teasing and playing with her, until she is open and wet, lying on her back with her legs wide. I take her slow and soft, holding my weight on my elbows and pumping gently until we both reach our climax.

A heated discussion brings our attention back to the football match unfolding in front of us. It's boys against girls, and the girls are playing dirty.

Savannah and Rose are in their teenage years now, and they are enjoying every damn minute. My heart is in my mouth every time they leave the house. Their dresses seem to get shorter each week. Bex tells me it's normal and to stop being an old fart. Girls are allowed to express themselves. But I would prefer they covered their ass properly.

Being concerned about boys was what I was preparing

myself for, but last week, Savannah announced she was into girls. So it looks like I will be beating all sexes off my cherubs.

Soon, I'm going to have to relinquish some control. Savannah heads off to university next September. She's chosen to study medicine like me and is hoping to be accepted for a place in Scotland. My little girl has excelled in school and is soon to set off into the big wide world. I'm devastated to let her go but excited to see her spread her wings and progress in this life.

Rose spends her days chatting on her social networks, meeting her friends at the shopping centre and generally giving me things to worry about. Her latest boyfriend is two years her senior and is going to drop out of school to become a pop star. My mind boggles as I rerun the conversation in my head, and I snigger to myself.

"What are you laughing at?" Bex asks.

"Oh, I am just thinking about our conversation with Rose last week regarding the up-and-coming Ed Sheeran she is dating."

She giggles, and it's the most beautiful sound in the world. I live for these moments with her.

Squeezing Bex's hand, I stand and go to join the game for a while. My kids are amazing, and I feel so lucky to have them all. The family I have is not the one I planned for when I was a trainee doctor. The path I took to get here is not one I would recommend.

But I wouldn't change them for anything.

After fifteen minutes, I'm exhausted and sweaty.

"Right, guys, let's head home," I shout, and we all start to pack up. "Thanks for a fantastic afternoon. All of you. I love you all very much." My emotions are on the surface.

The two boys stick their fingers down their throats and make gagging noises. I chuckle. Dropping off three of them at their mother's is always bittersweet, but the time that Bex,

Liam, and I have together is precious. It makes me even more aware that our time together is running out. We must savour it. Each time Bex wakes up unwell or is unable to do something else, my heart breaks a tiny bit more.

Kelsey ended up marrying her firefighter, and he's a good guy. George works hard and treats my kids like his own. I've never seen Kels so secure and happy. Our relationship is good, and we co-parent well together. It just goes to show that sometimes you just fall out of love with someone, but you can still care for each other while being a positive influence in their life.

Max hangs around like a bad smell. He still works at the school and keeps Bex up to date on the latest gossip. He visits at least once per week and normally brings something sweet as a treat. We don't see eye to eye, and I know he thinks Bex would have been better off with him. I tolerate him for her. He has been a huge support for her over the years, especially at times when I fell terribly short.

Giving up her career as a teacher has taken a terrible toll on Bex's mental health. But last year, after collapsing at home, she was forced to quit her part-time position. Between the children and her treatment, there wasn't enough left of her to go around. The day she handed her notice in, the tears had rolled freely down her cheeks, the devastation clear on her face. It truly marked the beginning of the end.

Bex is exhausted after our day out; these excursions take it out of her now. I know she will probably stay home for a few days. No doubt, both Katie and Amy will visit. They are like the three witches around a cauldron when they get started, gossiping and putting the world to rights. I'm grateful that Bex met Katie at the Cancer Centre. She has been a positive addition to her life.

When I can't make an appointment or must leave early, then Katie is there to support my wonderful woman. Katie's cancer is in remission, and she lives her life big and proud. Enthusiasm radiates from her. She's a joy to be around.

My parents have never fully accepted Bex into our family. Our relationship with them has improved in the past year, but they have never understood my preference of Bex over Kelsey. They always keep directly in touch with Kels themselves. Bex never mentions their coolness toward her and seems to have accepted it, but I know she hurts underneath her bravado.

In the beginning, she tried, inviting my parents for coffee and to our home. Their conversation was stilted and centred around the children. With every olive branch Bex would extend, my parents swiped it away. The pictures of Kelsey and I together are still displayed proudly in their home while there is not one of Bex.

Liam, however, they accepted with open arms, and they have been wonderful grandparents for the past few years. My threat to remove contact with them if they did not treat his mother with more respect was quickly dismissed by Bex. "Ben, my time is limited, and Liam will need his family around him when I'm gone," she said. Her understanding of their venom toward her is incredible. She kept their grandson from them until he was in school, and he was only discovered due to our chance meeting. Bex feels their negativity toward her is partly deserved.

My feelings toward my parents are not so forgiving, but I hold my tongue for the sake of my children and their mothers.

Time is not on our side. If I want to give myself to Bex entirely, I need to do it soon. That's why this weekend, I've arranged for all the children to be at Kelsey's. We are going away for a few nights, just the two of us. Because of her ongoing treatment, we can't go far, but I can make it special.

Friday rolls around, and I tell her to pack a bag for a couple of nights. She smiles at me.

"Where are we going?" Her voice is excited. I love it when she's animated like that; she looks like the Bex from years ago.

Tapping the side of my nose, I tell her, "Don't be nosey. It's a surprise." Then, I flash her a huge smile and wink.

She throws a selection of clothes, makeup, and shoes in a suitcase. "How long do you think we are going for?"

I laugh. "It's only two nights."

After flying the bird at me cheekily, she fakes a scowl. "Well, you won't tell me where we are going. I need to be prepared for anything. I mean, you might take me skydiving or something boring like that."

The car winds its way through the country lanes of the Cornish countryside. We are heading for the coast; I can already smell the sea. Our accommodation comes into view. It stands proud on the edge of the cliff, keeping watch over the waves.

Bex gasps as we approach the lighthouse. "We are staying here?" She squeals. "No way! You're amazing! I love you so much!"

I laugh at her childish excitement, but I must admit, this is remarkable. Our room is right at the top in the lamp room; the old lamp still sits pride of place in the centre. A balcony runs right around the room offering 360-degree views. The late addition of a lift on the outside of the building has made bringing her here possible. So many places have become unattainable since she was made to use her chair. It breaks my heart each time she is unable to do something which used to be normal. A little more of my Bex slips away.

The bed is huge and covered in red satin sheets. There are rose petals scattered everywhere and a bottle of champagne chilling on ice.

This is perfect.

Bex is sitting in her chair out on the balcony with her back to me, and the sun is setting over the water. The late summer breeze is gentle and warming on her skin. She's wearing a long, floaty gown in pale blue, and her wig is pinned high. I creep up behind her and wrap my arms around her, placing my head on her shoulder and singing her favourite song in her ear.

She turns and kisses me softly.

"I love you, Doctor Jones, but you're a terrible singer."

I kiss her fiercely, my tongue filling her mouth, and she replies with the same intensity. This woman still makes my blood sing with want for her; I harden instantly.

"Later," she mouths, and I wheel her toward the lift to go to dinner.

The restaurant is quiet; there is only one other table. But the evening is going as I planned. The waiter brings our desserts to the table, and on Bex's plate, there is a small pink box wrapped with a silver ribbon. Her eyes meet mine, curious.

"Open it," I encourage her, and she starts to untie the bow.

Lifting the lid off the box, her eyes pop open. Then, she sees me down on one knee beside her.

"Marry me, Bex. Please. I love you."

She sits, stunned. Then, a huge grin spreads across her face. "Yes! Yes! Yes!" she shouts.

I lift her up and spin her around. The few people in the restaurant clap in applause as I hold her tight in my arms.

This is the best night of my life.

Our wedding is booked for the following April. Bex loves the spring sunshine. She is dreaming of vases of daisies and soft white cotton dresses. It's going to be a small affair, just us, close friends, and family. There will be a short ceremony followed by a meal and then a walk down the beach to take photos in the setting sun. By this time, we know she will be too tired to do much more.

Savannah and Rose will be our bridesmaids while my boys are the best men. Rose has become incredibly protective of

Bex, ensuring she gets everything she wants for our special day. The arrangements are being organised in detail, and I know we are all counting down the days.

I cannot wait for people to refer to us as Dr & Mrs Benjamin Jones, for her to be officially mine.

After a wonderful family Christmas, Bex's condition quickly declined. There were a lot of extra appointments and drugs required to manage the growth. Her body began to lose the fight rapidly. She was struggling to eat and drink, barely able to stay awake for more than a few hours at a time.

Her unique beauty which I loved began to diminish as her weight dropped aggressively. Porcelain-white skin clung to her bones and bright eyes receded into their sockets. Every day, Bex became less herself and more of a patient. She tried to stay upbeat, but the pain tarnished even our happiest moments. The cancer was always there, sapping another part of her as I watched on.

By February, it was obvious she was not going to make it to our spring wedding, and she was moved into hospice care. Still wanting to make her my wife, I arranged for a celebrant to come to her room on a sunny winter afternoon to perform the ceremony.

The nursing staff was incredible, dressing Bex in her soft white wedding gown, arranging for her hair and makeup, and even organising her a hen party with a few of their younger residents. I believe one gentleman offered to do a striptease but was declined by the partygoers.

Being too weak to get out of bed, she was propped up on pillows as we said our vows to each other. The children surrounded us, wearing their wedding outfits, and holding bouquets of lilies and daisies, Bex's favourites. Our wedding was not what we had imagined or planned, but it was perfect all the same.

Eamon and his team did everything they could, but there was no stopping the cancer ravaging her body. She slipped away peacefully on the fourth of March 2018 surrounded by our family, with the winter sun streaming in the windows. I held her hands in mine and promised to love her always. She gave a final sad smile and closed her eyes.

One last time.

ABOUT THE AUTHOR

VR Tennent emigrated from Scotland to Spain in 2020. She lives in the Spanish campo with her husband, young daughter, and ever-growing animal family.

In January 2022, she decided to put pen to paper and write a book after joining the writer's group of her favourite author. Five months later she was offered a publishing contract on that very book.

She writes contemporary fiction filled with love, heartbreak, and spice. Never promising a happy ending but guaranteeing a rollercoaster ride of emotion. Her flawed characters will navigate their journeys through life often making controversial decisions in the process. Be prepared to laugh, cry, and scream in frustration as you read.

Find out more at http://www.vrtennent.com

Find me on social media

Facebook: https://m.facebook.com/vrtennentauthor/
Twitter: https://twitter.com/vrtennentauthor/
Instagram: https://www.instagram.com/vrtennentauthor/
TikTok: https://www.tiktok.com/@vrtennentauthor

Made in the USA
Columbia, SC
09 October 2023

24176388R00146